The Crusader's Heart

by

Kate Forrest

The MacKinnons of Mull, Book One

The Crusader's Heart

Cover Art by *Diana Carlile*

The Wild Rose Press, Inc.
PO Box 708
Adams Basin, NY 14410-0708
Visit us at www.thewildrosepress.com

Publishing History
First Tea Rose Edition, 2018
Print ISBN 978-1-5092-2132-5
Digital ISBN 978-1-5092-2133-2

The MacKinnons of Mull, Book One
Published in the United States of America

" 'Tis nice to know you lust after me, but I won't settle for being a poor crusader's whore."

The jab at his reduced circumstances made the lust disappear immediately. "Mary told you, did she?" Alex drew toward her, and Isobel quickly backed against the wall.

Isobel said nothing, but he'd seen Mary's jealousy of Isobel when they'd arrived. The love of his youth was beautiful, but she could be cruel.

"Alex, I did not mean…" She held up her palms, as if to push him away.

"Aye, you did. You meant exactly what you said." Alex pressed against her open palms, crowding her. "I may be poor, but at least I know my place in this world. Can you say the same?"

Now her cheeks were stained crimson with shame. At first, Alex felt satisfied. But then he saw the uncertainty in her eyes and his anger dissipated. *What am I to do with you?*

"What do you want from me, Isobel?"

"I do not know," she whispered.

"I think you do."

He cupped her face with his hands, lifting her chin upwards. He bent his head. Their eyes locked, but Alex hesitated. Then he felt Isobel's hands reach up and wrap around his neck, pulling him down to her.

"Kiss me, Alex," she whispered.

Dedication

For Tyler

Acknowledgements

The inspiration for *The Crusader's Heart* came from my first trip to Scotland in 2013. In touring Edinburgh Castle, I learned about Queen Margaret, who later became a saint. Visiting Dunfermline Abbey, the site of her burial, settled my interest in this fascinating woman. A second trip to Scotland the following year left me consumed by the beauty of the Western Isles, and I knew it had to be the setting for a story someday.

On moving to the Finger Lakes region of New York in 2015, I read every book I could find on Queen Margaret, intent on writing a story about her. But I was also desperate to write about the Western Isles, and a nagging voice in my head told me I should create distance between my protagonists and this iconic holy woman. And so I placed Margaret in the periphery and wrote a story that is threaded together with inspiration from my travels. It seems fitting then to first acknowledge the source of my inspiration: Queen Margaret and Scotland.

I started this project in July of 2015. I was settling into a new home and, truthfully, feeling a bit down after living two exciting years in England enjoying travel, rich history, and magnificent gardens. The Finger Lakes region of New York has a beautiful diverse landscape, but I wasn't ready to love it yet. My heart was still in the southeast of England, planted firmly alongside my Bishop of Llandaff dahlias.

My husband, Tyler, knew the only way to move forward was for me to write my novel. He gave me the love, support, and time I needed to get Alex and Isobel's story on the page. I fail to put into words exactly what that has meant to me, but it is why this book is dedicated to you, Tyler.

The person that helped me get this project off the ground is my good friend and fellow writer, Ryan Russell. His critiques of the manuscript, thoughtful advice, and enthusiasm were vital to me during my writing process.

I have been fortunate to learn craft from so many talented individuals, including the extraordinary Kathy Ayres, my writing mentor. Her guidance, wisdom, and encouragement are invaluable to me.

Thank you to all the authors, especially Susan M. Boyer, who gave me indispensable advice. It was a great kindness to share your time and knowledge with me.

More than once in my life, my family has told me, "Kate, do what you love. You love to write." They know me well, and their support of my creative work has never wavered. I am grateful to each of them.

Thank you to my dear friends of many talents. You critiqued, you inspired, you praised. It means the world to me.

A story isn't finished until it has an audience, and I am beyond grateful to my wonderful publisher, the Wild Rose Press, for giving this novel a platform. They also paired me with the perfect editor, Eilidh MacKenzie. I am thankful for her guidance and tremendous eye for detail.

Finally, I am thankful to all my readers. You complete my story's journey.

Chapter 1

Kingdom of the Scots, late spring, 1153

A twig snapped and a man said, "Dinnae move." Before Isobel Campbell could turn, strong hands grabbed her shoulders and pulled her backward to collide against the man's stomach. She bounced off him, but he pulled her back again—bringing her to rest against his full belly.

Isobel grabbed at her assailant's hands, clawing at them as the pressure on her shoulders increased from his crushing hold. As Isobel twisted and pulled away from him, she scanned the dark, empty forest. *Think, Isobel!* Instantly, her hands dropped to her side. *My knife!* She palmed beneath the satchel at her side for the *sgian dubh*. Carefully, she unsheathed the knife before he could restrict her hands.

"Turn to face me," he demanded.

His smell surrounded her. She inhaled slowly to steady herself, but his stench coated her throat. She coughed, her body convulsing as she tried to regain control.

"Enough!" her captor shouted, shaking her. The action only increased her coughing. He hauled on one shoulder, but her legs felt sluggish as she tried to keep up with the twist of her upper body. Her hands flexed, naturally wanting to steady her, but Isobel caught herself before she dropped the blade.

Finally, the coughing ceased as he released her shoulders. For a brief moment the awful pressure was gone, though quickly replaced with the feel of his bruising hands at her waist as he awkwardly pulled her around to face him. A rush of cool night air swept over her, sending Isobel's hair into a wild dance. She flinched, as though in pain, as her hair blew across her attacker's open mouth. He spat it out, the strands flying back across her face. The wetness from his mouth caused the strands to stick to her cheek; his terrible smell was now on her skin.

She wanted to attack, but she couldn't. *He still has too much control. I must wait for the right moment.*

She kept the blade of her knife concealed beneath her cloak.

"Your hair tastes as good as it smells," the fiend said, with a laugh of amusement. "Though I'd rather have it in my hands than down my throat!" He laughed again as he roughly brushed Isobel's spit-covered hair behind her ear. She ground her teeth in response, but otherwise remained passive as the fiend's hands came to rest on her upper arms again.

She knew from colliding with his stomach that he was portly. With him standing before her, she could also see he was short for a man, barely taller than her. Because of his weight, he would be slow to catch her if she somehow managed to escape.

Though he was no warrior, his strength was greater than her own. She would need to make a clean break.

"Too many fine things to be a peasant girl," he said, looking down at her wool cloak. "I wonder what riches ye have hidden away beneath this." He played with the fastening to her cloak and chuckled as his appraisal continued.

Isobel refused to show fear. She stood her ground—her chin lifted high as the disgusting examination continued. *Be patient.* She squeezed the knife's jeweled haft in her right palm, taking care to keep it hidden in the folds of her cloak, as she waited for him to relax his hold so she could make her move.

"A fine bag," he said, tapping his finger against her leather satchel. "I'll see what it holds soon enough." Her attacker whistled. "Look at ye! That face! Ah, I cannae wait to have ye! The lads will be sorry they missed this."

His words sent chills of warning down Isobel's spine. She knew what he meant to do with her. *The bastard is alone. Focus on that advantage.*

In his excitement, the man slapped his thigh. Isobel's right arm was momentarily freed.

Without delay, she rammed the knife straight into the middle of his belly. His laughter turned into a horrible scream as his eyes widened. When he grabbed for the knife, she pulled it from his swollen stomach and ran.

"Bitch!" His voice thundered in her ears.

Isobel raced along the rushing waters of the burn, jumping over fallen logs as she maneuvered her way up the hillside. The man panted and cursed as he chased after her. Despite his injury and size, he moved faster than she'd anticipated. The woods were too thickly forested, and she feared breaking her own neck if she ran into a tree in the dark. She needed to stay near the water so she could see by the moonlight, but that advantage worked for them both. The only thing she could do was wear him down. She quickened her pace as much as she dared, her satchel thumping against her hip as she raced over the mossy rocks on the stream bank. Isobel's own breathing labored and the muscles in her legs burned, but she kept moving. As the time passed, the sounds of her attacker became fainter and fainter. She ran until she was certain he'd given up.

Giving in to her own exhaustion, she leaned against one of the large boulders lining the stream and took several deep breaths. As the rhythm of her heart settled, she fought back the sting of tears that threatened to upset the calm she'd maintained since leaving Edinburgh. *That man deserves no tears. If he dies, so be it. One less beast on this earth.*

"If David could hear such thoughts," Isobel whispered. She should be repentant. David would demand nothing less if he knew she'd just mortally injured a man. And yet she could not find it in her to feel remorse for her actions. Stabbing that man had been her only course of action. It was survival. And she knew a great deal about survival.

Even though it wasn't the same, and she was no longer a helpless child, her present state resonated strongly with the past. *I've been on my own too long. I've had too much time to think. I must focus on the here and now.* She palmed her cheeks and forehead, wiping away the sweat from her run along the stream.

Despite tonight, she'd been lucky—too lucky since leaving Edinburgh. It had not seemed possible to pass through the city unnoticed, but she had. Then, when she was far from the city, she feared getting lost in the wilderness. She had traveled before by road between Edinburgh and Stirling, but David warned her to stay off the main paths and keep to the woods. She'd easily gotten turned around in the forest, and she had gone too far west, missing the easier route to Stirling. Isobel was angry for the time she'd lost. Only four days in, she was worn and weary. Still, that was no excuse to let her guard down.

She'd been careful of people and safely avoided several parties of traveling warriors and merchants since departing Edinburgh. Even at night when she slept, she devised traps around her so she would hear anyone approaching. She was rattled by her slip tonight in letting her guard down. Moments before the attack, she'd been busy making a temporary shelter for the night. She usually made camp earlier, before dusk, but she needed to compensate for lost time. In her exhaustion from walking all day, she hadn't heard any movement in the forest. A lack of awareness could be costly. She was fortunate to have escaped.

Realizing that her position by the water was still compromising, she made her way into the dark forest and found a large tree that afforded a good view of the burn and was wide enough to conceal her from behind. It wasn't ideal for the night, but it would have to do.

As she sat, Isobel flexed her right hand, trying to study it in the moonlight, but it was too dark. She gently touched her palm, flinching as she traced the indentations left from the jewel-encrusted handle of her knife. Beautiful and functional, the blade had done its job and, mercifully, the physical cost of the struggle would likely fade within a day. If she was in Edinburgh, a healer would tend to her sore hand, give her a dram, and she'd fall asleep in her warm bed.

Isobel closed her palm into a fist, willing herself not to miss her room at the castle. It did not satisfy to dwell on what was lost to her now, but she keenly felt everything that was out of her reach.

The first night in the wilderness had been the most trying. She'd wept freely at the isolation and questioned her strength to continue. The quiet was the most difficult part. Wherever David kept court, she was surrounded by people. While she didn't miss them specifically, she missed the noise and commotion. She missed hearing the men practice swordsmanship in the bailey at dawn, the sound of the fire crackling in the great hall, and the chorus of voices that rose up around her as everyone gathered to share stories and a meal together. She even missed the sound of children running down the castle corridors. In the wilds of the Lowlands at night, no noise reached her, save for what the passing breeze rustled from the stillness. Funny how sound had kept the loneliness from her life; now that all was quiet, she could truly see how empty her life was.

Isobel recognized early in her journey how thoughts like that could crush her. She fought against them, trying to focus on her true purpose—taking the relic to Iona. The first night she'd held the relic case tightly to her chest, finding strength in all it symbolized to her and the people of Scotland. David trusted her to find the relic a sanctuary, since it was no longer safe in Edinburgh. She recalled their parting words a few morns ago.

"I know you have struggled these past years to find where you belong in this world. I know I pushed hard for the church, but I saw in you what my mother saw in me—purity and light that is true." David looked down

at the case and then back to Isobel. "When she told me of its contents, I did not believe her. Not until after her death when I heard of the miracles surrounding her in life did I begin to trust what I now know to be true. It must be protected at all costs, and I fear, as I have feared for many months now, my time to protect it is nearly over."

He reached out, taking her hand in his, and placed the slim case into her palm. Isobel took it and carefully concealed it within the special pocket sewn into her cloak.

"The people of Iona will care for this as I have most of my life," he said. "I think you will also find what you have searched for all these years on this journey, Isobel."

She had felt in her heart it would be the last time they spoke. She wanted to say so many things to him, but there was no time to speak it.

Her departure from the city was hasty that morning, even though she'd known for some time she would be the one to move the relic. Plans were under way for a journey set for late summer, but everything changed a few nights ago.

David intended for a companion to accompany her, but such arrangements could not be made in time—not with someone they trusted. The morning she left, David assured her a crusader by the name of Alexander MacKinnon would escort her from Stirling to Iona. She hadn't considered what the man would be like; her mind had been preoccupied with other thoughts. During the day, she was filled with purpose and determination. The nights were different.

The nights exposed her thoughts beyond the

mission. *What will become of me when this deed is done?* She cursed her wandering mind and tried to relax against the base of the tree. *From a warm bed to the cold ground.* Court life had afforded her many comforts, and she was not ashamed to say she missed those comforts now. She knew the woman she was—and that woman missed her warm bed in Edinburgh.

In the morning, she would be who she needed to be. She would make for Stirling and pray her companion, the crusader, awaited her there.

****

Alexander MacKinnon had not been in Kirkcaldy one night before the missive from King David arrived. The king had given no mention to the mission when Alex saw him in Edinburgh just a few days prior. The task was unusual, but a request from the king would be met, no matter how strange it was. Any man—or at least any MacKinnon—would do the same. However, that seemed to matter very little to the man sitting across from him in the alehouse that evening.

"The earl will nae pleased with ye, MacKinnon," Angus said, setting his empty tankard down on the wooden table between them.

"I know it, but I must go west," Alex said. "If all is agreeable, I will come back when my mission is done."

"It may be too late by then. The earl's daughter is a fine prize; he will nae wait much longer for an arrangement."

Alex knew what the mission would cost him, but he could not deny the Scottish king. A wealthy bride would reestablish his clan's power and give Alex the means to build fortifications around his home. Much had been lost to the Viking raids on the isles of Iona and Mull, where his clan's stronghold was, but little had been replenished over the years. It was no secret the MacKinnons were in desperate need of coin. But when Queen Margaret had granted the stewardship of Iona to his clan half a century ago, other clans took notice. Even when the King of Scots lost his power over Iona to Somerled, Lord of the Isles, the MacKinnon stewardship of the isle remained intact. The MacKinnons were still favored by the royal family of Scotland, and that was worth a great deal on the mainland. It was how marriage talks with the Angus clan, which hailed from the north of Scotland, even came to be.

" 'Twould have been better for ye to have come to the earl a year ago," the Angus clansman continued.

A year ago, Alex was still away on Crusade. Though the war had ended in 1149, Alex and some of the men stayed on to travel the Mediterranean. Most were young and eager to explore like he was; there was no rush to return to Scotland. He'd been a fool looking for adventure. He wasn't ready to marry then, despite the push from his father to take the wealthy Angus bride.

"David's son was alive then. Now his kingdom is less certain, as is yer standing," he finished.

Alex's jaw tightened, and his hand flexed at his side as he tried to control his response. "King David still reigns, Angus. Take care with your words."

The older man's eyes flashed briefly with panic, but then he laughed. "I mean no offense, and ye ken it. But yer sway with the next king may not be as strong. Ye ken this, MacKinnon, as does Earl Angus."

"Then why does he consider me still?" *If the earl is*

certain my family has no power—or that what we have will soon be lost—why would he arrange this meeting?

"The spoils of war have been taken by men humbler than ye."

There it was. Why hadn't Alex seen it before? When he sent word to Angus weeks ago, he'd told him that he'd done well on Crusade. By that, Alex meant he'd been successful in battle—not in taking prizes. He'd returned home with the same coin in his pocket as he possessed when he left these shores years ago. Clearly, the earl thought the poor MacKinnon had returned a man of wealth.

"That may be, Angus, but I have brought home none." With that, Alex finished his drink and stood. "Give my regards to the earl."

"That's it, then?" the older man asked, standing across from him.

"Aye, that's it."

Alex headed out into the misty cool night and walked back to the village's inn, run by the father of a fellow crusader. The complimentary lodging would likely be his last night of comfort for some time, so he planned to enjoy a few hours rest on his straw bed before he rode out to Stirling. That alone made the effort to sail into Kirkcaldy to meet the Angus worthwhile. He shook his head and grinned at his misfortune, for what else could he do? He'd return home with no coin and no wealthy bride. How would he care for his people? He knew not, but he would find a way. His kin had always found a way.

Chapter 2

Isobel did not know what to do. She'd sat along the banks of Bannock Burn the entire morning trying to build up the courage to walk into Stirling. The water glistened in the sun, rushing past her on its way to the River Forth. She peered down over a calm pool along the stream bank, taking in her reflection. The pains of travel were beginning to show. Her brown hair stood at all ends, and smudges of dirt covered her face. She glanced around, checking to make certain she was still alone, and with the care of a red deer coming down to the burn's edge to drink, she splashed cool water on her face. She washed the dirt away and smoothed back her hair, keeping an eye on her surroundings as she did so. After a few minutes of work, she looked back in the burn and found her reflection much improved. *Now I will not give the crusader a fright when we meet.*

The plan, thin as it was, called for them to convene at the castle. *But when?* There was no set day to meet. How could there be? Everything was done in haste.

To make it all the more maddening, she had no idea what this Alexander MacKinnon looked like. She should have asked David for a description of the man, but in her rushed departure, she did not have her wits about her. It seemed a fool's errand to wander around the castle looking for someone she would not recognize. *Perhaps he will find me. If he's in Stirling.*

What if he never received King David's missive? Or he could have been detained.

Isobel took a deep breath, trying to quiet her fears. She could question it countless times, but there was only one path forward. She would go to the castle.

Around midafternoon, she finally forced herself to leave the burn and make her way into the city. She knew she was close when the stone fortress atop the hill came into view. One of her earliest memories of Stirling was when she was a child and David and his wife, Mattie, brought her with their family to keep court. That visit had been important, for it was when David oversaw the founding of Cambuskenneth Abbey—just to the east of the city. She'd been back countless times, but she'd mainly been confined to the castle. She knew very little of the maze of city streets she was now navigating.

The afternoon sun felt warm, but Isobel kept her wool cloak wrapped tightly around her. People eyed her strangely as she passed shops and markets. While she was not wearing her best, she was still dressed finer than many of the women in the streets. She did not look a peasant, and it bothered her. She felt a tingling at the back of her neck, warning her away, but she kept walking on with her head held high. She'd found many times in life that confidence was all one needed to seem as though you belonged. If you acted as though you should be there, people were more accepting of you. That was how she acted at court, among the peerage who looked down on the pitiful orphan child rescued by the pious king. Many felt David's religious convictions had brought him to rescue Isobel, so they accepted his decision. But they never accepted her. Still, Isobel found a way to walk the line between the worlds she lived in—the life of a royal and the life of a commoner.

Today, she knew she looked noble, and if she spoke, her voice would confirm what they all suspected—she was not one of them. And the temptation to speak was strong when the smells from a bakery wafted past her as she made her way up the street to the castle. She did need to restock supplies, though she hoped to do so after she found the mystery crusader who was to join her. But the ache in her belly proved too strong, and she hurried into the shop.

"We'll be closing soon, so be quick," the baker said, dusting away flour from his palms as he paused in his work.

His short temper did not bother her. A large selection of goods remained on display, which, for the time of day, was probably what had the baker upset. He hadn't sold much.

"Everything looks wonderful." Isobel eyed the gingerbread and tarts. She'd seen the seal on the outside of the building, which proclaimed he held a royal warrant. This meant he was a supplier of goods to the royal household and thus had ingredients other bakers may not, such as ginger. Isobel loved gingerbread.

"Forgive me, my lady. Please take your time."

Clearly, he'd taken note of her accent and attire. Isobel looked away from the goods and back to the baker. He'd straightened up and smiled at her.

"I'll take twelve oatcakes, two lamb pies, and—" She glanced longingly at the sweet selection beside her. Deciding any journey could use some gingerbread, she added, "—three gingerbread slices," for good measure.

"Of course, my lady!" The baker hurried into

action, gathering all of her requests. Once he'd collected it all, he looked at her expectantly.

A basket! Isobel forgot about the one thing every woman took to market—a basket! An unusual oversight, as the baker took note.

"No basket, my lady?" He frowned, as did she. Isobel only had a small satchel, where she kept her essential supplies. It would not do for her to present that to him. Sensing that she was unsure of what to do, he beamed back at her. "Not to fear—we have our own baskets. My wife makes them herself." He pointed to a selection of baskets in the shop's entryway, which Isobel had failed to notice in her rush to the counter.

"They're all so lovely." She examined the selection before her, choosing the most practical one: a basket with a woven lid to cover it. It was also the most expensive, which pleased the baker enormously. A short while later, with her basket filled, she continued her journey.

When she crested the hill, she took in the castle. The gray stone fortress contrasted against the vibrant green trees pressed up against the castle's perimeter walls. Through the gates that gave entry to the castle, she could see all manner of activity going on in the yard where crowds of people moved about. *How on earth will I find him?* More fierce warriors milled about than she'd expected. Any one of them could be Alexander MacKinnon. Isobel examined the faces before her, thinking perhaps intuition would guide her. Then she heard her stomach growl.

Blushing, as though the sound could be heard by others, Isobel retreated from the busy scene. Her nerves had left her appetite diminished, but the sweet and savory smells coming from the baker's shop earlier were tempting. She peeked into her basket. *Just one gingerbread slice, and then I will look for this Alexander MacKinnon.*

****

Alexander found her. It had to be her. What other God-fearing woman would sit alone in plain sight, perched on the castle walls, eating cake?

He rode out from Kirkcaldy early to arrive in Stirling midmorning and found no sign of the lass. He decided to give it time, so he made rounds every hour or so looking for her. He'd walked around the castle half a dozen times, checking out hiding places he knew around the perimeter, thinking perhaps she would stay hidden. He took notice of the lass sitting on the wall earlier, but he initially dismissed her. She seemed too at ease. Now, he realized, this Isobel Campbell was either fearless or just too comfortable with her surroundings.

He approached her cautiously. He could tell the moment he came into her vision, for she reached to her side where presumably she had a knife stowed away. *Good lass.* As he crossed the short distance to her, he took in her appearance. Her hair was dark brown. Her form was slim, but her thick wool cloak disguised her shape. She also sat facing the city below, so he could only take in her profile.

"I see you found the king's baker," he said, pointing to the crumbs in her lap.

She blushed and brushed the crumbs away with her free hand.

"David said the man makes the best gingerbread in Scotland. Would you agree?" Alex asked her.

When he used the king's name, she faced him. Her

brilliant violet eyes flashed with relief. She was breathtaking.

He stood dumbfounded as she asked, "Are you the crusader?"

"Aye. My name is Alexander MacKinnon, my lady." He almost stumbled over his tongue as he took in her appearance. *Pray to the kings of Alba, for she is beautiful!* Those intense violet eyes were accented by gently arched brows, a heart-shaped face, and the lips of a seductress.

"How can I be sure?" She was suspicious, as she should be.

Once he regained some sense, he reached into the leather pouch at his side and pulled out the missive King David had sent him. If she knew the king as well as he expected, she would know his handwriting. He passed her the note and admired the delicate hand that reached out to take it.

She read the note quickly—with little there to read—and looked back at him. "It has no description of me. How did you know it was I?"

Alex shrugged, not wanting to explain. "We need to get moving."

She stepped down from the wall and came around to face him. "What else do you know of this journey, Sir Alexander?"

"Alex."

"What else, Sir Alex?"

"Only what was written in the note." As she stood before him, the top of her head came to his chin. His large muscular frame contrasted with her slight form. The difference made Alex feel protective of her. *Is she used to be being around warriors, or does my appearance unsettle her?*

She frowned, looking back down at the missive. "But this only says you are to meet a woman named Isobel Campbell and take her to Iona."

He nodded, unsure of what she expected.

"Why are you doing this?"

"My king asked it of me."

Her violet eyes showed her hesitation to accept his answer, but he had no other explanation to give her.

"I hope I have not kept you waiting," he said. Given the unusual plans, he wasn't certain how long she'd been in the city.

"No," she said. "I arrived a short time ago."

"You came from Edinburgh?"

She nodded before explaining, "I should have arrived in Stirling sooner, but I will admit I lost my way."

"You had no escort to guide you?"

"No, I journeyed alone," Lady Isobel said.

"I am certain the king could have provided you with safe escort here." *How could the king send her off on her own?* She was clearly part of the peerage. She'd probably never walked more than a mile a day in her life. It did not make sense.

"It was not necessary," she said, tilting her chin up.

"Not necessary?" Now Alex was the one perplexed.

"I could have made the entire journey on my own."

She was so sincere; it took everything he had not to react to her words. If his sisters took to such a foolish notion, he'd laugh. And once he was done laughing, he'd tell them they were mad. He sensed Lady Isobel would not take such a response kindly. She had pride.

He wondered if it was a fool's pride or born from something else.

"Whether you find it necessary or not, you are now under my protection, Lady Isobel. I will see you safely to the shores of Iona," Alex said. "You have my word."

"I do not doubt that you are capable," she began, looking at his chest and arms. Color filled her cheeks as her perusal continued. Whether she was used to warriors or not, she seemed to enjoy the sight before her. He grinned at her response.

Her expression went from embarrassed to furious in a matter of seconds. "You clearly are a warrior, but I cannot trust you unless I know your motivation."

"Iona is near my home, Lady Isobel. The MacKinnons are the stewards of the isle and the caretakers of Columba's monastery."

With his father's failing health, Alex's return was all the more important. As the future chief of his clan, Alex knew what the failed marriage negotiations would cost him with his people. They looked to him for hope—for the renewal of his clan. They would not easily forgive the foolish son who had gone off for battles and victories on Crusade.

He studied the woman before him. *What is she to David? Why is she going to Iona? And why does she have to go in secret?* If she was someone from court, Alex would not know. Alex had been away too long to know the women there. She had spirit, but this woman was used to the fineries in life. The journey would not be easy on her.

"And you, Lady Isobel? What is your purpose in going to Iona?"

In truth, Isobel hadn't considered what David

would have imparted to the crusader. Upon seeing the note, she'd realized he had told this man nothing about her save for her name and their destination. And now he wanted to know her motivation. *What should I say? Should I lie?* It was only logical for him to want more answers. She wouldn't be able to trust the man if he didn't have wit enough to ask questions about this unusual arrangement. Still, she could not share the truth, and he would need something.

Isobel quickly thought over all she knew of Iona. She mulled over Columba and his monastery and then she thought of the nunnery. The daughter of Lord of the Isles, Bethoc, was recently instated as the first prioress of the nunnery on Iona. Then she thought of David's letter—the one she was to give to the prioress upon her arrival. The letter attested to the relic's authenticity and guaranteed she could take the holy vows, if she wished it. It also gave her the lie she needed.

"David is like a father to me," she began. "He has wished for some time that I take my vows. The wish has become more immediate now that he—"

"Now that he is an old man with an heir barely weaned," Sir Alex supplied dryly.

"Malcolm has just seen his twelfth spring, Sir Alex. He is not a babe."

"David knows his kingdom is uncertain in his grandson's hands. The Scottish nobles will control him or move against him."

"Nothing is certain." Isobel wanted to defend young Malcolm, but what the crusader believed was the reality that many feared. It also reinforced her purpose in traveling to Iona. "But you can see my need to leave. When David is gone, I will have no official purpose at court and no protector. It is time for me to go to the church."

Her words were meant to conceal her true purpose, and yet, Isobel realized she'd still spoken a truth. She would soon have no official purpose at court and no protector. The time had come for her to move on.

"You could take a husband." He moved to sit on the low wall, brushing past her as he did so.

A bolt of energy rushed through Isobel at the contact. The strangest sensation overcame her, and she could not help but look at him with curiosity. At court, Isobel spoke with many men. Most of these men, however, adorned themselves in finely ornamented clothes, possessed slim or vastly overweight figures, and were unremarkable in both stature and looks. She did not have fanciful thoughts about them, though she had waited for years to have such feelings. It took a crusading warrior for her to finally feel the disturbing flutter in the heart that weakened many ladies at court. She had never known such a dangerous feeling. *He's handsome. Of course I am attracted to him. 'Tis perfectly natural, but it does not mean anything. I am not weak because I can tell a man is clearly cut from a nicer cloth than most.* And, oh, he was cut from the finest cloth in Scotland. At over six feet tall, his stature demanded attention, and his muscular build told the story of countless hours of practice, labor, and battle. The gold strands of his light brown hair glowed in the sunshine, giving him a youthful appearance, but she could count the years in his eyes. Though a beautiful grayish blue like the stormy waters of the North Sea, his eyes were burdened by the worries only a man of experience could possess. The severe lines of his face appeared to have been chiseled from the granite Edinburgh Castle stood upon. His expression was void of any softness, but she found warmth in those troubled eyes. All this physical splendor and what attracted her most was his confidence. When she looked at him, she saw a sure man—a man with no insecurities or doubts. He knew himself. She ached to feel that kind of certainty in herself. He'd even spoken of her greatest uncertainty: should she take vows to Christ or choose another path?

She looked at the handsome man before her. She would not let him know of her worries.

"I could, but I will not take a husband." Isobel looked away from Sir Alex and out over the city before her, thinking on her freedom. She would not suffer an unhappy marriage and be used to gain favor with the king. Even after David passed, she would just be taken for her coin and lands. It was the way of things, but David had brought her up to feel she needn't do what was expected. Perhaps that was because he always intended her for the church. In all likelihood, the coin and lands would pass to the nunnery. She would have nothing in her name if she took the cloth, and she would have nothing if she married or tried for a life on her own. An impossible choice, but she knew by the journey's end, she would have to make a decision.

Looking back to the crusader, she said, "I know you want more of an explanation, but all I can offer you is the promise that this journey is important. It is something I must do, and I am grateful for your guidance along the way."

"And protection," he added. " 'Tis nae safe for a lass to journey alone. In truth, I am surprised you made it thus far."

"I have done what I must, Sir Alex. I am stronger than I look." She eyed the man before her, trying to contain her temper. She did not care to be looked upon as weak or in need. Sir Alex had probably never felt weak or needy a day in his life. His muscular frame exuded power and the weaponry strapped to his body looked as though it were part of him—an extension of his person. He was a formidable warrior. She knew it without having to see him in action. Though a wicked thought of him appeared in her mind—his muscular arms flexing under the weight of a battle-axe as he swung it through the air, his skin glistening with sweat from the exertion of battle. She bit her lip and whimpered before she could catch herself.

"Lady Isobel?" Sir Alex approached her, and she hastily retreated. "Are you well?"

"Perfectly." She nodded to the horizon. "Should we journey on then?"

"Aye, we should. We shall stay in Doune this night. My horse is nearby," Sir Alex said.

Isobel followed him to his horse. In a matter of moments, her belongings were secure, and they were seated and riding off. Isobel glanced back at the castle, trying to capture it in her memory. This could be the last time she ever saw Stirling. The last tie to what she knew, and seeing it fade into the distance was bittersweet. She looked ahead and realized the path before her was all new. She was covering ground she'd never seen before. The idea made her smile and, for the first time in five days, she did not mind the idea of the unknown.

Chapter 3

A bath! I will have a bath at long last! Isobel felt the hot sting of tears in her eyes. How worn she was by the travel to make a bath overwhelm her. Once the maid emptied the last bucket of hot water into the soaking tub, Isobel nearly pushed the woman out of the way so she could jump in. The maid said she'd forgotten a drying cloth and excused herself from the room to retrieve it.

Common sense made Isobel touch the water with a toe first, to make certain it wasn't too warm, before sinking down into the tub. She sighed with contentment as the sweet floral smells of the lavender sprigs and rose oil reached her nose. It was kind of the mistress to perfume the water. Her worries from the day vanished as she soaked in the tub. Isobel's concerns over going into Stirling were for naught. *The crusader found me, and I even got to enjoy my favorite treat and now a bath! Ha!*

They'd traveled the ten miles to the fort at Doune in near silence, which was just as well. Isobel was exhausted and hadn't felt like conversation. She was, however, delighted they would be staying the night at the fortress. Once they arrived, Alex immediately saw to her care. She wasn't surprised, exactly, as she knew very little of this man and his ways, but to see the caring side of a warrior felt strange. In truth, she'd known few warriors by name, let alone how they treated women, but when every inch of his body seemed built for destruction, it didn't seem possible for him to have a caring side. Wherever it came from, Isobel was grateful for his attentiveness and for their hosts', the Stewarts', obliging nature.

The Stewart mistress even took Isobel's garments to be washed. The idea of having a fresh gown made her smile, but then she frowned at the thought of not knowing when she'd have such luxuries again. Perhaps the crusader had many associations they could appeal to on the journey to Iona.

The wooden keep at Fort Doune was small but well maintained by the Stewarts. Their modest guest room afforded the luxury of a small fireplace. The room also had a narrow window, if it could even be called that, for the keep's archers. From it, she could view the River Teith in the pink light of the evening sky. This time of year, darkness didn't fall until the wee hours of the morning. It would give them more daylight to travel by, which would aid the journey west.

As Isobel scrubbed away the dirt and grime of travel, she contemplated if she wanted the passage west to be quick. She glanced at her cloak—the one thing she'd refused to let the mistress of the keep launder. For the sake of the precious relic she carried, she should try to reach Iona as soon as possible. But the quicker she went, the less time she had to decide. Perhaps she should ask Sir Alex of the life there. He had grown up around the religious community. Surely he would have insight into it.

Just as she finished washing her hair, a knock came at the door.

"Come in," she called, assuming the maid had returned with a plaid for her to dry off with. She stood up and poured a bucket of clean water over her body, washing away the perfumed water and lavender.

Had he not spent the last few years on Crusade, Alex was certain he would have closed his eyes and shut the door immediately. But he did not do either of those things. He was transfixed and incapable of looking away. Lady Isobel was standing before him naked, water dripping down her delicate back over her perfectly shaped bottom and down her slender legs. She bent and lifted a pail of clean water. He sucked in a deep breath as she poured the water over her body.

She hadn't looked at him yet, and while he knew it was wrong—she was for the cloth and he'd be damned to hell for it—he had to look at her. She was perfection. Standing in the water as she was, she looked as though she'd just emerged from the sea like a selkie. *Aye, a selkie that could lure a man to his death.*

"How dare you! Why are you here?" she cried, and the moment was shattered. Her eyes blazed as she watched him from over her shoulder. Alex straightened his spine and shook his head, trying to clear the lust from his mind. *Why am I here?*

Belatedly, he turned his back to her and firmly closed the door so no passersby could see into the room.

"I thought you'd finished your bath by now," he explained.

"And so you just barged into the room?" Her voice steamed with outrage.

Alex winced. "I did no barging, Lady Isobel. You bid me to come in."

25

"I bid you to—" She was beyond outraged now, but Alex had knocked and she did tell him to come in. "I thought you were the maid. She was supposed to bring a plaid for me."

He looked around and saw a plaid folded neatly on a stool by the door. "You must have been distracted when she came; she left it here." He pointed to it but was careful to stay facing away from her.

He heard the water slosh over the brim of the bath as she stepped out onto the wooden floor. "Will you leave while I dress?"

"Open the door when you have finished," he said, doing as she asked.

While Alex waited in the hallway, the master of the keep, Ian Stewart, walked by. "Kicked ye out of the room, aye, laddie? My wife was always doing the same when we first married. She despised me something awful."

"What changed?" Alex asked, curious.

"Not a damn thing!" He chuckled and slapped Alex on the shoulder. "In time, they just put up with ye, rather than shut ye out. Plus, I got a bit more skilled with my loving." He winked, chuckled some more, and continued down the hall.

Old Master Stewart was a character, but Alex could trust the man as he did his own kin. Stewart would not betray him or Lady Isobel for a boat full of riches. Alex's father had fostered Stewart's son many years ago and trained him to be one of the greatest warriors in Alba, but that title was short lived. Alex was but a lad when the Stewart son died at the Battle of the Standard when King David was trying to extend his kingdom southward into Yorkshire. Stewart was beside himself and fell into drunkenness until, through the MacKinnon connection to the king, he was granted the stewardship of Doune. Since then, the Stewart felt indebted to the MacKinnons, and Alex and his kin were welcome anytime at the fortress—no questions asked.

When he'd arrived a few hours earlier, Stewart did not inquire over the lass at all. He'd asked his wife to see to her, but clearly, he assumed Alex had taken a bride. Alex didn't deny it. In fact, he planned to travel as husband and wife for the journey. It would make them less suspicious when they were guests or when staying at inns along the road west. He'd yet to tell Lady Isobel this, and he had a feeling she wouldn't be pleased with the idea.

He waited a few moments longer, hoping she would come to the door on her own accord. He'd come to her room for two reasons. The first was to use the bath when she'd finished. He didn't want to ask the maids to carry more water at this hour, and he hesitated to leave the fort to wash in the burn. He usually bathed in the lochs and rivers, especially in the summer when the water didn't chill to the bone. But he needed to protect Lady Isobel, and he would not leave her side for long, which was the second reason he was there—to share the room for the night.

****

He's seen me naked! Isobel was furious and embarrassed with equal measure. No man had ever seen what Sir Alex had just seen. While mortifying to think about, Isobel reasoned it was an accident.

Once she was dressed in the linen shift and robe Mistress Stewart had left her for the night, she opened the door and peered into the hallway. Alex stood with his back to the door, his arms crossed over his chest, looking down the corridor. He was on guard.

"Sir Alex," she spoke quietly. Most of the keep was asleep by now.

He turned at her voice, and she bade him to come inside.

The room, which was once large and spacious, now felt much too small to contain both her and the crusader. She looked around and waved him to the stool by the small grate in the corner of the room. She remained standing as he took a seat.

"What is it that you wanted?"

He nodded to the barrel-shaped tub sitting in the center of the room. "You've come to remove the tub?" she questioned.

"Nae. I've come to take a bath."

"In here?" Now he was just mad. He couldn't bathe in here—not with her in the room. "Surely there is another room—"

"This is the only room free in the keep, Lady Isobel. I cannae leave you to go wash in the burn."

"Of course you can." *Why couldn't he?* The Ardoch Burn ran just on the other side of the fortress. They had ridden along it on the way to the keep.

"I cannae leave you for long. I will not argue on this."

He sounded unmovable, so Isobel tried another tactic. "You smell perfectly fine to me. Surely a few more days without a wash would not hurt."

He laughed. "Are you so sure, Lady Isobel?" He stood and prowled toward her like a wild cat. Isobel inched her way backward, trying to create some respectable distance between them. He smelled of sweat and horses, but he also smelled of leather and gingerbread. He must have eaten one of the baked treats earlier. Isobel retreated until she collided with the bed.

"I see your point, Sir Alex." Frowning, Isobel looked down at her state of dress. She couldn't very well stand in the corridor in her robe. Then she eyed the bed, a surprisingly grand piece of furniture, considering the otherwise spare surroundings. It was a four-posted bed made of iron with draperies tied to each corner, allowing the bed to be completely enclosed. It would keep in the warmth on winter evenings but also afford some privacy for them both.

"I'll wait on the bed with the draperies closed while you bathe," she said evenly and went about untying the cloth panels.

"As you wish." Before she'd finished pulling the cloth panels together around the straw mattress, Sir Alex started to undress. Hastily, she jumped onto the bed and closed the draperies. She couldn't help but listen as he sat down in the tub and washed himself. The water was probably cool, but it would be warmer than the burn.

Isobel sat there fidgeting, something she prided herself on never doing, but she could not control it. There was a naked crusader in her room. Though a naked man was unremarkable in itself (she'd seen men in various states of dress at the castle, a natural consequence of living among warriors), the fact that this naked man was handsome and they were alone together was an entirely new experience. She could not fault herself for playing with the linen mattress covering (another luxury) over and over again. At least she was trying to distract herself, and she didn't have to do it for long. The bed curtains muffled the sounds of splashing and dripping, followed by a great rush of falling water. *He must have poured the second pitcher of water over himself.* The maid had brought her two, but she'd only needed one for rinsing herself off.

He paced on the floor, gathering his garments she assumed, and then all went silent. *What is he doing?* Perhaps he'd left, though she hadn't heard the door open and close. *Surely it would not take him this long to dress.* Unable to control her curiosity, she opened the panels and stepped onto the floor. She found Sir Alex with the drying plaid wrapped loosely around his waist, his face downcast as he eyed something on his side. The rippling bands of muscle across his stomach flexed, and Isobel shuddered. He was built exactly like the rendering she'd seen of Ares, the Greek god of war. He was slightly shadowed, but she could still see how sculpted his body was—a body designed for battle, and he had the scars to prove it.

As he continued his examination of his side, Isobel stepped closer, trying to see what he was looking at. The floorboards creaked from her movement, and his gaze snapped to hers.

Mortified once more, Isobel spun on her heel. "Forgive me. I thought you'd dressed."

"Give me a moment." The floor boards moaned as he moved around, then he bid her turn. She found him wearing a fresh linen tunic and trews. His hair glistened from the water. He tucked it behind his ears, and the long locks reached his shoulders. He looked younger than he'd appeared when she'd first met him. She wouldn't put him but a few years past her in age now—perhaps five and twenty, but no more.

A lock of hair fell loose from behind his ear, and as if on her body's own accord, she crossed the short distance between them and reached up to gently tuck the hair back into place. His blue eyes penetrated hers, and heat radiated off him. The air suddenly felt heavy, and she had trouble breathing. His eyes grew dark with desire; the reaction was mirrored in her own, but whatever it was could not be. Lust had no place on their mission.

"Isobel." The single word floated on the air, enveloping her like a spell. His voice was deep, and the sound of her name on his tongue sent a shiver down her spine.

This had to stop. "Did you hurt yourself?"

His eyebrows knitted together. "What?"

"Your side," she said, pointing to where he'd been looking earlier. "I thought you might be injured."

"I broke some ribs about a month ago. They are nearly healed, but I still feel some pain. It is naught for you to concern yourself with, though."

"This was in battle?"

He shook his head, studying her as though she was some sort of puzzle he needed to work out. After a few moments, she saw something flash in his eyes— disappointment? She couldn't say for certain, but he looked dissatisfied. Perhaps she was reading into his expression too much. After all, she hardly knew him.

"I had a disagreement with a crew member on my way back to Scotland." He moved toward a table near the doorway. There sat a bottle of ale and two cups. With quick efficiency, he helped himself to a drink. He raised the empty cup to her.

"No, thank you." Isobel preferred wine over ale;

besides, she would not drink in his presence. She needed her wits about her. "What was the disagreement over?"

He shrugged.

"You won't say?" Isobel asked, intrigued by his secrecy.

Instead of responding, he drank the ale and turned to gaze at the fire. Isobel waited patiently, unsure of what to do. Sir Alex muttered something about the Stewart's poor choice of ale, then looked to her. "Why the rush to reach Iona?"

"What do you mean?" Isobel asked. *Why is he bringing this up?*

"You must have been in a great hurry to leave Edinburgh without an escort to Stirling."

"David is unwell," she began, but Sir Alex didn't let her finish.

"David's health is failing, but he is nae on his deathbed."

"Even if it weren't for the king's health, I've been planning to go to Iona for some time. I did not leave in a hurry." She kept her eyes on his. Averting one's gaze implied deceit.

"I know the king. He would not have sent you alone to Stirling without cause."

Isobel laughed. "You are determined to find a lie, Sir Alex, but you will not find one. As I told you when we met this afternoon, I did not require an escort."

"I see." He smiled briefly, which Isobel found to be a strange response, and took another sip of his ale. "And the new nunnery on Iona will be your home?"

"It is David's wish," she said firmly.

"There are nunneries closer to Edinburgh. I'm

surprised you would not wish to be closer to the place you call home."

For all the thinking Isobel did in a day, the thought to justify why Iona over other nunneries never came to mind. While the monastery and church of Columba were known beyond the shores of Scotland, the nunnery was still in its infancy. There were other holy locations closer to Edinburgh. Sir Alex was right. Their proximity to Edinburgh is what made them poor choices for the relic's continued safety. Iona was the safest choice. *But why would it have been my choice?* It wasn't, so she need not lie.

"You must know of the great love David's family has for Columba's church. When his mother, Margaret, visited there, 'twas said she never saw a place more beautiful or holy. David couldn't have chosen a better place for me."

"As you say, Lady Isobel."

Isobel did not like how he spoke those words to her. He did not trust her. *Is it of consequence?* He said he would see her safely to Iona. It was of little importance what he thought of her, so long as she and the relic reached the nunnery. *If it doesn't matter, why do I care what he thinks of me?*

Before she got lost in her thoughts, Sir Alex spoke again. "We'll share a room this night and any night we stay at an inn or keep. We must appear as a married couple. 'Tis the best way to blend in."

"Is that so?" Isobel challenged, her thoughts on his distrust of her now gone.

"Lady Isobel, you know I have the right of it. How would it look to the Stewart if I were to sleep in the hall with the men when I could be fast asleep next to my wife?"

He was right, of course. Isobel could see that plainly. But how on earth could she spend a single night with him in the same room? She eyed the bed warily and looked back at Sir Alex. He downed more ale. *Looking for courage?* Isobel wanted to smile. He was nervous. Though he need not be. Nothing would ever happen between them. She needed to remember that as much as he.

"I do not share my bed, Sir Alex." She spoke the truth, but Isobel could feel the color in her cheeks rising at the idea.

"Then it is good I dinnae expect you to share your bed, Lady Isobel." He pointed to the floor. "That's where I'll sleep."

"On the floor?"

"Aye," he said, as he set to work making a bed for himself. He unrolled a plaid and laid it on the floor near the door. "The floor is good enough for me." He sat down and stretched out.

"That cannot be comfortable, Crusader."

"Crusader?"

"You are a crusader, are you not?"

He smiled at her. "Aye, lass. I'm a crusader, and I need no comforts."

"You sound arrogant, Sir Alex, but I will not argue with you." She climbed into the large bed and closed the panels. The mood had lightened, and she was grateful.

"Good night, Lady Isobel."

"Good night, Sir Alex."

She let out a deep contented sigh, not caring if he heard her. She would enjoy her night of comfort and pray that nights such as this were not scarce on the journey ahead. She had proven she could survive in the wilds of the Lowlands alone, but she was relieved to be alone no longer. David had chosen well. From what she could garner of him in such a short time, Sir Alex could defend her, and based on what had just transpired, he seemed to respect her. She did not have his trust, but that was not to be. She knew he would see her and the relic safely to Iona.

Chapter 4

Holyrood Abbey, Edinburgh, later that night

Robbie MacDonald stood in the back of the abbey awaiting the arrival of the bishop. Regret soured his stomach. He should be with Agnes and Murdoch, not doing the bidding of a greedy old man. He stretched his back, twisting side to side to loosen his muscles. He'd spent the day teaching his younger brother swordsmanship, something Robbie was late to do for the lad. He tilted his head up into the abbey. The Norman arches disappeared into the darkened ceiling above; only a few torches lit the perimeter of the church. At well past midnight, the spring sun had finally set, giving way to the blackness.

Robbie was familiar with the blackness. It had crept inside him and refused to leave. When his parents had been cut down by thieves before his fifteenth summer, a little blackness bled in. But he'd done what was needed to care for his younger siblings, Murdoch and Agnes. Within a few years, he'd noticed Agnes's health was beginning to fail. Without the means to seek the help of a physician, she'd only received care from a few local healers who would take furs in payment. It wasn't enough, and none of the healers could tell him what was wrong with her. That's when he took up the sword. Robbie had always been muscular, and with some practice, he'd learned he wasn't bad with a blade. He began contracting himself out as a mercenary. The work made him question his morality, and the blackness inside him grew. Yet with his skill and efficiency came more jobs and more coin to get better physicians for Agnes. Yet, of all the physicians he'd been to, no one could heal her. That was why he'd agreed to meet with the bishop. The bishop said he could change all that.

"You came." It was the bishop. Following behind him was a servant carrying two velvet covered chairs.

Robbie stood tall as the man approached from the front of the church. "You knew I could not refuse."

The old man nodded, waiting for the servant to place the chairs. Once he seemed satisfied with their placement, the bishop dismissed the servant and took a seat. "Sit and we shall talk."

"I will stand," Robbie said. Only the king sat in the abbey; no man would disrespect him, present or not, by sitting in his church. No man, it seemed, except for the bishop. Folding his arms across his chest, he carefully watched the man who had summoned him. He was more ornamented than a crown. His fine gown sparkled with golden threads, and his hands were covered with gemstone rings. Even his finely made shoes reflected his wealth. The bishop was rich and powerful. Some claimed he had more power than the king himself, but the king was too preoccupied with his works to take notice.

"Do you know why King David built this church here?"

"Nae," Robbie said.

"Some years ago, when the king was a young man,

he stood on this spot and had a vision of a stag and a cross." The bishop nodded toward the altar. "He prayed there for days and days until he heard God's voice speak to him and command that he build an abbey here, an abbey grand enough to house Scotland's most treasured relics." The bishop's eyes filled with fire. "One particular relic has been kept here under the watchful eye of a dedicated few for a long time, but five days ago it was taken."

"Stolen?"

"No. The king gave it to the orphan girl, Isobel."

"For what purpose?"

"I fear the king's mind is not well. He doesn't know himself, else he would have never let her take it."

"Where has she taken the relic to?"

"I do not know her journey's end, but I heard word she was headed toward Stirling," the bishop said. "I have asked you here to find the girl."

"And retake the relic?"

"Yes. Bring it back to me, and I will send the best healers in the kingdom to see to Agnes's condition."

Robbie's spine tingled. He looked sharply at the bishop. *I never told him Agnes's name.* Robbie felt uneasy about this mission, but he had no other choice. "You want the relic back so it can be protected?"

"Precisely. Who knows what this girl intends to do with it? It has been safe here for decades, and I will see to it that it remains safe for many years to come."

"And you swear to send someone to help Agnes."

"I have the best healers in my charge, MacDonald. They will make her well again."

Though he knew the bishop lied about his intentions for the missing relic, Robbie could not walk away. He needed to help Agnes, and he'd exhausted all other options. He would take this mission and pray his sister would finally be well again.

Chapter 5

The next morning, after they'd broken their fast with their Stewart hosts, Alex and Lady Isobel set out on their journey. A chill hung in the air, but the sun was bright. Alex welcomed the favorable weather.

"We aren't going on horseback?" asked Lady Isobel, as they walked down to the River Teith.

"We'll walk and ride, as needed. The mare isn't young. She is not built for carrying two all day." Alex had bought the horse when he arrived in Kirkcaldy. She was sturdy enough for the journey, but he didn't want to overtax her.

Lady Isobel nodded and bundled into her cloak. The one garment, he'd noted, she had not allowed the Stewart mistress to take for laundering.

"What is our goal this morn?" she asked.

"We'll reach Loch Venachar by midday," he said, as he walked ahead with the mare. "We'll follow the water straight there."

As they walked on, Alex thought on what had also happened the night before. If only Lady Isobel had stayed on the bed with the panels closed. Instead, she'd stood looking at him while he dried himself with a flannel. He was trained to listen—to always be aware—and yet, he hadn't heard her approach. Then he'd looked in her eyes and saw desire. It was unmistakable. It was also illogical. How could there be such a connection between them? He'd known the woman less than a full day, and yet, standing there in the room last night, he'd ached for her.

I've been too long without a woman. Standing there last night, he had studied her carefully trying to understand it. Thankfully, he'd had the sense to clothe himself. The tension faded some, but he still needed the drink to steady himself. While trying to cool his blood, he thought about the unusual circumstances he found himself in. He thought on their conversation at Stirling. He was still surprised she'd journeyed alone to the castle. Though she was unusually well kempt given the days she'd spent traveling, she still looked exhausted. It made him angry the king hadn't supplied her with an escort to the city. With so many in his service, someone could have been spared to accompany her.

It also made him question why he was chosen as the escort from Stirling. There was something odd about this business. *Why must she travel to Iona in such a way? Why not go on horseback with a party or by ship?* For a woman of means, traveling alone or with a single male companion was not done. It made Alex consider the woman herself. *Is she running away from someone or something?* Her story provided more questions than information, and he did not like being deceived. He would take her to Iona, but he would not put himself at undue risk. Not until he learned this woman's secrets.

Even with his innate distrust of her, he genuinely enjoyed her company. He liked her and saw no reason not to be agreeable with her, but he would be on his guard.

"The weather is favorable," Lady Isobel said,

pulling Alex from his thoughts.

"For now, but it can change in an instant," Alex noted, glancing behind him. He stopped midstride, nearly tripping over a rock, as he took in Lady Isobel. There she stood by the water, her eyes closed and her face lifted to the sun, soaking in the morning light. She looked so peaceful and content. A breathless sigh escaped her lips; he focused on her mouth. Her lips were a soft rose color, like the flowering sea pink that covered the cliffs and shores on Iona and Mull. He lingered over her heart-shaped face, noting her high cheekbones, which were slightly flushed, and her winged eyebrows. He'd observed her beauty yesterday, but seeing her in the sunlight was different somehow. She was beautiful—too beautiful—and he was painfully aware of it.

Damn. He turned away quickly so she couldn't see his arousal.

"Are you all right?" Lady Isobel approached his side, so he continued along the shoreline, staying ahead of her.

"Aye."

"It's just that I thought I heard you mutter something," she pressed.

Apparently, he'd spoken aloud. He felt like a damned fool. *Mission for the king. She's going to be a nun. What am I doing?* He cleared his throat and spoke as though nothing happened. "From Venachar, we'll journey on to Loch Katrine, where we'll spend the night."

"You take this route often?" she asked.

Alex shrugged. "Often enough." When Alex was younger, he'd travelled from Iona and Mull through the

Trossachs and Lowlands with his father to meet with and maintain alliances among the clans. On their journeys, he learned the terrain well and set it to memory.

"This will be a big homecoming for you, will it not?"

Alex tensed. He was returning home without the means to restore his family to their former glory. There would be no grand homecoming, for he'd failed his people. Knowing that saying anything less than "Aye" would stir up more questions, Alex nodded. "I'm eager to return." He'd be more eager if he'd secured the marriage contract with the Earl of Angus's daughter or returned from Crusade with the coin many expected he'd possess. He could not dwell on the things that were lost to him now. He needed to move forward. *And right now moving forward means getting Lady Isobel to Iona.*

As planned, they stopped for their midday meal along Loch Venachar. Just as they were finishing their biscuits and cheese, a clap of thunder sounded in the distance. Alex peered up at the ominous black clouds moving in from the west.

"We'll need to seek cover. The skies will open any time now." Alex scanned the forest for shelter. "I'm afraid the trees are our only refuge."

The thunder roared again, getting closer. Alex knew they had only a matter of minutes before a torrent of rain hit them. He gathered up the remnants of their food and placed everything into the leather bag he wore strapped to his back. He helped Lady Isobel off the driftwood they'd been using as a bench, and along with the mare, they hurried up the rocky shoreline into the thicket.

"What trees make the best cover?" Isobel asked. She was peering up at the thin pine trees that dominated the forest.

"Unfortunately, not these pines," Alex said, taking her and the mare deeper into the woods. The rain was spitting now, and soon they would be soaked to the bone. This part of the forest was ancient, and the tree limbs were over fifty feet above them. They needed to find newer growth. He quickened his pace and cut in so they ran parallel to the loch. If his memory was correct, farmland lay ahead. With any luck, they'd find shelter there.

A few minutes later, the rain was coming down in a steady stream, but they had gotten lucky. They'd come into a clearing, and ahead Alex could see a plum orchard.

"There," he said, pointing ahead of them. They raced under the cover of the trees. A few pink petals clung to the branches, but for the most part, the trees were blessedly full of leaves. He guided Lady Isobel under the cover of a tree situated a few rows into the orchard. He tied the mare under a taller tree beside them and returned. He had to bend to avoid brushing against the branches. Kneeling down, he held out his open palm waiting to see if any water droplets fell into it, but none did. "No rain will get through. We'll be fine here for a while."

"I wonder how long it will last," Lady Isobel said, sitting down against the trunk of the tree.

Alex shrugged. Storms could last for minutes or days. He would wait as long as he could before he pushed them onward.

****

Isobel couldn't take the silence between her and the crusader anymore. They'd sat under the plum tree for what seemed an hour without speaking a single word to each other. After listening to the steady hum of rain falling, her other senses focused in on the warrior sitting beside her. Today, he wore a fresh short-sleeved linen tunic, and he smelled of something masculine, yet floral, like wild roses. *Roses? How odd.*

"Why do you smell of roses?" Isobel asked.

Sir Alex grinned. "Noticed, did you?"

"It's not every day that a man smells of roses."

"Indeed," he said. He reclined with one knee bent and the other leg crossed; one palm was planted firmly on the ground while the other toyed with a twig. "It's the rosewater I brought back from Crusade. I put a few drops on my tunic."

"It's nice," she said.

He nodded in thanks, still reclining. The muscles in his arm flexed from supporting the weight of his upper body.

Unconsciously, she licked her lips. When she finally drew her attention away from his arms, she studied his face. His profile was to her, highlighting his firm jaw line and how his wet hair clung to his neck and the side of his face. An impulsive thought entered her mind: she could reach over and touch him.

Nervously, she looked away and closed her eyes. *Control yourself, Isobel. 'Tis just a man. Like any other man. Except this one smells like...cloves, wild roses, and...* She searched for the other scent. She couldn't describe it exactly, but it was heady and distinctly masculine. *Surely it is a sin for a man's smell to create such need.* Her eyes snapped open.

"What is it like on Iona?" she shouted. Clearly, she'd startled Sir Alex because he'd jumped at the sound of her voice.

"What?" His eyebrows arched, and he looked alarmed.

She straightened her back and primly swept out her skirts, making sure every inch of her legs were covered. "Forgive me. It's just that I'd like to know about Iona, since it is soon to be my home."

"Of course." He relaxed into the position he'd been in for the past hour. The seconds stretched out into minutes, and Isobel feared he wasn't going to talk about it, but then he spoke.

" 'Tis a small isle. It would only take a few hours to circle it on foot," he began. "There are some hills, but the land is mostly flat. It's good for some farming, but we do most of the farming on Mull. A number of seabirds call the isle home, and all varieties of wildflowers grow in our fields. On a clear day, the sea comes alive, and every shade of blue and green reflects in its glassy surface."

He had a wistful look on his face, and she could tell he'd thought often of his home while he'd been away.

"But the rainy days are many, and the wind cuts across the land." He glanced back to her. "The nunnery and monastery are on the eastern shoreline, where you can look out at Mull and see the red granite boulders jutting out into the water.

"We've had many raids over the years, but that has slowed since the Vikings have come to settle around the Western Isles. We have nae had a raid in over a decade, so you needn't fear for your safety at the nunnery."

She nodded. "David told me about the raids."

"We lost a great deal. We're still trying to rebuild, but it will take time." He frowned and looked away.

Sensing this was not a subject he wished to discuss, she asked, "And what of Mull? You said you can see the coastline from Iona."

"Aye, the isles are separated by a short distance. You can swim between them."

"And Mull is where the MacKinnon stronghold is?"

Sir Alex nodded. "We keep men on Iona to protect the monastery and nunnery, but over the years we've had less of a presence since the threat of invaders has decreased."

The thought of seeing him often, even after they reached Iona, made her smile. She'd just met this crusader and knew nearly nothing about him, yet she was drawn to him. Such feelings were inexplicable.

"I have not met the new prioress yet, but the daughter of the Lord of the Isles is said to be an enchanting woman."

Isobel wasn't sure what to make of that. *An enchanting prioress?*

Suddenly, Sir Alex rose and stepped out from underneath the cover of the plum tree. "The rain has stopped. We should keep moving." He reached for her hand, and Isobel gingerly placed her palm in his; awareness flooded through her at the moment of contact. The tension between them was like a current sweeping down the River Teith. It seemed to consume them both. They looked to one another with shocked expressions. Sir Alex recovered first, planting a stern look on his face, but his heavy breathing gave him away. He was as affected as she was, but Isobel pushed it from her mind. She stood quickly and then released his hand and walked several paces ahead into the grass.

This is dangerous. She had one purpose, and her mission could not be compromised by fanciful feelings of infatuation. She needed to create distance between them. She would not be distracted.

Chapter 6

Doune, later that afternoon

Robbie MacDonald eyed the small fortification at Doune from across the River Teith. He'd gone to Doune direct from Stirling after his encounter with the king's baker earlier that morning. The man bragged the lass (the presumed Isobel) bought "two dozen gingerbread slices." After Robbie offered him a few coins, the man explained he'd watched the lass go up to the castle and meet a warrior. Robbie was even lucky enough to learn the direction they'd traveled in: northwest. After considering the roads in that direction, Robbie chose the one that led to Doune, the most logical route.

It was just past midday, with no visible activity outside of the settlement. That was likely due to the torrential rain storm that had blown in minutes before Robbie had reached the cover of the trees along the river. Rain was common this time of year, and though inconvenient for travel, it served his needs just now. He encouraged his mare, Coira, into a gallop, taking her across a shallow spot in the river and over to the fort's gated entrance. A few moments later, a guard asked what his purpose was there.

"I'm returning home to the Western Isles," he explained. "I seek shelter from the storm."

"What's yer name?" the guard demanded.

"MacDonald," he said. "Robbie MacDonald." No need to lie.

The guard gave him entry into the courtyard and pointed to the stables, where Robbie took Coira to dry off. There he was greeted by two young stable hands.

"She's a fine horse," the older of the two boys said in awe.

"That she is," Robbie agreed. Coira was a rare breed. He'd found her on Crusade and refused to leave her behind. It had been worth the effort to get her back to Scotland. She was a fine horse, with a beautiful black coat.

Robbie picked up a handful of fresh straw and wiped Coira down, though they'd be back in the rain soon.

"Were you on Crusade?" the older boy asked.

"Aye. I returned a few years ago." Robbie continued drying Coira as he regaled the young boys with a tale of victory in battle. When he was finished, he added, "I wouldn't be surprised if more warriors like me came through Doune."

"They have!" the younger boy exclaimed. "Just yesterday there was—"

"Ssshh!" the older boy hushed him. "You are not supposed to say such things."

"But he was a crusader, and his wife was so bonny!"

Sensing the older boy was uncomfortable with how much the younger had revealed, the lad quickly excused them both and ran from the stables.

Wife, aye? A good ruse. Knowing they'd come through Doune confirmed his suspicions. They were taking the relic to the Isles—Iona or possibly even Ireland. He'd take the river west and catch up with them. It would be an arduous ride for Coira, but she could do it. He'd have the bishop's work done and get help for his sister before the week was through.

****

Alex made camp for them along the southern banks of Loch Katrine. It had been a long day, but Lady Isobel had braved it well. Not once had she complained, and she'd even tried to hide her exhaustion, though he could tell she was relieved when he suggested she ride the mare for a few hours. He watered the horse, then tied her up to graze.

"We'll make a fire and eat," Alex said, as though he felt he should explain the process.

"Can I help?"

"There is bread and cheese tied up in the plaid."

"I also stocked up while in Stirling. I got more than gingerbread," Lady Isobel said, holding up a small parcel.

"Is that what you had in the basket yesterday? What happened to it?"

"Yes, 'twas a lovely basket, but it seemed impractical for the journey. I gifted it to the Stewart mistress in thanks for letting us stay the night."

"That was kind of you," Alex said, sitting down next to her to start a fire.

"Can I ask you something?"

"Aye," Alex said, building up small pieces of driftwood into a pyramid.

"How did David know you'd returned from Crusade?"

"Most of the crew planned to travel on from

Edinburgh, so our ship stopped there for a few days. Several of us had an audience with the king."

"I do not recall seeing you at court, but then there are always many men waiting to meet with David."

"Perhaps you were preparing for the journey?" Alex offered. He did not remember seeing Lady Isobel at Edinburgh Castle either.

"Perhaps," Lady Isobel said.

"We were only there for a few hours, but the king did show me the chapel he built in his mother's memory."

"Margaret's Chapel?"

Alex nodded. "Aye, 'tis a small but peaceful place."

"I agree. I have spent many hours there." A wistful yet pained look crossed her face.

He wanted to ask how she came to be there, but he hesitated. If she wanted to tell him, she would.

The silence stretched between them as they ate, but Alex did not mind. While on Crusade, he'd had little quiet. He learned to be grateful for the silence when it came, for it was always short-lived.

Alex could not help but think back on his time at Edinburgh, just over a week ago. He and some of the other men from the ship met the king. King David had asked about Lisbon and their time spent traveling after the Crusades ended. Then the king had taken Alex aside to speak to him about Iona.

"How is the monastery?" the king asked.

"I understand from my family that all is well, Sire."

"Is there still great influence from the Lord of the Isles?" King David asked.

Alex was unsure of how to respond. Mull and Iona were part of the Inner Hebrides. They were islanders, but they were not as tightly under the control of Somerled as the Outer Hebrides. Still, many clans were allegiant to him.

"His daughter was installed as the prioress of the recently founded nunnery, but he lays no claim to Iona or Mull, Sire."

"But he is more present than your Scottish king?"

Alex shrugged. The king knew the answer to his question.

"I see," said the king. "Does Somerled also hold the allegiance of Clan MacKinnon?"

Alex needed to be careful. The king was searching for an absolute, but control over the inner isles was complicated. He was certain the king knew this, but he also saw the king wanted reassurance that his hand stretched west of the mainland.

"We respect and trade with the Lord of the Isles, but we are allegiant to you, Sire."

How could Alex's people not be? His clan had great love and respect for the late Queen Margaret, though he himself had never met her. That loyalty extended to her descendants, even if the Scottish royal family's influence in the isles was not as strong as it was on the mainland.

"Then I have your sword, should ever I need it?"

At first, he assumed the old king spoke of battle, but something in the king's eyes told him that was not what he meant. Even so, only one response existed.

"Of course, Sire."

Kind David held his gaze for a few moments, as if to assess the truth behind Alex's words. Then the king smiled and patted Alex on the shoulder.

"Now tell me where you go next. West to Stirling?"

"Nae, Sire. I must travel first to Kirkcaldy. I expect to be there for a few days before I begin the journey home to Mull."

"Then I bid you farewell, MacKinnon, and a safe journey."

Alex had thanked the king and immediately departed the castle. He never suspected at the time he'd be called upon again so soon, but here he was on a mission to take Lady Isobel, someone of import to the king, to the holy island.

After they ate, he laid out plaids on the ground and offered Lady Isobel her choice.

"I'm afraid there is no soft ground to be found, Lady Isobel, so the choices are fairly equal."

She settled on the plaid that paralleled the water and faced the fire. Alex lay on his own plaid and bade her a good night. After he had inhaled a few deep breaths of the June air, Lady Isobel stirred. He opened his eyes to find her wide awake, looking up at the sky.

"You should sleep. 'Tis a long day's travel ahead of us."

"I will, just not yet."

"What are you thinking on?"

"Everything," she said quietly.

"Would it help to talk?"

"About?" she asked.

"Anything you like," he offered.

"I'm sure you have been asked countless times since you reached the shores of Scotland, but—"

"But what was it like on Crusade?" Alex finished for her. "It was war, and then a small crew of us stayed on to travel the Mediterranean."

"You were in Jerusalem?"

"Aye, a rare opportunity to travel there during a relative time of peace. None of the battles fought were in Jerusalem."

"Why did you stay so long? I understand the campaigns ended four years ago."

"I wanted my freedom. I wanted to see places I'd heard tales of from others. I wanted adventure before I became the MacKinnon chief."

"Do you not wish to be chief?"

"I am prepared for my duty now. I had just seen my nineteenth summer when I left to join the fleet in 1147. I'm a man now. I know my duties to my people. I will not fail them." He prayed his words were true, that he would find a way to rebuild his clan.

"Did your father encourage you to go?"

"Nae, well, he did not want me to go, but he understood why I had to leave. He gave me his blessing to go and do battle."

"And did you enjoy it? Doing battle?" she asked.

"There is no joy to be found in battle. I'm just built for it."

Alex saw her eye his arms and could not help but flex his muscles under her scrutiny. Still, he wanted to be clear. "I do not just mean I have the physical strength for it. My mind is suited for it as well."

"What do you mean?" Lady Isobel asked.

"I have seen atrocities, and I carry them with me. I always will. But I can look past them. Some of the men I knew could not look past the blood of battle. Their minds became poisoned by what they'd done."

"I know of what you speak. I have seen the toll of

war on a man's soul."

"You witnessed this in David's court?"

"No. But the wives would come to see Mattie—I mean, the queen, and she would pray for them. The stories they told, especially of their husbands' fitful nights of sleep. They were haunted, the wives would say."

"Aye, that's a good word for it. Haunted."

"But you are not haunted?" she asked.

"I can sleep," Alex said. "I am at peace with what I have done."

"But you won't tell me how you came by that bruise and broke your ribs?"

Alex sighed. *Of course she wants to know. It's a nasty bruise.* "It is nae because of bravery, so you can put your hopes of a hero's story to bed."

"You fought with another man?"

"Aye."

"What did you fight over?"

"My father," Alex said. "Another crusader criticized my father's care of clan MacKinnon, calling him a weak chief. I could nae let it go." The man had called his father more than that, but Alex wouldn't recount it.

"Why would the man say such a thing?" Lady Isobel asked, propping her head up on her hand.

Alex could see the concern in her violet eyes. He found her care oddly welcome, but he would not tell her of his clan's woes.

"I've said how I came by the bruise, Lady Isobel. Now it is time to rest."

She frowned but lay back down on her plaid. After a few moments, her breathing steadied, and he knew she was asleep. Alex thought back on the fight with his father before he'd left. When Alex was young, he looked up to his father. He was an honorable man and a fierce warrior. Food always covered the table at the evening meals, and even though the keep's fortifications were in disrepair, his father always spoke of plans in the works to repair them. He always assured Alex and his sisters that he'd rebuild the keep. He'd find the coin, and he'd do it. Only he never did.

Alex had been too young to understand that his father had mismanaged the clan's funds. Precious little of his mother's fortune was left, but Alex's father could never account for it. At least not to him or his sisters. When Alex declared he was going on Crusade, the chief argued with him.

"Ye need to marry and soon, Alexander," the chief stated.

"I am young yet, Father. A few years on Crusade will not hurt the clan."

"I never wanted the clan's finances to be on ye, but we've little left and I need ye to make a good match. I met with the Earl of Angus when I last journeyed to Stirling, and he is interested in a match between ye and his daughter."

"And the match cannae wait a few years? How old is his daughter?"

"Young enough that he may consider waiting a few years," the chief said. *"But I dinnae ken we can wait that long."*

"But mother's coin. There must be enough left to keep the clan for a few years yet."

His father looked away, and Alex could see the man's cheeks turn pink. He was embarrassed, Alex realized.

"Father, what has happened?"

"That is nae yer concern. Ye just need to do yer duty, and all will be fine."

"None of my concern? You will not tell me the cause of the problem, only that I am to be the solution?"

"Ye'll do it for your clan."

Alex's jaw tightened at the memory. His father had been right. He would be the solution, but it wasn't by the means his father had planned. He would find a way without the Angus bride.

He glanced once more at Lady Isobel. Her face was calm with the peace of sleep. He closed his own eyes and prayed for the wisdom to manage his own path forward, for every step brought him closer to home and closer to his duty.

Chapter 7

Easby Abbey, York, the same night

In the small confines of Easby Abbey refectory, the Bishop of Edinburgh and the Duke of Lincoln sat in conversation in the empty communal dining hall. This was not a meeting between friends. It was a meeting between two men holding an uneasy alliance. The purpose of the alliance was to gain power and access to the King of England. However, the bishop's delay in acquiring the relic meant their shared goals would not yet be attained.

"You have failed," the duke said.

"I have not failed," countered the bishop. "My man is working to retrieve it as we speak. His Majesty just needs to be patient for a few more days."

"He has been patient with us, Bishop. If we cannot deliver this to him, he doubts how either of us will be of service to him at court."

"I have great influence; there is much I can do for the king," the bishop said. "I do not think the same can be said for you."

The duke scowled at the insult to his worth. "I have value beyond delivering the relic. I have not failed in my endeavors, as you have."

"As I said, it will just be a few more days," the bishop explained.

The duke snapped his fingers, and two men appeared in the shadowed entrance to the hall.

"This is Rolf and Watkin. They are soldiers in my personal guard," the duke said. "They will go and retrieve the relic."

"There is no need," the bishop said. " 'Tis likely my man is already in possession of it."

"If that is true, then we've nothing to fear. Since we cannot know if your man is successful, sending another team would be prudent." The duke dismissed his men so they could continue their conversation in private.

"If my man fails and your guards do retrieve the relic, then have it brought to me at Edinburgh," the bishop said, looking his companion in the eye to deliver his warning. "If you go behind my back, you will regret it."

"We are still in this together. You have my word," the duke said, extending his hand to the bishop.

"And you have mine." The bishop grasped the duke's hand.

Chapter 8

Isobel woke early and broke her fast with Sir Alex. The sky was gray, and a chill hung in the air. Isobel tightened her wool cloak around her, trying to find some warmth. Sir Alex watched her with interest, and she had to stop herself from reaching for the relic.

"We should start our journey," Sir Alex said. "We'll camp near Loch Lomond this night, and I fear storms will hinder our progress."

"The wind is picking up," Isobel noted, as she helped him ready their belongings.

"We'll cover as much ground as we can before the rain falls," he said.

Isobel sat atop the mare, at his insistence, and he guided the horse, setting a fast pace. The wind blew Isobel's hair across her face, so she pulled up the hood of her cloak and carefully tucked her hair beneath it. As they continued on, Isobel took in the rolling hills speckled with the golden yellow and green foliage of heather. Late spring blooms of pastel pink and rosy purple filled out some of the shrubby evergreens, with much of the heather yet to flower.

The bleak gray sky above only magnified the natural beauty around them. Isobel feasted on the rainbow of green in the landscape—there was every shade of green imaginable. Moss blanketed parts of the earth in muted and dull shades. The moss was complemented by pops of vibrant emerald grasses and deep dark pines that towered together, protecting the world beneath their canopies.

"Can I ask you something?" Sir Alex asked, as he helped navigate her and the horse through a narrow valley.

"Of course," Isobel replied.

"Your speech. It's just you sound English."

"It is unusual, isn't it?" Isobel was surprised he hadn't inquired about it sooner.

"Unusual for a Scot, I think."

"I do not know if you are aware, but David spent most of his youth in England. The accent remained, even after returning to Scotland, and he brought several scholars and tutors with him from England. They taught me, so I was exposed to the accent at a young age. I suppose when you grow up around it, that is how your own voice comes to sound. Even at court, I spent limited time among the Scots and Gaelic speakers, so I confess my accent makes me even more foreign than I truly am."

"More foreign?"

Isobel wasn't sure how much to reveal of herself. Her past was no secret. She was not ashamed of it, nor did it make her vulnerable. It was her past—her story.

"I was an orphan taken in by the king. I came from nothing into a world of everything." She paused as he nodded. "That made me strange to those at court and a stranger from what I knew. I never belonged there."

"You can share a common name with an entire clan and not feel as though you belong," Sir Alex said.

Isobel wondered then, if he, like her, had always struggled to fit in.

"When I return home, I will be a stranger to my people. But in truth, I was a stranger to them before. I didnae do my part to be included—to be one of them—and I will have to fight to gain a place among my people." Seeming embarrassed by his admission, he quickly changed the subject back to Isobel. "I hope Iona will become the place where you belong, Lady Isobel."

Isobel nodded, but she wouldn't say if she held the same hope.

"We should stop for the midday meal and let the mare rest," Sir Alex said. He guided them off the path and into a thicket of trees. "This will give us some cover if the rain starts."

Isobel went to climb down from the saddle; Sir Alex was by her side in an instant.

"Let me help," he offered.

Isobel took his extended hand and slid off the saddle into him, awkwardly colliding with his chest. His hands were at her sides, helping to steady her. She knew the moment he found the case, because his eyes locked with hers.

"What is that?" he asked, as his eyebrows knitted together.

She pushed away from him and straightened her cloak and gown. " 'Tis nothing."

Sir Alex arched a brow in response. "Oh, aye, I can see that it is nothing by the shape of it."

"It is just some jewelry." Isobel was pleased she'd thought of something quickly. "David felt it'd be safer if I had it sewn into my cloak."

He studied her for several moments, and Isobel was afraid he didn't believe her, but then he nodded and untied their supplies. To reveal the secret of the relic was to put it in danger. Though David trusted the crusader with her care, she could not confide the truth of the relic to someone she had known for such a short time.

She was lying. Alex was certain of it. *If jewelry isn't in her cloak, then what is it? Could whatever possession she carries be the cause of her journey to Iona?* He did not understand the need for secrecy. *Did she steal something?* Alex conceded Lady Isobel hardly seemed like a thief, but intuition told him something was wrong with this situation. The woman did not seem keen on taking vows to the church, and her close relationship to the king suggested whatever she was doing, she did on his behalf. She was an orphan taken in by a king. Nothing could make one more indebted than being saved by another. He'd seen it himself in battle. While not saving Lady Isobel from a sword (at least he assumed not), King David had given her a new life.

Alex thought on the old pious king. King David was firm in his rule but always fair. Alex never heard of or witnessed cruelty from him. The man would not force his adopted daughter to do something for him, but that did not mean she would not offer to help. *What sort of difficulty is the king in?* Their conversation in Edinburgh made Alex believe something troubled the king; he was looking to confirm that he could trust Alex. *Did the king know then he'd set me upon this mission? If so, why not just ask me to stay and take the lass from Edinburgh? Why did she need to start the journey alone?*

Alex considered all this as they sat and ate their meat pies. Lady Isobel would not supply the information he sought, at least not yet. She did not trust him, just as he did not trust her. One could argue trust was not gained in a matter of days, but Alex always prided himself on his intuition. He was able to judge and determine the trustworthiness of most people within a short period of acquaintance. He could trust a man he'd known less than a day or know to distrust him just as quickly. In the times when it could be proven, Alex was right in his judgment.

Still, Alex acknowledged not everyone had such abilities. Perhaps she was uncertain of him because their time together had been brief. Otherwise, Alex knew he did not merit her distrust. Either she was genuinely unsure of his character or she lied for another reason. Either way, she was keeping the truth of this mission to herself.

He would do his duty to King David, but he would no longer involve his allies or friends. Not until the full truth was revealed. That meant they would not stay the night with his dear friends Tom and Katy. In Edinburgh, he sent them word of his return and intention to visit on his journey home. Indeed, it would have been a perfect and safe place to stay the night, but he was wary of Lady Isobel's secret. Should that secret prove to be dangerous, he would not risk involving his friends.

"We should keep moving. We have some distance to journey yet before we can make camp for the night," Alex said.

They gathered their things, and Alex helped Lady Isobel onto the mare. Once she was situated, he let his hand slip over the hidden object in her cloak. The motion resulted in Lady Isobel's sharp intake of breath, and her violet eyes widened with worry. *Jewelry, my arse.*

"Is everything all right?" he asked, moving his hand away from her side.

"Perfectly." She smiled brightly.

A beautiful smile to mask her discomfort, but it was still a mask. Alex would learn the truth. By the journey's end, he would learn the real reason Isobel Campbell was going to Iona.

****

Alex stretched his legs, enjoying the warmth of the fire on his feet. Isobel was sound asleep on the plaid beside him. They were camped outside of Inverarnan on the northern tip of Loch Lomond. At daybreak, they would make for town, and, after a night's rest, journey onward to Oban. Once on Mull, they'd be safe, and his duty to King David would nearly be at its end.

His eyes narrowed on Lady Isobel, examining her face as she slept. She looked at peace now, not worried and tense like she was during the day. Something weighed on her. He knew it involved King David and whatever lay hidden in her cloak.

"Why has David sent you to Iona?" Alex whispered to himself. He reclined against a low boulder and took a swig from the skin. The bitter taste of ale coated his throat. He scanned the perimeter, looking into the darkened woods. The faint sound of a twig snapping carried on the breeze. The skin on the back of his neck prickled as his senses took over.

Something didn't feel right. Alex reached for his gallowglass sword, a treasured gift from his uncle, an Irish mercenary considered one of the fiercest warriors in the Western Isles. It was the sword Alex trained with and the one he'd taken into battle on Crusade.

Alex listened carefully, blocking out the sound of the breeze in the trees and the crackle of the smoldering wood on the fire. If someone was there, they'd give themselves away eventually. Alex strained to distinguish the sounds buzzing around him. Then he heard it again—a faint snapping of twigs. It could be an animal—a badger or a fox on the prowl—but his gut rebelled against that reasoning.

Alex snuffed the fire. With his sword in hand, he shuffled over to Lady Isobel. With his back to the loch, he placed his free hand on her shoulder and gently squeezed.

"Lady Isobel," he whispered, his gaze to her face, but, in his periphery, he was aware of the forest. "Isobel, you must wake."

After a few moments, she mumbled and sighed.

"Lass, please." His voice became more urgent, and he tightened his hold on her shoulder.

Suddenly, her eyes snapped open. "What's wrong?"

"I need you to remain calm and not react. Can you do that?"

She nodded.

"Thirty paces ahead of us, in that grouping of pines—" He nodded toward the forest. "Someone or something is watching us."

"What?"

Her voiced was raised; Alex quickly covered her mouth with his hand. "We're being watched."

Her eyes were alive with worry, but she took a deep breath, and nodded once more. When Alex was satisfied she was calm, he moved his hand away.

"An animal?" she whispered.

"I dinnae think so," he said. " 'Tis likely a man."

"How can you be certain?" She tried to sit up, but Alex kept her down, placing his hand once again on her shoulder.

"I heard twigs snapping," he whispered.

She looked up at him questioningly with those deep violet eyes, and he could tell she thought him mad, but Alex knew he was right.

"But how?"

"I cannae explain how I know, but I know."

"What do we do?"

With a grim line set across his face, Alex glanced at the forest and then back to Lady Isobel's delicate face. It pained him to see her frightened. If he was by himself, Alex would have gone on the offensive, but he couldn't leave her alone.

"We wait for them to come to us."

"Wait? Surely there is something—" she began, but Alex shook his head to silence her.

"If I were him, I'd wait until we'd gone to sleep, and then I'd come forth." He motioned to his plaid, laid out above where Lady Isobel rested by the extinguished fire. "I'm going to lie down and pretend to sleep. I need you to do the same. When someone approaches, I'll attack." He paused, studying her solemn expression, finding courage in those sharp violet eyes. A wisp of hair blew across her cheek, and he reached down. Before he could think on it, he gently tucked the loose hair behind her ear. *I'll keep you safe*. Alex abruptly dropped his hand and crawled back onto his plaid and waited.

He lay still and kept his breathing slow and steady

as he watched the trees. Minutes slipped by.

The glint of a steel sword shone in the moonlight as a man broke through the forest. *A crusader? Perhaps a mercenary?* Most men in these parts carried a bow or axe. Alex pulled his plaid up close to his face to keep the moonlight from reflecting in his eyes as the man stalked closer. The intruder was now twenty paces away from their camp. He prayed Isobel would keep still, but her breathing hitched. Alex knew she was afraid, but he needed her to trust him.

After the cloaked man took a few more steps, Alex reacted with the speed and skill of a seasoned warrior. In seconds, he was standing on the loch shore with his gallowglass sword drawn. The cloaked figure stopped suddenly, seemingly startled by Alex's quick movements. Alex held the sword out beside him at full arm's length with the three-foot blade pointed away from him. He walked slowly across the rocky shoreline, approaching the cloaked man, sword never wavering to show his opponent his strength. Alex hoped the man would turn and run, but the cloaked man regained himself and raised his blade above his head, hilt gripped in both hands like a crusader. Alex held his sword low, angled down from his side.

As the distance between him and the man dwindled to less than five paces, Alex could make out the Celtic scrollwork along the side of his opponent's blade. *A crusader and an islander.* He knew the craftsmanship well.

"If you are looking for coin, there is none to be found here," Alex said.

"Coin is not what I'm after," his opponent replied.

Alex stopped with only three paces left between

him and the cloaked man. As though orchestrated, Alex and the man simultaneously started walking again, this time circling the other. Alex was measuring his opponent for a weakness, but he found none.

"Then what have you come for?" Alex would have preferred a simple thief. *What else can the man be after?*

"I've come for the woman."

He knows of Isobel? Alex was shocked but recovered quickly. The cloaked man stopped, firmly planting his feet into the pebbled beach. The sound of crunching stones stopped as Alex stood to face the man, both of them with their swords still raised.

"She is not for bargaining."

"I am here to take back what belongs in Edinburgh," the cloaked man said, standing fast.

Before Alex could consider his words, the cloaked man kicked out with his foot, showering Alex's face and chest with stones. Alex hopped back, as his opponent's sword descended. He swung up to meet the man's blade; the clash of the weapons reverberated through the night air.

They met blow for blow, each man using movements executed countless times in battle.

The fight shifted with a surprise move from Alex's opponent. From his boot, the cloaked man produced a knife and threw it straight at him. With a single graceful movement, Alex swung his sword up and struck the knife out of the air, the metal ringing as it landed on the rocky beach. He rushed his opponent and swept his sword down overtop the cloaked man's head. *Yes! This is it! He's done for!* But the victory was premature; the man sidestepped the death blow just in time. The tip of

Alex's blade crushed only stone.

They circled one another once more. Alex's muscles burned from exertion, and his heart thundered in his ears. With his senses on edge, he focused on the ragged breathing of his opponent. *I'm tired, but so is he. I can wear him down.*

The cloaked man raised his sword to strike. Alex met his blade in the air above their heads. They were locked in a battle of strength. The force given was met with equal force. Alex's teeth clenched as he tried to gain the upper hand, searching his muscles for the strength to overwhelm his opponent.

Just then Lady Isobel screamed.

Another assailant? Alex turned to look at her, leaning his weight off his attacker. The next few moments were a blur as Alex toppled forward and his head collided with a rock. His vision narrowed as though he was looking through a sea cave. Just before blackness swallowed him, the cloaked man picked up his sword and turned toward Lady Isobel.

Chapter 9

Isobel took refuge behind a stack of driftwood as soon as the fight broke out. She was stunned to watch as the men circled each other and clashed swords. She could imagine David saying, "The warriors are well matched," and he would have been right. She'd seen David's soldiers practice at the castle enough to know when the best were on the field together. The intensity of the battle made her pulse race, and fear for the outcome left her stomach in knots.

The action continued with Sir Alex's sword locked against the assailant's. He wore his short-sleeved tunic again, so Isobel could see Sir Alex's muscled arms flex as he pushed against the man. The assailant seemed to push back with as much force.

She couldn't bear to look, but she had no choice. Her eyes remained firmly fixed on the scene before her, the moonlight outlining everything.

The men stood with swords locked. They seemed to be at a stalemate for the longest time; neither one was losing or gaining ground. But then it looked as though Sir Alex was leaning back, instead of into the attacker. *Is his strength giving out?*

Fear flooded her body, seeming to completely encase her from head to toe. *What if he fails? What if the other man wins? He'll die!*

Isobel screamed.

As soon as the cry escaped her lips, she wished it back again. Sir Alex's eyes flashed toward her, concern filling his face. For a moment, time was suspended. It was just her and the crusader, and the chaos around them stilled.

But the chaos flashed back in, time sped up, and in the next moment, Sir Alex crashed to the ground, slamming his head against a rock.

"No!" Isobel cried out in horror as his body went limp. Her first instinct was to run to him, but then the attacker fixed his gaze on her.

Cold sweat trickled down her back. Isobel's heart thundered in her chest as the cloaked man approached. *He will kill me. I must flee!* The words formed in her mind and yet her feet stayed firmly planted, even as the man stalked her down. The driftwood barrier provided no protection. *You must keep the relic safe; you promised David.* Finally, she forced her body into motion, and she ran. She dashed into the woods, narrowly avoiding the logs and brush that covered the forest floor. She ran until she could no longer make out the edge of the trees along the shoreline and hid behind the trunk of a pine. Then she listened. The seconds passed by, and yet she heard nothing. Surely, he followed her into the woods. Unless he meant to finish Sir Alex off before he came after her. The thought made bile rise in the back of her throat. *Oh, God, what have I done? Was it my fault?* If there was one thing David insisted on, it was that his men stay focused in battle. "Being distracted could cost you your life," he'd warned.

The warning was a reminder for her now.

She didn't know the terrain and hadn't the physical

strength or skills to take on such a warrior. Her limited training from David only went so far. It had saved her from an overweight fiend days before, but a skilled warrior was not something she was prepared for. Her best hope was to stay hidden until daylight.

She wrapped the cloak tightly around herself and leaned back against the tree, taking a slow deep breath to steady herself. She closed her eyes and took another deep breath. As she exhaled, the cold tip of a blade pressed into her neck. Snapping her eyes open, she saw her attacker.

The wind had died down, and the forest was silent. All she could hear was her breathing and the attacker's labored inhale and exhale as he recovered from his altercation with Sir Alex. *Alex! No, I cannot think of him now.* The pressure of the blade increased, taking her back to the present. She leaned as far back against the tree as she could, but the pressure from the blade followed.

Isobel studied the figure before her. He was imposing, and his fight with Alex proved his skill and strength. In the darkened forest, his features were hidden. He stood in the shadow of another tree, so she could not make out his face in the moonlight. But she did not need to read his face to know his intent—the blade made that clear.

Instead of collapsing in tears of defeat, she straightened her spine and flexed the muscles in her arms. *It's not over yet.*

"Easy now. No quick movements." His voice was surprisingly gentle, as if his intent was not sinister after all.

But why have the pretense? Why the effort to calm

me? "What do you want?" she asked, still leaning away to escape the press of the metal against her skin.

"The relic." The two simple words hung in the air, but they had more impact than the press of his blade. Isobel had feared for her life before, but now her fear was even greater.

He knows of the relic! I cannot react to his words. Pretending to be ignorant was her and the relic's best chance.

"What are you speaking of?"

"You know of what I speak. Do not pretend otherwise," he threatened.

" 'Tis not pretending if it's the truth," she said. "I am just a bride traveling home with my husband."

"Course you are," he said. "And I'm the King of Scots."

Isobel studied the assailant. He relaxed his arm slightly, which moved the blade off her neck. She did not mistake his relaxed stance as an opportunity to escape. She could not outrun him.

"Time to hand it over, Lady Isobel."

"My name is Mary. Mary MacKinnon." She could have kicked herself for how her voice wavered.

"I tire of this talk. Give me the relic, and I will be on my way."

"I'm afraid I cannot give you what you want."

"That is unfortunate." He hesitated for a moment, as if deciding the next course. "Turn and face the tree."

Does he mean to slit my throat? If he's going to kill me, he can face me. She held her ground and refused to turn.

"I said turn. Now." His tone was firm, and she was certain many a person, man or woman, obeyed that voice when it gave commands. Yet, she would not.

"If you mean to kill me, then do it. But do not expect me to make the task easy for you."

He did not respond. Instead, he grabbed her by the shoulder and spun her around.

Isobel awkwardly stumbled against the tree as he pressed her face into the bark.

She tightened her hold on her *sgian dubh*. The small blade was barely longer than her middle finger, but it was sharp. He would kill her, or perhaps he intended to bind her wrists. Before he could do either one, she had to act.

He temporarily moved his hand and sword away from her body, and she took the opportunity. Isobel spun around and swung with all of her might into him, ramming the small blade into his side. He staggered back, pulling Isobel's cloak with him.

"No!" she screamed, as the cloak tore off her shoulders into the assailant's hands. She reached for the cloth, trying to grab for the pocket that held the relic, but the man bundled it up against his chest.

"It's in here, isn't it?" He held his blade back up, pointing it at Isobel, and tucked the cloak under his arm. He grunted in pain as he pulled the blade from his side, tossing it to the ground.

Isobel went to reach for it, but the man's blade pressed against her side.

"That would be foolish," he said. She could hear the pain in his voice, but she had no doubt the attacker had plenty of strength left in him. She backed away from her knife.

"Hidden in the cloak, aye?" he asked, as he felt through the cloak with his free hand. When he found the hidden pocket, he stilled. "I'll be on my way then."

In an instant, he disappeared into the forest. She thought of taking chase after him, but she knew what she had to do. Retrieving her knife from the ground, she turned and ran back to the loch.

Once she made it into the clearing, she found Sir Alex. He was on his hands and knees, trying to stand.

"You're alive!" she shouted. She ran to him and knelt on the rocky beach, reaching her hand out gingerly to touch his head. He hissed in pain, and she quickly moved her hand away.

"Alex, are you well?" she asked.

"I seem to be. The damn rock knocked me out cold." He leaned back on his heels, his hands pressed to his face as he opened and closed his eyes slowly, as if testing them out. He looked at her. "Did he hurt you?"

"No, I'm fine. I wounded him." She explained how the attacker found her in the woods and she'd stabbed him in the side. Alex's eyes fixed on the forest behind her.

"I am sorry you had to do that, Isobel. I did not protect you the way I should have."

"Alex, you fought bravely. It is nothing to be ashamed of. He's a very skilled warrior."

Alex's jaw set in a grim line, and she sensed her words had not soothed him.

He studied her more closely and frowned, reaching out to touch her arms.

"Where's your cloak?"

"He took it."

"Why would he take your cloak?" Alex asked. Then he quickly added, "What was in it, Isobel?"

"If you are able to run, we must catch up with him.

Can you track in the woods at night?"

He stood all the way up, blinking as he touched the side of his head. Then he fixed his gaze firmly on her. "Isobel, what was in your cloak?"

"I must get it back!" she cried. "Can't you see? There isn't time to explain."

She ran for the thicket of trees, but Alex called after her.

"Isobel, stop!" His voice thundered in her ears, but she wouldn't stop. She reached the line of the forest but hesitated to go in.

"You cannae go in there!"

"But I have to!"

"Have to? What did you lose?" he yelled, as he jogged over to her.

"Something of great value," she choked out.

Alex reached for her, pulling her to stand in front of him. Isobel felt frantic as she looked up at the crusader. *Why is he wasting time?*

"What was in the cloak, Isobel?" he repeated.

"It is something David entrusted into my care. It is very important, Alex. We must get it back."

"I will help you, Isobel, but first I want to know exactly what it is."

She took a deep breath and looked Alex in the eye. Keeping it secret didn't matter, now that the relic was lost. "Hidden in my cloak is the Holy Rood of Scotland."

Chapter 10

It took Alex a moment to understand what she said. The bastard that bested him had stolen the Holy Rood of Scotland, the relic that was claimed to have come from the True Cross of Christ. The most cherished relic in the country, representing Scotland's importance to Rome, the Pope, and the Almighty himself.

Queen Margaret's greatest gift to the Scots was the Holy Rood. *But why was Isobel in possession of it?*

"You owe me an explanation, but if what you say is true, then I'll need to chase him down."

"Yes, we must hurry!"

"Nae, not we. Me." He started back toward the loch. "I need to get our supplies."

Isobel trailed behind him. "You're a fool if you think you're going without me."

Alex didn't respond as he approached their camp site. He strapped his weaponry to his body. After sheathing his sword and slinging his pack over his shoulder, he turned to Isobel.

"There is a cottage not far from here. The family there are friends of the MacKinnons. They'll keep you safe while I track down the man who's taken the Rood."

"No. I'm going with you," she said, squaring her shoulders. She looked like the fiercest warrior who ever went into battle, but she could not come.

"Isobel, I know how much this means to you, but I must do this task without you." He reached for her and gently squeezed her palm. "In truth, I am stronger, faster, and more skilled in tracking."

"I've yet to see your tracking skills, Crusader, and I don't see why you feel you are better suited for the task. I'm the one who wounded him."

Alex had heard many things over the years. He'd also taken his fair share of criticism. But he'd never been taken to task like this before, and he had to admit it cut him, even more so than her applause of his bravery in fighting a "very skilled warrior." A man could only take so much.

"Had I not feared for your safety, I wouldn't have fallen, and you wouldn't have needed to wound him."

"Clearly, your strength was giving out," Isobel said flatly. "I'm not going to flatter you to restore your ego. We don't have time for this."

"My strength was not giving out," Alex countered. "And I don't expect anyone to flatter me!"

She cocked an eyebrow at him, and Alex could no longer think. *This argument is not getting us anywhere.* He took a deep breath. *Be rational, and she'll be rational.*

"I cannae fight the way I need to if I have to worry for your safety." He'd been distracted by her presence when he'd fought the attacker. He would not make such a foolish mistake again. "I know you are capable and strong-willed, but you must see I am right in this."

Her eyes no longer looked crazed, but he could sense she was on edge, and he felt certain she'd argue to hell and back to go with him.

"I promise I will bring it back," he said, looking

The Crusader's Heart

her straight in the eye.

She seemed hesitant still, but after a few moments she said, "All right."

"And when I return, you will answer my questions."

"Agreed. Now you need to hurry, so take me where you must."

Alex ushered her and the mare into the forest, taking care as the undergrowth was dense and the forest canopy blocked most of the moonlight. His mind raced over what he'd just learned. The mission was more complicated now, though in truth he hadn't known what he was getting himself into when he'd received the king's missive.

"How did he know about it, Isobel?" he asked, as he navigated them through the woods.

"At the start, David and I were the only ones who knew I was taking it out of the city. But things got complicated."

"There is a good deal to this story, isn't there?"

"Yes," Isobel said, as they raced onward. "I promise I will tell you all I know when you bring the Rood back."

"I'll hold you to that," Alex said, as he quickened their pace.

As they hurried through the forest, Isobel contemplated the alarming fact that the attacker had intentionally been looking for her and the relic. David had sworn her journey would be kept secret, but the bishop must have found out sooner then they imagined.

"Keep up. We're nearly there," Alex called back to her. He ran ahead with the horse at his side.

Isobel regained her focus and hurried to catch up.

Within minutes, they came out into a pasture. Standing alone in the field, save for a few oaks, stood a tiny farmer's cottage. Though predawn, smoke rose from the chimney and candlelight could be seen in the windows.

"This is it," Alex said.

"If it was so close, why did we not stay here for the night?"

"Because I did not trust you, and I would not put my friends in needless danger."

Until the attack, she had not considered that the Rood put them at risk. Assuming the relic's whereabouts were still a secret, she only feared for the things anyone traveling would, such as being set upon by thieves.

"Just answer me this, Isobel. Did David entrust you with the relic?"

"Of course. It's destined for safe keeping on Iona. I am but its escort."

" 'Tis as much as I suspected, but I wanted to know for certain."

"Surely you do not think I stole it." *How could he think such a thing?*

She must have worn her emotions on her face, for Alex reached for her hand, taking it in his, and whispered, "I know you are no thief, Isobel. I never thought you were, but I wanted to hear the truth from your own lips."

She nodded.

"Come," he said, his hand still locked in hers. They continued on; the mare trotted beside them.

Before they reached the cottage, Alex whispered for her to hold back and handed the reins of the mare to her. He walked several paces ahead of them and whistled. He repeated the same notes twice before the door to the cottage opened and a man holding a lantern whistled back.

"Let's go," Alex said. They walked up to the timber house, and he clasped hands with the man at the door.

Isobel watched intently as the men greeted each other and then a woman appeared in the doorway. She looked to be no more than a few years older than herself, with blonde hair and a broad smile covering her welcoming face. She embraced Alex with a hug and kissed him on the cheek.

"This is Isobel," Alex said, offering no more information.

"Greetings, my lady," the woman said with a slight bow. "I am Katherine, and this is my husband, Thomas."

"It's a pleasure to meet you both."

Katherine moved aside and invited Isobel in. Isobel obliged her and stepped inside the cottage. The kitchen and seating area were close to the hearth, which was centered in the room. The furnishings were plain but well built. Aside from a single painting on the wall near their table, the only decoration was a grouping of small ceramic vases on a shelf. They held a collection of dried wildflowers. The mint-laced scent of hyssop and the floral notes of lavender wafted from the dried herb collection hanging from the rafters. Another shelf near their straw bed brimmed with small bunches of herbs. At first, she thought they were for cooking, but with such a number and variety, it seemed more likely they would be used in the healing arts. *Is she a healer?*

"Sit, please." Katherine waved her to one of the thatched stools near the fireplace. "I'll prepare some food and drink."

Isobel said her thanks, and Alex remained by the door speaking with Thomas. Seated, Isobel took stock of her hosts. Katherine's pale blonde hair was tied back in a bun. She brushed a loose strand behind her ear before she lifted the kettle over the fire. Isobel shifted her stool back, so Katherine could work freely before the hearth. In the light of the freshly stoked fire, the woman's warm hazel eyes sparkled and her fair skin glowed.

Her husband's hair was dark brown, and he bore the tanned skin of someone who labored outdoors. The contrast between the two men was evident as they stood talking together. Thomas had some attractive qualities, but she wouldn't say he was classically handsome. Not like Alex. Thomas was the listener in the conversation with her companion, nodding his head and only speaking a few words here and there. He was reserved, she decided, as Alex approached her.

"You'll be safe with Katy and Tom," he assured her. He set his leather bag on the floor then said his goodbyes to Thomas and Katherine and walked out the door.

Her hosts looked at her expectantly, and Isobel felt an unbearable pressure in her chest. *He didn't say goodbye.* Isobel tried to ignore that gnawing feeling in her heart. *It doesn't matter. We don't need to say goodbye. But what if he doesn't return?*

"I forgot to tell him something," Isobel said to Katherine and Thomas before rushing out the door. She caught up with Alex in the middle of the pasture.

"What's wrong?"

She felt foolish for chasing after him, but she wouldn't back down now.

"You're going into battle," she began.

"I'm nae going into battle, Isobel. I'm going after one man." Alex frowned.

"I know, but after what happened by the loch—"

"A man could do without so many reminders of his failings."

"I didn't mean to—" All she wanted to do was say goodbye, but somehow she kept saying the wrong thing.

"Isobel, the thief could have traveled miles by now. I must hurry if I'm going catch him."

"Of course, I just—"

He shifted on his feet and glanced to the woods before looking back at her, showing his impatience. Isobel knew she was wasting precious time, but she couldn't leave things like this. She launched herself against his chest and wrapped her arms around his neck, dangling nearly a foot off the ground. Almost instantly, his solid arms wrapped around her waist, and she was surrounded by his warmth.

She held onto him as though he was a lifeline, the only thing keeping her grounded to the earth. He smelled of cloves, pine, and something intrinsically male—a powerful combination. Isobel savored his scent as she pressed her cheek to his neck.

"I'll be fine, Isobel. I'll come back," he assured her.

"I know," she whispered. He still held her tightly, but she needed to let him go. Before she could think on the repercussions, she kissed his neck, letting her lips linger against his warm skin. He stiffened and she wondered what could happen next, but the moo of a cow brought her back to the moment and the urgency of their mission. She quickly released him, as though she'd touched fire, but he held on, gently setting her back on solid ground. She looked up at the fierce crusader before her; his expression was unreadable, but the tension between them was easy to recognize. Before she could do anything else foolish, she fled.

Chapter 11

Alex stood dumbfounded as Isobel ran back to the cottage. She'd kissed him. Yes, on the neck, but she'd still kissed him. *What the hell was she thinking? And what the hell was I thinking?* He had that bastard to catch up with, and he was standing in a field looking longingly after a woman.

Alex was grateful she'd agreed to stay behind. He needed to focus on the new mission, not be distracted, and Isobel was definitely a distraction. He wouldn't fear for her safety either—Katy and Tom would take good care of her.

The grazing cow nearby snorted as it munched on the dewy morning grass. The interruption cleared Alex's mind and reminded him of the immediacy of his duty. With one final glimpse at the cottage, he turned and ran into the forest.

****

Robbie could run no farther. The pain in his side had left him weak, and the forest seemed to spin around him. He recognized the signs that he was going to pass out and managed to hunker down against the trunk of a tree before he fell. He finally allowed himself to inspect the wound. His tunic was matted down with blood. Bracing for the worst, he pulled the fabric back and examined the wound on his stomach. She'd stabbed him with only a small dagger, but he could tell the cut was deep. The blood was still pulsating from the wound; he needed to make the bleeding stop.

Robbie grabbed for the knife he kept at his side and cut through the fabric of his tunic. Once he'd cut several strips, he folded one into a square and pressed it against his stomach.

"Christ."

He inhaled and exhaled sharply as the pain intensified. As he swallowed back a wave of nausea, he made quick work of binding his side. With one last look around the forest floor, he succumbed to the blackness.

****

Alex was in luck. He'd picked up the trail easily back at their campsite along the loch and followed it several miles east through the forest. Initially, he'd regretted leaving the horse behind. He could have traveled faster, but he might have missed the trail. He needed to be on the ground to track. At first there had been no blood, but into the third mile, he'd spotted drops on the underbrush and ground. As the drops became closer and closer together, Alex slowed his pace. *The thief must have stopped to tend the wound. He couldn't keep going like this.* Alex searched the trees for signs of the man. Just as he was about to move on, he heard a soft moan. He listened carefully and heard it again. *'Tis not a moan. It's a snore.*

Alex cautiously walked around the trees, following the sound of the sleeping thief. He found him out cold, with his tunic soaked in blood.

Alex searched around the man and found Isobel's cloak tucked under his legs. With extreme care, Alex pulled the garment out from underneath the wounded thief and inspected it for the Rood. His breath caught when he found the box tucked safely inside an inner pocket.

"Thanks to God."

Alex silently backed away from the man, preparing to turn and run, but something made him stop. He glanced back at the warrior. Judging by his looks, the man appeared close to his own age. His clothes were worn, but his weaponry was well made. It confirmed his suspicion that the man was a mercenary. Not many would respect a hired sword, but Alex did. Alex's uncle was an elite gallowglass warrior, part of an army of Irish warriors contracted by feuding kings and clans. His skill with a sword was unmatched by any other MacKinnon; Alex had strived to become his equal. Something he still couldn't claim to have achieved.

"Ah, hell," Alex muttered, running a hand through his unkempt hair. *I could leave him for dead.* On Crusade, he'd seen countless warriors cut men down but not finish them. The sight was worse than seeing the dead. The horror in the eyes of those close to death would carry with him all his days. He'd not leave a man near the end. He'd kill him or help him.

And Alex could not justify killing him. He'd stolen the Rood and given Alex a good beating, but the man did not harm Isobel and he hadn't mortally injured Alex, something he could have easily done when Alex was knocked out cold at the campsite. The man was a thief, but he was no murderer. Though the penalty for stealing in David's court would land your head at the Mercat Cross, Alex never felt the punishment was equal to the offense.

Alex sat down on a fallen log near the man and studied him carefully. He checked the wound on the thief's side. The man was fortunate the bleeding had stopped.

Alex would learn why he'd come for the Rood and who betrayed David. With resolve, Alex bound the thief's hands and waited for him to wake.

****

Isobel was nervous. Nearly midday, and Alex was still gone. *What if he can't find the man? What if the Rood is lost forever? What if he does find the man and the man kills Alex?*

"Lady Isobel," Katherine called, interrupting her thoughts.

Isobel turned as her hostess approached carrying a tray covered with bread, cheese, and two tin cups.

"Please, call me Isobel," she offered and helped her set the tray down on the ground. After being cooped up inside all morning, Isobel had excused herself for some fresh air, promising Katherine and Thomas she'd keep to the kitchen garden off the side of the cottage. She'd found a lovely spot near the corner of the garden where she could watch the cows graze and keep an eye on the forest.

Katherine sat down beside her on the ground. "I thought you would be hungry."

"I confess I am." She helped herself to bread and cheese, savoring the taste of the freshly baked loaf and the soft blue cheese.

"Your garments are nearly dry," Katherine said.

Isobel nodded as she ate. Katherine had taken her and Alex's clothes and laundered them.

"I am ever so grateful, Katherine," Isobel said, after swallowing her food. It had been several days since her hostess at Doune washed her clothes, and she ached for a fresh gown. Normally, her dresses would not need washed so frequently, but the travel took its toll on everything.

" 'Tis nothing," Katherine said, waving her hand. "They'll be ready soon with all this sunshine and the breeze."

"I am sure Alex will be grateful too."

"Forgive me," Katherine began, "but I have to ask—" Katherine was giving her a rather peculiar stare. "What are you to him?"

"To Alex?" Isobel asked.

Katherine nodded.

"Well, he and I—" *What am I to him? Nothing. Just a task.* "He's my escort to a nunnery."

"Oh, goodness. I had this all very wrong." Katherine blushed. "I imagined you were his bride."

"No, no. I'm not—we're not." Isobel felt herself blushing too.

"Ah," Katherine said, an easy smile spreading across her face. "I see."

"See what?"

"There's clearly something between the two of you, but I suppose if you are for the cloth, then that's that."

"I am for the cloth," Isobel said. "Besides, Alex doesn't seem the marrying kind." In truth, she hadn't considered whether he was or wasn't, but she wanted to know what Katherine thought.

"He'll marry and soon. He must."

"Must?"

"He's to be chief soon and our clan—" Katherine paused, and her eyes clouded over. For one brief moment, Katherine looked as though her heart might break. "I meant his clan…" Katherine had once been a MacKinnon but was no more. "His clan is in need of—" Her eyes went wide. "I should nae speak of it."

"Speak of what, Katherine?" *What did his people need?*

"Nothing." She shook her head. "But a future chief needs a wife. He'll need heirs. Of course he will marry."

"No doubt someone has already been chosen for him then."

"Indeed, someone has been. But if you are here, I dinnae think a contract was made."

Had the mission for David cost him a bride? "I do not understand."

"I just mean Alex was to visit his betrothed before returning home. That's why I asked what you were to him. I thought you were his intended."

"Perhaps he plans to return for her later," Isobel said, trying to conceal her interest.

Katherine shrugged. "Perhaps. From what I hear, she is a fine catch."

Isobel did not know what to say. *Is Alex in love with someone? Or perhaps this woman can give his clan whatever they are lacking.* It should not matter to her, but Isobel was curious. She hated to think this mission could cost him a wife. The thought brought a lump to her throat.

"With the way he was looking at you, I wasn't certain what had passed between you both."

How does he look at me? Most of the time when he looked at her, he appeared perplexed. She did not consider herself to be a complicated woman, so those peculiar looks he gave her did not seem warranted.

Though, the other night at the fort in Doune, that look had been clear—he'd wanted her.

"Nothing has passed between us," Isobel assured her. "I've only known him a few days."

"Sometimes that is all it takes," Katherine said. "That's all it took for me to know Tom was the one."

Katherine's face transformed. Her eyes twinkled, and she wore the happiest smile Isobel had ever seen. *This woman is utterly and completely in love.*

How Isobel envied her. "You are fortunate. I know few women who would have that look upon their face when thinking on their husband."

"Is that why you have chosen the church? You have seen too many unhappy marriages?"

"No, that's not why I intend to take my vows. The church suits me," Isobel said.

"I hope it's what you really want," Katherine said. " 'Twould be awful to spend your life yearning for something that could have been."

"As I said, I've only known Alex a few days."

"It was out of place for me to say anything. I apologize for being intrusive. Alex used to always tell me I spoke too freely."

"You were curious," Isobel said. "I can understand that."

Katherine nodded and reclined against the garden fence. "Let's enjoy this fine day. I have some time yet before I need to help Tom tend the animals." She closed her eyes and tilted her face toward the sun.

While Isobel understood Katherine's curiosity, she still felt conflicted about their conversation. *She does not know me or anything about my situation with Alex.* Unfortunately, Katherine's words only affected Isobel because there was truth in them. There was something between her and Alex. She knew it from the first time they met. But falling in love with the crusader was not part of her mission. The Rood came first, and then she would decide her path forward. Besides, Alex already had someone waiting for him, didn't he? How could she let her feelings grow for a man betrothed to another?

Chapter 12

Stirling, the same day

The Duke of Lincoln's men, Rolf and Watkin, stood with the king's baker, listening to his tale of serving, they assumed, Isobel Campbell. They had needed only a few well-placed inquiries with the merchants and craftsmen to find someone who had interacted with her. The blacksmith said the king's baker spoke of a noblewoman stopping by his shop some days ago. "Brags about how much gingerbread the damn lass bought," the smith said. He wasn't wrong.

"Bought twelve dozen gingerbread slices," the baker claimed.

The English soldiers glanced at each other skeptically but urged him to continue the story.

"She then went up to the castle and met some warrior," he finished.

"How do you know the man was a warrior?" asked Rolf, the senior guardsman to the duke.

"By the way he was dressed," the baker explained. "He was a few yards off, but I could tell he carried a large sword strapped to his back. They headed off together, going northwest."

Rolf and his partner, Watkin, nodded.

"Is there anything else?" Watkin asked.

"Mayhaps," the baker said, looking down at the table in the bake shop where Rolf and Watkin had placed a few coins.

Rolf arched a brow but sat another coin down beside the rest.

"You aren't the first to ask after this lass." The baker took the coins off the table and hid them away in a pocket on the front of his apron. "Another warrior was also asking after her."

The guards knew he spoke of the bishop's man.

"Have you seen him pass by here again?" Rolf asked.

"Nae," the baker said, shaking his head.

"We thank you for the information," Rolf said, nodding to his companion. Watkin went to the shop's door and closed it. He remained facing the street, standing guard so no one else could enter.

"What's he about?" the baker asked, looking to Rolf.

Rolf ignored the question and approached the baker.

"What are ye doing?" the baker shouted.

Rolf put a hand over his mouth and reached into his apron pocket, fishing out the coins he'd just given the man. Once he'd put the coins away, he stared down at the frightened man before him. Rolf crowded him, holding his hand firmly over the baker's mouth, and backed him into the corner of the shop.

"Do all Scotsman lie?" Rolf asked, moving his hand away so the baker could answer.

"I didnae lie to ye," the baker explained, his eyes wild with fear.

"Why would a woman buy twelve dozen

gingerbread slices?" Rolf asked.

"That was just a wee bit of an exaggeration."

"What else was exaggerated?" Rolf demanded.

"Nae a word," the baker said. "I swear it."

Rolf stared down at the man for a few more moments, finally deciding that the man spoke the truth. He backed away and returned to the front of the shop. Watkin opened the door, and the men left. Climbing onto their horses, they galloped up the street heading northwest.

Chapter 13

In the forest near Loch Lomond

Around midday, the man finally came to. He struggled against the bindings but stopped when Alex pressed his sword to the center of the man's chest.

"I want answers," he said evenly, when he had the thief's attention. "Who are you?"

The man said nothing but looked Alex straight in the eye.

"Your name," he demanded.

Again, the man said nothing. Instead of pressing him for more information, Alex reclined back on the log and waited. He kept his blade out but did not extend it toward the thief.

"That's rare," Alex commented, nodding to the sword that lay beside the man. "I have not come across such fine craftsmanship since I left Skye."

The man tensed. Alex knew a few clans who called Skye home. Alex had fostered there as a child with the MacLeods, who happened to have some of the finest blacksmiths in the Isles. The man's sword also bore some Celtic ornamentation, like Alex's own sword. The Celtic design was more common in the Isles than in other parts of Scotland.

"An islander on a mission, but for whom and why?" Alex leaned forward on the log and studied the man. The man stared back, unblinking and focused. Though he fought exhaustion, he did not show any weakness. Alex admired him for it, but he was also tired and he wanted to know who was after him and Isobel. All signs pointed to Edinburgh, but he needed to know exactly who was coming for the Rood.

"I know a healer who can mend that," Alex offered, pointing his sword tip toward the man's wound. "Or we can sit out here for the rest of the day and night and let it bleed and fester until the blackness takes you."

Alex didn't expect the words to have any impact, but it seemed the injured warrior had the sense to recognize defeat and his own need for help, for he looked to Alex and said, "My name is Robbie MacDonald."

"Of the MacDonalds of Skye?"

Robbie nodded.

"Why were you after this?" Alex asked, holding up the black case that held the Rood.

"It belongs in Edinburgh."

"Who sent you?"

Silence stretched out between them, but Alex knew to be patient.

"The bishop," Robbie finally said.

Alex had never seen or met the man, but he knew he was a powerful figure in Scotland.

"You did not finish me off or kill the lass. Why?" His gut told him this man was not evil, but something was pushing him to help the bishop.

Robbie shrugged.

"What is he offering you in return for bringing this back?" If Alex hadn't been watching carefully, he would have missed the flash of pain in the man's eyes. *It's personal.* "You've put me in a difficult position, MacDonald."

In battle, Alex did not question whether his enemy was a good man or a bad man. He was commanded to destroy, and he destroyed without pause. But now Alex could ask questions, and he could see that this MacDonald of Skye was not a bad man.

Alex's hands were stained with the blood of too many souls. He promised himself when he returned from Crusade he'd be different. He would no longer kill without justification.

"You will not die by my hand today, MacDonald. But I will have your word that you will not try to take this case again."

"I cannae make that promise."

"What does he have on you?"

Again, he was met with silence. His first priority was to safely deliver Isobel to Iona. Having learned of the Rood, he had the added duty of protecting what she carried. This man fully intended to take the Rood. It was simple: Alex needed to remove the threat. He frowned back at the injured man before him.

"I can help you. I'm Alexander MacKinnon of Mull."

"You cannae help me."

"I know someone who can help." Just then, a horse neighed nearby. "Is that yours?"

Robbie nodded.

"It would be painful to ride with that injury. You wouldn't make it very far."

Alex waited as Robbie seemed to consider his options. After a few moments, Robbie asked, "Who is this healer you spoke of?"

****

"He's returned," Thomas called from outside. At his words, Isobel dropped the gown she'd been folding and rushed out the door. Katherine followed.

"Where?" she asked him, scanning the horizon.

"There." He pointed to the forest's edge.

In the distance, Alex and a man on horseback approached. The man held his side. He was the one who'd taken the Rood.

When Alex and the man crossed into the garden in front of the cottage, Alex said, "This is Robbie MacDonald of Skye." He helped the man down from the horse and seated him on the low stone wall surrounding the garden. Tom took the reins and tied up the horse.

"Tom and Katy, I have a favor to ask." Alex took them a few paces away.

As they spoke, Isobel studied the man. *He's young.* She wouldn't put him past her by many years. When he'd fought Alex and captured her, she hadn't assessed any of his facial features. She could barely remember what he'd looked like—it all happened so quickly. Now, in the calmness of the late afternoon, she took in his appearance. From the look of his physique, he was a warrior, like Alex. His hair was black, and he wore it short, just past his ears. What she noticed most about him were his eyes—a silvery blue. They looked cold and remote.

The MacDonald of Skye glanced at her briefly but looked away and grasped his side. *That's where I wounded him.* Before she could think more on that, Thomas and Alex returned to take the MacDonald inside the cottage, and Katherine hurried in after them. Isobel stayed behind, uncertain of what to do.

In a few moments, Alex came back outside.

"He's staying?" Isobel asked.

"Katy is going to see to his wound."

"We're helping him?" *Why on earth are we helping a thief?*

"Aye, we are," Alex said. He reached into the leather bag at his side and retrieved the black case.

"Here," he said, handing it to her. "I'm afraid your cloak was ruined; we will buy you a new one in Inverarnan."

Isobel clasped the case to her chest, feeling the weight of it in her hands. She didn't care about her cloak; she only cared that the Rood was safe. She opened the outer box to make certain the inner box that housed the relic was secure. David had sealed the Rood within the inner case for added protection. Once she was certain the Rood was as it should be, she asked, "Why did you bring him back? Why didn't you—"

She didn't say it, though she felt her meaning was clear.

"He didnae deserve it, Isobel," Alex said. "On our way here, he told me he was tasked by the Bishop of Edinburgh to return the relic. He says, in return the bishop will help his sister. She is ill."

"I see," Isobel said. "And what will become of his sister now?"

"When we reach Iona, I plan to send a healer to treat her."

"And the bishop?"

"He'll likely send someone else, but we have some time." Alex stepped closer to Isobel. "Do you know what the bishop plans?"

"He and David fought about where the Rood should be kept. David feels its rightful place is in Scotland, but the bishop wants to give it to King Stephen. He claims it will be safer there, but David thinks he is scheming for a seat at the English court."

"Aye. I asked Robbie, and there is talk that the bishop is worried about his place when David no longer reigns. It is believed he is trying to gain favor with the English king."

"The King of England is deeply religious. The Rood would be important to him. If the bishop took it to him, I am certain he would gain much favor with Stephen," Isobel said. "That's why I had to leave Edinburgh so quickly. The night before my departure, David caught someone in Holyrood Abbey. The person was cloaked, but the trespasser was trying to break into the vault that housed the Rood. David frightened him off but was unable to catch him. He felt the person was sent by the bishop, though he had no proof.

"David and I discussed concerns over the bishop before. He desired more power. David knew the Rood needed to be moved. We just didn't anticipate it happening so quickly," she explained.

"That is why you left on your own," Alex said.

"We couldn't trust anyone," Isobel said. "That's why he sent word to you. He trusts you. He trusts me too, and I nearly failed him."

Alex took her free hand and held it gently in his palm.

It feels so natural to touch him this way.

"He knew the Rood would be in danger on this journey," Alex said. "It is my duty to protect you and, by extension, the Rood. I am the one that nearly failed him. Not you."

"You almost died," Isobel said, squeezing his hand.

Alex shrugged. "My ego is more bruised than my head. Both will heal."

Isobel smiled, though she still worried for what could have been. *He's alive. I'm alive. And the Rood is safe for now. That is all that matters.* She glanced across the garden, the beautiful black horse catching her eye.

"She's a fine horse."

"Aye. She was tied up near where I found Robbie. He must have stashed her away before he approached our camp."

The mention of their campsite from last evening made Isobel's stomach sour.

"Do you think I was wrong in defending myself?" she asked. It had not occurred to her the man stealing the Rood was doing so to save his sister; now the pain of her actions was sinking in.

"Nae, lass. You were right to defend yourself. You did not know his intent or the cause for his actions. He was a threat."

"I could have killed him," Isobel said. Even though she'd likely taken the life of that man in the forest near Stirling, this felt different.

"He was trying to take the Rood, Isobel. You were protecting it at all costs, as you should."

"But if he's just trying to help his ill sister—" The situation was so muddled. She could not see a clear right or wrong, but surely someone was right and someone was wrong. *Perhaps I could have used less force with the man. I could have stopped him without the knife.* "I did not know."

"It is all right," Alex said.

"No. It's not. He isn't some evil henchman. He's a man trying to help his sister."

"Did he tell you that when he was trying to steal the Rood?"

"Of course not," Isobel said, perplexed.

"Nae, well, you were acting on a threat. On Crusade, I fought against countless men. Men who were husbands, sons, brothers, and fathers. Honorable men," Alex explained. "When we do battle against the enemy all we can see is the threat. We dinnae ask questions nor do we judge. We act. That's battle, Isobel. It may not be moral or right, but that's how it is."

"Is that how you justify what you've done? By saying that it is how things must be?"

Alex didn't respond. He took a deep breath and looked up at the sky. "We've a long journey yet. Get some rest, Isobel."

He left her then and went back into the cottage. Isobel remained outside and looked out into the pastureland. Around her, all was calm. She envied the stillness of the grazing cows and the distant rose-purple heather blossoms that swept across the ground like a wave at sea. She wanted to feel as peaceful as the landscape around her, but inside she felt worn and confused.

****

Later that night, Alex sat with Robbie outside the cottage. They shared a skin of ale and gazed up at the pink and purple sky as the sun reached for the darkness.

"It's the Holy Rood of Scotland," Alex said, handing Robbie the ale.

"Scotland's most cherished relic."

"Aye, it is," Alex agreed.

"More men will come for it," Robbie said. "The bishop is greedy, and his pockets are deep. You plan to take it to Iona?" Robbie took a swig of ale and handed the drink back to Alex.

Alex nodded. "That is the plan."

"It won't be safe there."

"I know it, but we have nowhere else to take it."

"He'll come for it with more force next time," Robbie added.

"I expect so. We'll do what we must to protect it." Once Alex returned to Iona, he was certain the Lord of the Isles's daughter, Bethoc, would know of a safe haven for the relic. Somerled was profoundly religious, as was his family, and they would find a way to protect the Rood. Then the concern would be in someone else's hands, and he could focus on rebuilding his clan's home. With that thought, he eyed the warrior beside him. Robbie had proved himself and Alex knew he could trust the man. He couldn't explain the connection, but he knew to rely on his instincts.

"We could use a warrior like you on Mull," Alex said.

"I don't know that a life back in the Isles would suit me, MacKinnon."

"Aye, well, you'll never know unless you try." Alex reached out, and the men clasped hands in solidarity. "The offer stands, should you ever wish for something more permanent."

Robbie nodded.

"And I'll send a physician as soon as I return. You have my word." Alex knew physicians remained at

MacKinnon Keep, for, in his last letter from his sisters, they'd written of the healers tending to his ill father.

"Thank you, MacKinnon. I am in your debt."

They walked to Robbie's horse. Alex knew the man was eager to leave, but Robbie's injury would make the ride painful.

"I think you should stay on with Tom and Katy. At least until that wound heals."

"Nae, I must be getting back. Besides, the mistress did a fine job of stitching up my side. She also gave me some medicines she thinks will help my sister. I am anxious to return to her."

"Katy worked with the healers of our clan for many years. She could be a healer in her own right."

"I think she already is. Please thank them again for me."

Alex nodded. "How will you handle the bishop? When you return to Edinburgh, he will expect a meeting."

"I'll tell him I was wounded and you both escaped," Robbie said. "Unless there is another tale you care for me to spin."

"Nae, I won't complicate things for you, but I fear his displeasure at your failure may have consequences."

"I've thought on that," Robbie said. "If I must, I'll take my family and leave Edinburgh for a time."

"Send word of where the healer can reach you. I should be back on Mull by week's end."

Robbie agreed and mounted his horse, wincing in pain as he climbed up. He held his side for a moment but recovered.

"Good luck, MacDonald."

"The same to you and Lady Isobel." With a final

nod, he cantered off into the field and disappeared into the forest.

The moon was bright, so he'd be able to see to travel. Alex and Isobel would leave soon as well. They needed to take advantage of the clear night to get closer to Oban.

He went back into the cottage and found Isobel asleep on the bed Katy had prepared for her. He gently shook her shoulder, trying to wake her, but Katy interrupted.

"She needs to sleep, Alex. You both do," she said.

"We need to journey on."

"Well, you can journey on in the morning." Her tone made it clear it wasn't a suggestion. Instead of being upset, he just smiled. He'd missed his bossy friend.

"Very well, Katy. One night and then we'll be gone in the morning."

"And I'll be happy to be rid of you, MacKinnon." She turned her face and pointed a finger at her cheek. Alex obliged and gave her a quick peck.

After saying goodnight, Alex settled in on the bed Katy had made for him in front of the hearth. Isobel was a short distance away with her feet peeking out from underneath her plaid, seeking the warmth of the burning embers in the fireplace. The fire would die soon, so Alex reached over and tucked her feet back under the plaid. A long day was finally at its end. He still couldn't believe what he'd learned. Isobel Campbell was on a mission to protect the Holy Rood of Scotland. The woman was willing to risk so much for the safety of Scotland's most cherished relic. She had great courage and unwavering determination. She was a wonder. *Aye, she is a wonder.*

****

After they broke their fast, Alex and Tom went into the garden. The ladies followed. Katherine wanted to give Isobel herbs for some basic medicines, should they have need of them on the remainder of their journey. While Isobel and Katy huddled in the kitchen garden, Alex drew Tom aside.

"I want you to take the mare, Tom."

"Why?"

"I cannae take her across to Mull. There will only be room enough for me and the lass in the boat," Alex reasoned.

"Then you'll sell her at market in Oban," Tom said.

He was a hard man to argue with, but Alex pressed on. "Tom, you know as well as I do there is little market for mares in the Isles. You'll fetch a better price for her."

Earlier, while Katherine was preparing the morning meal, she'd spoken of the rough season they'd had with the crops last year. They needed the coin, but his friend was stubborn. Tom would not take charity. To be fair, nor would Alex.

Tom glanced at Katy then back to Alex.

"Then I'll sell her and pay you on your next visit," Tom offered.

"For the trouble, you should take at least half the coin," Alex said.

" 'Tis a deal." The men reached out their hands and shook on it.

Alex gave Katy a hug and thanked her for her kindness. Isobel said her goodbyes as well. As they approached the garden gate, Katy pulled Alex aside.

"Have a care with her, Alex."

"What do you mean?"

"I mean, she has a fragile heart, and you are sure to break it if you keep looking at her the way you do."

Alex nodded, but explained, "She's safe from me, Katy. Dinnae fear. I'm not going around breaking maidens' hearts. Especially not ones destined for the church."

"She may not be as resolved for the church as you think," Katy said with a pointed look. "You need to take care."

He didn't need the warning; his journey back home was reminder enough.

Chapter 14

The sunrise was just illuminating the sky when they departed the cottage. To the east, the pink and orange hues of morning reached out from the horizon, pushing the remnants of night away. It was enough to light the trail before them. They followed the path north, which led to Inverarnan. Without the horse, it would take longer to finish this part of journey. When they broke their fast earlier, Alex explained it would be a two-day walk from Inverarnan to Oban. Katherine assured her the trail wasn't demanding; she had taken the same path when she'd come to settle near Loch Lomond many years before. Thinking back on that conversation, Isobel could no longer ignore her curiosity over Katherine's life.

"I wanted to ask…" she began, getting Alex's attention.

"Aye?" Alex glanced at her, and then focused on the path ahead.

"Katherine was a MacKinnon, wasn't she?"

Alex paused a moment, but continued walking and said, "She was the daughter of the keep's cook, and we became good friends as children."

"What caused her to leave?" Isobel knew full well it was none of her concern, but she had to know what could have separated this kindly woman from her clan.

"Katy didn't take to cooking like her father, but she

had a love for the kitchen garden. She learned how to use plants for medicine at a young age. She was gifted in healing. Some felt she was too gifted, and rumors spread of witchcraft. They thought she summoned dark spirits to help her mend the ill."

"How on earth could anyone believe such foolishness?"

"The foolishness of man knows no bounds. They could nae understand how such a wee thing could be so bright and gifted. Instead of thinking Katherine was skilled in her own right, they thought something evil gave her magical powers." Alex shook his head. "I cannae think on it without feeling angry. My father, the chief, decided the best course was to send Katy away. He turned her out from the clan when she hadn't yet seen her twelfth summer."

"Why would he abandon her? Why didn't he fight to suppress the wrongful accusations against her?"

"I pleaded with him to help her, but I was too young and my words meant nothing to him." Alex stopped walking and Isobel came to stand in front of him.

Alex's eyes were filled with emotion. It still pained him. It made her chest ache, knowing how much he cared for this woman and how he'd been unable to help her when he was a boy.

"She was cast out, along with her father, and for years I could not find a trace of them. Eventually, I learned that my mother's family, the Grahams, had brought them into their home. I had no idea Mother had worked behind Father's back to ensure Katy and her father's livelihoods."

"Your mother is a brave woman." Not many

women would go against their husband's wishes, let alone the chief's wishes. She was bold and determined, but it also spoke to Alex's mother's sense of justice and kindness.

"Aye, she was."

Isobel took that to mean she had passed.

"I never knew it until that day, but I've appreciated her for it all the days since," he said. "Thomas is a Graham as well. The clan is based nearby; I know him from when we both fostered on Skye. He and I became good friends and, as it turns out, he and Katy fell in love. They married just before I left on Crusade. Even though it has been many years since I've seen them, they are like my own kin. They'd do anything for me and I for them."

"Such friendships are rare," Isobel noted. In fact, she had never known that kind of friendship. In all her years at court, she had never found a true friend. She could laugh with the other women and make jokes with the men, but she'd never had a confidant. She envied what Alex had with Thomas and Katherine. Still, there was something curious about his story.

"You said Thomas fostered with you on Skye?" she asked.

"Aye."

"But he is a farmer now. I thought boys only fostered when they were being raised as warriors."

"Aye, well, Tom was rather terrible with a blade. In truth, he nearly cut his own limbs off a dozen times or so. Thankfully, he has a gift for growing things. I think his interest in gardening is one of the things that brought him and Katy together."

"It is a nice when a couple can share a common

bond," Isobel said. David and Mattie had shared their strong religious faith, but Isobel knew countless couples at court who seemed to share nothing between them. Save for mutual disinterest in one another.

"Aye, they have something rare," Alex said. "You'll not need to worry over that though, will you?"

"What do you mean?"

"I assume you still intend to take your vows when we reach Iona," Alex said. "Or was that part of the lie intended to keep the Rood safe?"

"Yes and no," Isobel said. Thinking of it created knots in her stomach. "It's complicated."

"Always is," Alex said, walking on. Isobel joined him. "If you're willing to tell me, we aren't lacking for time."

"I did say I'd tell you the whole truth."

"I believe you did."

"David has been preparing me to go to the church for some time," she began. "He knew once he was gone, I would have no place at court. I was not prepared for marriage, so he felt a nunnery was best. We discussed several choices, but when he learned of a new nunnery being built on Iona, he felt strongly about me going there. I wasn't prepared to take the vows then; in truth, I still don't know whether I am. But I did not want David to worry about my future. There was never a set time of when, but we both agreed sometime over the summer would make the best traveling conditions. I was meant to go with several women and guards for protection. David never intended for me to travel alone."

"But that all changed when the bishop tried to take the Rood?"

"Yes."

"Why did David not have the bishop arrested?" Alex asked.

"Several reasons, I think. The bishop is a powerful man with great influence, especially now with the council. David is also powerful, but he relies on the council for support. With his failing health, I think he worried this was something he could not resolve in time. We decided I should take the Rood and go alone to Iona."

"And then the king asked me to escort you."

"Which wasn't made known to me until the morning I left."

"Preferred to have gone it alone?" Alex questioned.

"It was enough to see I could survive on my own, but I will admit I was glad of your company after Stirling."

"You are strong, Isobel. I dinnae doubt you would have carried on well enough on your own."

Isobel was surprised to hear him say such a thing.

"But the question remains...will you take the vow?"

"I should," she said. "And you? What will the crusader do when he returns home?"

"I will return to my family's stronghold. My father's health is failing. Word reached me some months ago that I needed to return, but I could not gain passage home immediately. I've had no news of his health since returning to Scotland."

"Perhaps he is well again," Isobel offered.

Alex nodded, but Isobel could tell he doubted his father had recovered.

"You reconciled after what happened to

Katherine?"

"I never forgave him, but in time we spoke again," Alex said, adding, "We are not close."

Isobel nodded, curious about their strained relationship. "Does he have the love of your clan?"

"He has men loyal to him. As to the rest, I do not know," Alex said. "What of your parents? You have spoken little of your past."

"There is little to tell. I don't remember my parents." Isobel did not want to speak of her painful past. She'd never told it all to anyone before, not even David. Though she liked the crusader, she would not share her sad tale with him. "Was Robbie well recovered?"

Alex slowed his pace and glanced at her, noting the shift in conversation, but then his pace resumed. "Aye. Katy did a good job sewing up his side. He should be fine."

"I'm glad of it," Isobel said. "I was worried I'd seriously injured him."

"Nae. He'll mend," Alex said. "I told Robbie we could use a warrior like him on Mull. I think he'll consider it, though God help him if my sisters ever catch sight of him."

"He is handsome," Isobel admitted, then had to keep from laughing as a deep scowl appeared on Alex's face.

"Nae."

"I don't think it's a matter of opinion, Alex. The man would be considered handsome by anyone."

He looked positively disgusted. *He's jealous!* The thought delighted her to no end. As handsome as Robbie was, he wasn't for her. Alex didn't know that though, and she was enjoying the moment too much to tell him so.

"That's not what I was thinking of anyway," Alex said. "With being in charge of his siblings, including one who is ill, they'd just see him as a project. They'd want to help him."

"Would that be so bad?"

"You haven't met my sisters. I wouldn't wish their attention on anyone."

"I'm sure they mean well," Isobel said.

"I've no doubt they do, but their good deeds always end in trouble." Alex shook his head. "Especially my youngest sister, Flora. I can only imagine what she has gotten up to while I've been away."

"Perhaps she'll surprise you."

Alex shrugged. "We're nearly to the village. Remember, if anyone asks, we are married."

"Yes, husband," Isobel said, meaning to make light of things, but somehow she'd sounded perfectly serious. Alex must have noticed, because he stopped walking. Isobel turned to face him. He was looking at her in the most peculiar way.

"I was practicing," she offered, trying to make the uncomfortable tension go away.

"Right," he said, but there was something strange in his voice. "We best get a move on. All this talking has slowed us down."

He then marched ahead of her with the purpose of a warrior going into battle. His behavior couldn't have been any odder, but Isobel followed along.

Alex was flustered. *Aye, that's the word for it: flustered.* He could not figure out this woman. What was most perplexing was her response to his question about taking the vow on Iona. She'd said, "I should," not "I will" or "yes" or "I am taking my vow." Katherine was right. She wasn't as resolved for the church as he'd previously thought. It changed everything, and yet it changed nothing. Then she'd called him "husband," and it was like a punch to his chest.

It felt right, which was wrong. It shouldn't feel right. *What has this woman done to me?* He wasn't thinking clearly. If he was thinking clearly, he wouldn't be thinking about her at all. *I am on a mission for the king. Finish it and be done with her. She isn't for me.*

He was allowing himself to become distracted, which could prove deadly. Robbie wouldn't be the only one the bishop sent. As far as he knew, more men could already be on their way. Alex needed to keep vigilant. They both did for their sake and for the Rood.

Learning about the Rood was surprising. Of all he could have imagined Isobel keeping secret, it was not that she carried with her the Holy Rood of Scotland. Though few had ever seen it, almost everyone in the Isles knew the tale of how it came to be in the hands of the Scots. That tale originated with David's mother, Margaret, who came to Edinburgh as a wealthy Saxon princess seeking sanctuary from the newly installed King of England—the Duke of Normandy. Margaret was the granddaughter of Edmund Ironside, King of England, and daughter of the exiled Edward Atheling. With her father exiled, she was born and raised as a princess in Hungary, but her mother wished her for a life of devotion to the Christian faith and so she was taught by Benedictine nuns. Eventually, she and her family returned to England for her brother, Edgar, to claim the English throne. The legend was, when she came to the Isles she possessed part of the True Cross, though how it came to her in Hungary was unknown.

Alex recalled the events that led to Margaret seeking sanctuary in Scotland. No doubt it had a great deal to do with politics and power and the Duke of Normandy's fear of an uprising of support for the young Edgar. What was more of a mystery was how Malcolm Canmore, King of Scots, won over his future bride. One of Margaret's ladies claimed the princess refused the king a dozen times, but in the end, she took him as her husband.

He guessed Isobel would know more of the story. He slowed his steps until they walked in unison once more. "I was thinking of all I know of the Rood, and it has me wondering about something."

"What is it you want to know?"

"Why did Margaret marry Malcolm?"

"She loved him," Isobel said.

"She loved him?"

"Yes."

Alex came to a halt; Isobel stopped beside him.

"That's the only reason?" Alex was dumbfounded.

"Is that not reason enough?" Isobel gave him a sideways glance and continued walking.

"That's not why people marry," Alex said, catching up with her. "People marry for land, for coin, or for alliances."

"Is that why Thomas and Katherine married?"

"I'm not talking about them," Alex said.

"Are they not people?"

"I meant to say people in power. Tom and Katy

119

could marry for love. Margaret was a princess. Princesses don't marry for love."

"She did," Isobel said. "And what about you, Alex? Will you marry for love?"

The question surprised him, though with Isobel nothing should have surprised him. He'd stopped walking again and found himself standing a foot away from her. Isobel had paused on the trail as well, fixing those violet eyes on him. He wanted to look away from her scrutiny. Even when he was certain his face would give nothing away, the grin in her eyes told him she saw everything.

"I don't know," he said and walked on.

Isobel was not a romantic. At least, she had never considered herself to be one. She did not believe in the fairy tales Mattie told her as a child, and she had never dreamed of a wealthy nobleman falling in love with her or she with him. But she did believe in love, and she believed that people should marry for love.

Margaret married Malcolm for love, not for safe sanctuary (as many assumed). David married Mattie for love, not for her dowry (as some assumed). Isobel knew what love looked like between husband and wife. Even so, she understood many people did not marry for love. Still, Alex's admission saddened her. *Is he uncertain because his mission for the king could have spoiled the contract with his intended? Is their journey costing him marriage to the one he loved?* She could not stand the idea of being the cause of someone's unhappiness.

I don't even know if the man is in love. I am assuming too much.

But then she thought of what Katherine had said or, rather, what she almost said. Alex's clan needed something. It may not be a love match at all. After his talk of people in power not marrying for love, it would make sense. He, a son of a chief, would soon be head of his clan. He would then be in a position of power. "People marry for land, for coin, or for alliances," he'd said. Which of those did his future bride offer?

Chapter 15

Inverarnan

Isobel sat watching the commotion on the muddy street below the window of their tiny room at the inn. They had arrived a short time ago, and Alex was at the market gathering supplies for the remainder of their journey into Oban.

A knock sounded at the door. Alex wouldn't be back so soon.

"Who is it?"

"The maid, ma'am. Yer husband asked to send up mead before he left."

Isobel opened the door cautiously; a maid with a serving tray greeted her on the other side. The petite woman swept into the room and gently sat the tray on a small wooden table near the hearth.

"The biscuit bread is fresh. Cook just baked 'em," she said and smiled.

"It smells wonderful," Isobel said. "Thank you."

"Ye are verra welcome," the maid said but didn't move for the door.

"Is there something else?"

"Nae, ma'am. Sorry. I should be on m'way." She hurried for the door but paused again.

Isobel waited expectantly, curious about this woman's behavior.

"Been a maid here fer going on three years, and I ne'er had a husband request mead fer his lady. Lucky to hae him, ye are," she said, her heavy accent could not mask her wistful tone.

Though the maid's words would be out of turn if Isobel was a princess living in David's court, she couldn't help but agree. "He is thoughtful."

"And handsome!" the woman gushed. "Oh, nae! I've said too much. Begging yer forgiveness. I'll be on m'way." With an awkward bow, the maid dashed out the door, banging it closed behind her.

Isobel shook her head, wondering if Alex had left lovesick maidens across the Mediterranean. That, of course, prompted her to wonder, *Have I left anyone lovesick?*

As she sat down by the fire to pour herself a cup of mead, she thought back on the men who could have been considered suitors at court. A few men had taken a liking to her, but they were all motivated for reasons other than genuine interest. Some thought her connection to the king made her a useful pawn. Even though no one knew of the dowry and lands attached to her (something David insisted on keeping private for her own protection), some men sought to use her to gain favor with the king. Others wanted her for her physical attributes. Isobel knew she was attractive. She didn't boast about it, but it also seemed silly to pretend she didn't realize her features made her appealing to men. She knew an attractive woman at court who pretended she thought herself ugly to gain flattery. Isobel would have none of it. She did not need the honeyed words of conceited men to know her true value and qualities. Nor had she used her feminine qualities to manipulate others. She honestly didn't know how, and she didn't desire anything of the men at court.

Isobel was sure of many things, but she had to admit life in David's court had been surprisingly sheltered. She didn't just mean in the sense of male and female interactions. She did not know much about life in Scotland. There was so much she wanted to learn. Would she be able to learn it all from a nunnery? Nuns were secluded from society; they were not out among the people. She wasn't even certain if they were allowed to read, and reading was her greatest passion. Leaving Edinburgh had meant parting with David's priceless collection of books. In choosing the church, she would also forfeit her dreams of travel—of exploring the Isles.

Two thoughts struck her: *How much of myself must I give up? Should I not yearn for the life of a nun if it is my destiny?*

Isobel had reasoned for a long time that uncertainty was natural. Fear of the unknown and of making a lifelong commitment made her hesitant. That is what she told herself when David spoke of his hopes for her in the church.

Yet, it had never felt right. Did it make it a sin to take the vows without truly knowing if it was right for her? But what if it felt right in time? What if the sacrifices were worth it? Only time would reveal the truth. The question was if she was willing to move forward with hope for a change of heart later on.

Sighing, she slumped in her seat. Isobel finally lifted the cup to her mouth and took a sip. The cold drink felt unsatisfying. She reached for the biscuit bread, but it had gone cold. She sat the cup down on the tray and looked back out the window into the gray afternoon sky.

****

Alex returned from the market in time to catch the evening meal being served in the downstairs of the inn.

"Plenty more for ye and yer wife, MacKinnon," called the innkeeper.

"We'll be down together shortly," Alex replied, heading for the steps. The smell of roasted mutton followed after him, causing his stomach to growl. He'd spent so long at the market, he'd lost track of time. But his efforts were rewarded in finding exactly what he wanted.

He knocked on the door to the room he shared with Isobel. Moments later, the door swung open, and Isobel welcomed him back.

"Did you get all the supplies we'll need for the journey to Oban?"

"Aye." Alex sat his acquisitions down on the floor but kept one item tucked under his arm. "I'm sure it is not as fine as the one you had, but I hope it will do." He handed the cloth wrapped article to her.

"Is it a new cloak?" Isobel asked.

Alex nodded as she carefully unwrapped it. At first, he couldn't read her expression, but then her lips parted and her eyes widened. *Is she shocked by its ugliness?* While Alex knew very little of female garments, he thought the cloak was fine.

"Is it to your liking?" Alex asked. "I'm sure we can trade it for another if it displeases you."

"It's beautiful," Isobel exclaimed. " 'Tis the color of wine."

"I thought it would bring out the violet of your

eyes," Alex said.

"You noticed my eyes?"

"How could I not notice such rare and stunning eyes?" He immediately regretted his words when he saw her eyes light up from the compliment. Alex remembered Katy's warning. He needed to be careful. "Anyone would notice them," he added. "Not just me."

"I see," she said.

"I had them add a special pocket, like you had on your last cloak for the Rood." He stepped forward and reached for the cloth. "See here," he said, pointing it out.

"Aye, 'tis very thoughtful," she said. "Thank you, Alex."

"Aye?" he asked. "Is my Scots Gaelic rubbing off?"

"I suppose it is." Isobel smiled.

Alex couldn't help but grin. *By the journey's end, she just may pass for an islander.* The thought of reaching Iona left him feeling strangely empty. When their journey was over, he'd no longer have cause to see Isobel. He enjoyed her company. He would miss her.

She is part of the mission, he reminded himself. *I cannot have feelings for part of the mission.* He was a warrior. Alex knew better than most how to keep his heart out of the mix.

"We should go down for the evening meal." *And for a few glasses of ale,* he thought, as they walked downstairs.

****

After their meal, they returned to their room, and Isobel set about organizing her belongings. Alex watched with interest as she shook out her garments and refolded them with precision, tucking in sprigs of lavender as she went about the task. Katy must have given her the lavender. A clever way to keep her clothes smelling fresh. When she came to the cloak, her hands swept over the decorative needlework around the collar. It had cost a small fortune. Alex knew he should have kept the money for his clan. He did not know what conditions he'd return to, but he felt certain circumstances would be as he left them or worse. Yet, when he'd gone to the market and looked at all the cloaks the dressmaker had to show him, that purple cloak caught his eye. He imagined Isobel standing on the sandy beaches of Iona, the purple cloak tied around her, and her violet eyes sparkling as she gazed out over the sea.

Isobel tucked the Rood's case into the hidden pocket, and then carefully laid the cloak over the stool near the hearth.

"We should rest," she said. "You planned for us to leave early in the morn. The better rested we are, the greater progress we shall make."

"Agreed," Alex said, taking one last sip of ale from the flagon he'd brought up to the room.

"I'd like to change." She twirled her pointer finger in the air, and Alex took her meaning. He turned and faced the wall. A few moments later, he heard her climb on top of the bed.

"You can turn back now," she said. She'd pulled the blankets up to her chin. One would think winter was upon them and not the start of summer.

Alex reached for his bag and pulled out his plaid. He eyed the floor of the small room with a frown for there was no space for him to lie down.

"You might as well sleep on the bed too," Isobel said.

"Nae, the floor is fine. I just need to move the furniture around a bit."

"It'll be our last night of comfort until we make the crossing to Mull," she argued. "It makes no sense for you to sleep on the floor."

"All right." Alex took off his boots and pulled out the knives he had tucked around his waist but left his clothing on. He climbed onto the narrow bed, the straw compressing beneath his weight and stretched out alongside Isobel.

"You don't want to lie underneath the blankets?" she asked.

"Nae. I'm not cold."

They lay together in silence for some time before Isobel spoke.

"When I was younger, David taught me to read in many languages," she began. "I can read English, Scots Gaelic, and Latin. Even some Italian."

"That's impressive." He knew no other woman with such an ability. "I must admit I can only read some English."

"You speak it well," Isobel said. "I noticed you use a mix of Scots Gaelic and English when you talk."

"I suppose that's a result of keeping company with so many English on Crusade," Alex said. "But speaking it is different from writing it."

"It is," she agreed. "In my case, it seems a waste. I can read like a scholar, but I cannot be one."

"Is that what you wish to be?"

"I wish to be useful," Isobel said. "I wish to use the bounty of knowledge I have learned under David's tutors and be a help."

"Can you nae help as a nun?" Alex asked. "I know little of the new nunnery—it wasn't even there when I left—but I know the monks at Columba's monastery are well educated. They even transcribe books."

"Nuns are not like monks in that regard. I have met many in my travels of religious sites with David, yet I know few who are educated or skilled with languages."

"You could be the exception then," Alex said. "And if they don't want your knowledge there, you could come teach my sisters. I can think of nothing else they desire more than an education."

Alex turned onto his side so he could face Isobel, and she turned to face him.

"I would not be allowed to teach your sisters as a nun, Alex."

"Why not?"

"Nuns on Iona are cloistered. They are not allowed among the people. Once I go there, I will never be permitted to leave."

"That cannae be true."

"I'm afraid it is," she said.

"Perhaps you could transcribe books, as the monks do."

"Perhaps," Isobel said, turning away.

Alex could tell by how she spoke she did not believe it would happen. A woman of her knowledge should not be kept away from society. She could do so much to enrich the lives of the people around her.

"I wish Margaret were alive. She would know how to counsel me, just as she did David."

"Aye, I'm sure she could have."

Queen Margaret had passed before Alex was even

born, but his grandfather met Malcolm and Margaret in Dunfermline, when the abbey there was consecrated. Alex could still remember his grandfather's description of the fair queen. "She glowed, like the sun, and I never saw light in a person like that before or since," he'd told Alex when Alex had been but a wee lad. There were so few memories he held of his grandfather, but the old man's reverence for Queen Margaret stuck in Alex's mind.

"You won't dishonor him, if you choose another path," Alex offered.

"What do you mean?" she asked, turning to face him once more.

"I mean, just because this is what King David wants does nae mean he will be disappointed if you decide this isn't your path."

"There are few paths for a woman, Alex. Trust me. I thought of this often enough."

"Think on it some more. You need to be certain."

"I will," Isobel said. "Deciding one's future is never easy, is it?"

"Nae, I don't think it's supposed to be."

"And what about you?" she asked. "Have you decided on your future?"

"What?"

"Have you decided what to do about your intended?" she asked.

"My intended?" Alex was confused.

"Katherine told me you were intended for some woman. She said you were meant to see her before returning home. I feared this mission ruined your chances with her."

Leave it to Katherine to tell Isobel tales of the

Angus bride. Though she is not my Angus bride anymore. Knowing Katherine had spoken about her, Alex was concerned about what all she'd revealed.

"Did she tell you why I was marrying her?"

"No," Isobel said. "Though, she may have implied this woman could provide something your clan needed."

"But she did not say what?"

"No."

At least Katherine had spared him the humiliation of confessing his clan's dire situation, though he should be angry she had divulged anything about it. He did not need Isobel knowing any of this, but now that she had some knowledge of it, he was unsure of how to reply.

He could tell Isobel the truth—the Angus woman was no longer his intended—but letting her believe it kept much needed distance between them. His clan was without means. What could he offer her besides hardship? *Better to let her think I have someone.*

"She may yet wait for me," Alex said. "But there is nothing to be done about it until I return home."

"I hope you can find happiness, Alex," Isobel said. She sounded so sad. It was all Alex could do to keep himself from telling her the truth.

Stay firm, Alex. It is better for her to believe this.

"I hope you find happiness as well, Isobel." He wanted to reach out and comfort her, but touching her would do neither of them any good. Before he could change his mind, she turned and faced away from him.

After several minutes passed by, her breathing steadied. Certain she was asleep, he reached out and gently placed his hand on her arm. He inhaled her scent—heather and lavender—and sighed deeply, letting his eyes finally drift closed.

Chapter 16

Edinburgh Castle, late that same evening

Robbie stood in Margaret's chapel waiting for the bishop. King David had built the chapel as a private place of worship for his family and later dedicated it to his mother, Queen Margaret. The space was small but peaceful. He used the quiet time alone to contemplate his words to the bishop. He risked his life in coming empty-handed, but he had no choice. Failure to make an appearance when summoned would rouse suspicion, and the bishop would send more men when he learned of Robbie's failure. In truth, he probably already knew Robbie did not carry the Rood. Guards had searched Robbie upon entry to the castle. He brought nothing with him, save for a knife.

The door to the chapel opened, and Robbie straightened his spine. The bishop had arrived.

"My men told me you were unsuccessful," the bishop said.

Robbie nodded.

"I'm disappointed." He was eerily calm and even toned, but the man radiated displeasure.

Robbie explained what transpired, leaving out all the details he could. When spinning a lie, it was best to keep as much truth as possible. Robbie even showed him the wound on his side, which was healing well thanks to Katherine.

"Bested by a woman? Most men wouldn't believe you."

"Most men wouldn't own up to it," Robbie countered.

The bishop nodded. "That is true." He paced around the small stone room, then paused to say, "Considering where you caught them, it seems they mean to take it to Iona. 'Tis well then I sent two more men after her. They were only a few days behind you. 'Tis likely they have found the Rood."

"You thought I would fail?" Robbie hadn't expected another team to be sent so quickly. The MacKinnon and Lady Isobel were in danger.

"I plan for mistakes," the bishop said simply. "I'm afraid this means I won't be able to help your sister after all."

Robbie nodded. He knew what he sacrificed, but he also trusted the MacKinnon. He would send a healer, as he promised.

"You may also have trouble finding anyone else to hire you."

"What do you mean?" He narrowed his eyes at the bishop.

"You should have known there would be repercussions for failure. I suggest you leave the city. There is no hope of finding someone that will hire your sword in Edinburgh."

The threat was clear. Robbie needed to get his family out of the city and soon.

Robbie wasted no time getting home. He rented rooms above the tailor. They were humble lodgings but safe, and that mattered a great deal when he traveled for work. Once inside the door, he called for Murdoch.

"How's Agnes?" he asked, when his younger brother appeared.

"Better. Her breathing is steady, and she hasn't coughed since you gave her that medicine earlier."

"That's good to hear," Robbie said. "I think she'll be well enough to make the journey."

"Make what journey?"

"We need to leave the city."

"Why? What's happened?"

"Nothing," Robbie said. He didn't want to alarm the lad, but they needed to leave as soon as possible. "We're moving back to the Isles. There is a healer there that can help Agnes and a clan that has need of my sword."

"And me? What about me?" Murdoch asked.

"You'll train with the clan's men," Robbie assured him. Murdoch had wanted this for years. Because of their situation, he could not let Murdoch go off and foster. The lad was determined to be a great warrior, and it infuriated him that he could not train as one. He'd just seen his fifteenth year. He was young yet, but old to be begin training.

"You mean it, Robbie? You'll let me train?"

"Aye, you'll train with the best warriors in the Isles."

Murdoch launched himself against Robbie's chest. Robbie embraced him in a hug and laughed. He'd never seen him so happy before.

Pulling away, Murdoch's brows knitted together in concern. "I don't have much to pack, but I best get to it. Will you see to Agnes?"

"Aye, get going. I want to leave at daybreak."

Robbie gathered his and Agnes's possessions and tucked them into a few bags. Aside from his weaponry and some clothing, Robbie had very little to his name. Agnes had a few simple gowns and her needlework, which she worked at most days. Everything else in their rooms was rented from the tailor. Though never easy to start again, they would do it, as they'd done before.

When Murdoch and Agnes were ready, Robbie loaded up Coira with their belongings and they began the journey west to Mull. Once they were safely out of the city, Robbie would ride ahead to warn MacKinnon. He prayed it would not be too late.

Chapter 17

The two-day journey between Inverarnan and Oban was uneventful. They'd spoken very little, and a solemn cloud seemed to hang over them both. Alex was quiet, with a furrowed brow. He was conflicted, and she felt certain his turmoil was over his intended bride. She yearned to discuss it with him, but she could find no cause to do so. *He is my escort to Iona. His marriage does not concern me. But what if he is conflicted over his marriage because of his interest in me? Surely the tension between them was not one-sided. Perhaps it is just physical attraction and nothing more.* Isobel sighed deeply. *How could something unspoken be so complicated?*

The town was a welcome distraction from the flurry of thoughts consuming her. The seaside village was brimming with activity, but there was little time to explore. Isobel stood by the dock, where their newly chartered boat waited. The air was salty and fishy, and the wind cut off the water, but Isobel drank it in. They were close now. Soon the relic would be safely in the hands of the nunnery's prioress. She felt relief, and yet her insides fluttered. The sooner she reached Iona, the sooner she had to make a choice.

She looked to Alex. He stood bartering with a baker. He returned with a loaf of bread for their journey across Mull, and something else wrapped in cloth.

"I was surprised he had it," Alex said, as he handed the cloth to her.

Curious, Isobel unfolded it and found two slices of gingerbread.

"I thought you liked it," he said, sounding uncertain.

"It is my favorite." Isobel couldn't believe his thoughtfulness. "But why?"

"We should all have some comforts from time to time."

He wanted her to be happy. "Thank you, Alex. 'Tis very kind."

"You are welcome, Isobel." Alex smiled, before letting the warrior façade fall back into place. He looked to the sea. "The winds are favorable; we should depart soon for Duart Keep."

****

"Surely you cannot row straight for three hours," Isobel said in shock as Alex helped her board the small watercraft.

"I'm an islander. I can row all day."

"Are you gloating, islander?"

"*Glotta*," Alex said. "That's the Old Norse word for it, and aye, I am." He grinned as he pushed the boat into the water and jumped aboard.

"You won't be grinning at the midday meal."

"I'm sure you are right, lass, but for now, I'm doing just fine."

And he was, to Isobel's astonishment, doing just fine. He cut through the waves as though they were nothing. Favorable winds were something to be grateful for, though, and aided their journey considerably. Isobel admired the green-blue sea around her. Though she'd lived close to the North Sea in Edinburgh, she was rarely by the water. The beauty of the landscape here was unparalleled by anything she'd seen before. Distinct from the eastern shoreline in so many different ways. She was also surprised by the relative calmness of the seas.

"I thought the waves would be bigger," Isobel commented, after observing the breaks in the water.

" 'Tis the inner seas. They are usually much calmer than the waters out beyond the Inner Hebrides."

"What are the Inner Hebrides?" She'd never heard of them before.

"Mull, Iona, Staffa, and Skye—along with some other isles, make up the Inner Hebrides. The Outer Hebrides consists of Uist, Lewis and Harris, and a hundred or so smaller islands."

"Have you been to all of them?"

"Nae," Alex said. His muscles flexed as he lifted the oars out of the water, taking a break.

"How far west have you gone?"

"Ireland," he said. "Though it is southwest."

Isobel knew Columba had come from Ireland to create a religious community on Iona, but she knew very little of Ireland itself.

"What is it like there?" Isobel asked, interested to learn more.

"Like here but different."

Isobel frowned. That didn't tell her anything at all. "What do you mean?"

Alex relaxed his arms, pulling the oars up higher out of the water. He seemed to be thoughtfully considering her question, but then he shook his head, shrugged and continued to row.

"You should go there and learn about it for yourself," he said, after several minutes passed.

"Maybe I will," Isobel said. Once the Rood was delivered to Iona, her life was open. Anything could happen. Deep down inside of herself, she knew joining the church was not what she desired. An impossible decision, but perhaps there was another path—Ireland.

I could go west and make a life for myself there. If only she was able to obtain the land and funds promised to her if she wed or joined the church. She could not travel without means, and she would not be able to build a life for herself without coin. *I've gone mad. I cannot go off on my own in this world. I dream of foolish things that cannot be.* In truth, the idea of going off on her own was not appealing. She did not wish for isolation. She wished for a meaningful life to be shared with someone she loved. A fairy tale of the highest order, she supposed, and she was not one for fairy tales. The only problem was she'd seen the fairy tale brought to life. She had witnessed true love between two people. Seeing such happiness only made her crave it for herself.

If only she knew someone like Alex. He was kind, loyal, determined, and brave. *That's what I need. I need a man like Alex.* Isobel bit her lip. *What about Alex himself?* There was a spark there. There was no sense in denying it. *But he is intended for someone else.*

Isobel inhaled deeply and exhaled, trying to calm her thoughts. A storm brewed in her mind, yet all around her the water was calm. She looked longingly out over the sea. Birds cried and flew out beyond her sight. The gray clouds hung over them as they progressed toward Mull. Isobel turned to look back and was surprised that she could no longer glimpse the village of Oban. She faced forward once more and studied Alex. *He cannot keep this up.* Alex's breathing was loud, his face was red, and his arms were slick with sweat. She was about to tell him to slow down when he spoke up.

"We're nearly there," he said with a labored breath, nodding his head over his right shoulder.

Isobel looked beyond him. In the distance, she could make out the northeastern shoreline of Mull. Perched high above the water sat Duart Keep. The fortification was wooden, like Doune, only the keep here was nearly twice the size of Fort Doune. It afforded perfect views of the water way, which was no doubt intended.

A short time later, their boat was docked and guards escorted them to the keep. As they entered the great hall, the chatelaine greeted them.

"Mary, it is good to see you again," Alex said.

"It is good to see you too, Alexander."

The blonde woman offered him her dainty hand, and Isobel had to keep from frowning as Alex placed a light kiss upon it.

"And this must be your new wife!" The woman stepped around Alex and approached Isobel. "How is your father, the Earl of Angus?"

Isobel stood, mouth agape, looking between their hostess and Alex. *His betrothed is the Earl of Angus's daughter?* The Earl of Angus had wealth and power in the northeast of Scotland. She'd seen him in David's court on several occasions, though his daughter had never accompanied him.

"Nae, Mary. This isn't the earl's daughter. This is

Isobel," Alex said, quickly.

"It's a pleasure to meet you, Mary," Isobel said, feeling awkward.

"My apologies." The woman seemed confused, but she smiled and said, "You are very welcome here, Isobel. There is a room prepared." She turned to face Alex. "Or should I have another room readied?"

"One will do, thank you," Alex said. Isobel could have sworn his cheeks turned pink. *Is he blushing?*

"Alex, my father wants a word with you in his solar." Mary then looked to Isobel. "I will take you to the guest quarters. I'm certain the journey was tiresome."

"Indeed, though Alex did all the work bringing us over from Oban." She still marveled at his strength in rowing for hours.

"It is good those muscles you have grown have purpose beyond fighting," Mary said to Alex.

The woman took in his appearance and then, without a care for Isobel's presence, she winked at him. Winked!

"Aye, I'm no longer the lanky lad who left these shores six years ago." Alex seemed to genuinely beam at her observation of his strength.

"Nae, you are not," Mary said.

Oh, good heavens. Isobel did not want to hear what Alex would say to that, so she cleared her throat and asked, "Our room is ready, Mary?"

The woman glanced at Isobel. "Aye. I'll take you there now." Of course, that couldn't be the end of it, for she called, "See you at the evening meal," to Alex as he strode off to meet with Mary's father.

Isobel did not like the woman. Even though she

and Alex were not wed or betrothed or anything to each other, this woman did not know that. Yet, she shamelessly flirted with him in her presence. Clearly, the two had some history together. Though, Isobel reminded herself, it was just that: history.

"You must be of great import," Mary said, as they took the steps up through one of the keep's towers. "For years, everyone around here assumed he'd take the Angus daughter as his bride."

Isobel didn't respond, though she found it surprising earlier that this woman knew of Alex's betrothal. *Apparently, such things are common knowledge around here.* Mary's jealousy was evident, and she meant to take aim at Isobel.

At court, Isobel had been treated in all manner of ways. Mostly, she experienced indifference. Yet, there were a rare few instances when she had the displeasure of experiencing jealousy. Some women envied her or perceived her as a threat to their potential suitors (though her value was much less than that of David's children—after all, she was the orphan girl). There were a few ways one could react in such circumstances. Normally, Isobel would rise above it. With her temper already stirred up from the interlude in the great hall, it did not seem that today would be one of those times.

"I am of great import," Isobel said, boldly.

They continued up the stairs, walking side by side. From the corner of her eye, Isobel could see Mary's eyebrows arch.

"Then I guess you'll be the one to save his sad impoverished clan," Mary said.

Sad impoverished clan? What is she talking about? Isobel paused on the steps; Mary came to stand on the step above her.

"Oh, he didnae share that with you?" Mary grinned.

Even if what she said was true, why should she delight in it? "I am certain you are wrong," Isobel said, staring up at the woman. "The MacKinnons enjoy the favor of the king. He would reward the stewards of Iona handsomely."

"The king's had nothing to do with Iona in years. Somerled lays claim to the Isles."

"That cannot be true." Iona was holy, and David cherished all that was holy in Scotland. He would not abandon its stewards. Nor would he let someone else claim his lands.

Mary shrugged and resumed her progress up the steps. Isobel followed her. They reached the landing off the stairs, and Mary led her down the corridor to a room. Pushing open the door, she said, "You will see it with your own eyes soon enough." With that, the hateful chatelaine excused herself.

Isobel marched inside her room and closed the door firmly behind her. *Is Mary lying?* It didn't seem likely, given the pieces of information Isobel had obtained from Katherine and Alex himself. And yet, the idea of David leaving the stewards of Iona in such a state rebelled against everything she knew of the king. She would have to look into the matter once they reached Iona. Something had to be done to help Alex's clan. Once the king learned of their situation, he would do something. Yes, once she reached Iona, she'd send word to David, and all would be well.

****

Alex stood in the Maclean chief's solar rereading

the missive.

"It arrived by messenger not an hour before ye docked," the chief said. "With yer family's connection to the crown, I thought ye should know."

"I cannae believe it," Alex said. But there it was in writing. King David was dead.

"He'd been ill for some time; I think we've all been expecting it."

"In truth, he seemed well when I saw him not a fortnight ago in Edinburgh," Alex said.

"I've heard he was good at hiding it," the chief said. "His young grandson will have a hard time keeping power. It will also mean a loss of power for the MacKinnons, will it nae?"

The Maclean is digging for something, Alex thought, studying the old chief. He was around Alex's father's age and had seen at least fifty or so summers on this earth. Alex had mixed feelings about his island neighbor, but he knew the value in keeping a steady alliance with the Macleans of Duart.

"What do you mean?" Alex asked.

"I'm told ye did not bring home the Angus bride," the chief said, ignoring Alex's question. "But a woman did accompany ye. Who is she?"

Alex did not like his host's questions, so his response was evasive. "You'll meet her at the evening meal." He did not know if the chief even knew of Isobel's existence. Alex hadn't known of her, but the Maclean could be better informed. Though, if memory served correct, the Macleans never had much interest in the politics of Edinburgh nor the Scottish king. In fact, sharing the news of David's death was the first time he'd ever heard a Maclean even mention the king.

"I look forward to it," the chief said, offering Alex some wine.

Alex accepted it and raised his glass. "To the king."

"To the king," the chief repeated.

Alex downed the wine in one drink.

****

Alex went directly to the guest quarters; he did not know which room they'd been given, so he knocked on all the doors, but no one answered. He'd crossed through the great hall on his way to the stairs, so he knew Isobel wasn't down there. *Perhaps she sought fresh air,* Alex thought, heading back downstairs.

The guards in the bailey pointed him toward the sea. "She walked out there," one of the men said, pointing at the gate that led out of the fortification.

Alex nodded his thanks and hurried out the gate. He found Isobel on the cliffside overlooking the Sound of Mull. The wind blew her hair back in waves, like the sea. Her purple cloak floated in the breeze behind her, and her gray dress clung to her curves as the wind pushed against her—over her—blowing inland. He drank in her appearance, her calmness, for he knew as soon as he spoke she would no longer be at peace.

"Isobel," he called to her as he approached.

She turned and looked at him, concern instantly filling her eyes. "What is wrong?"

Her reaction was proof of how easily he let his guard down in her presence. At home, among his clan, he knew to never show anything but control. Even when times were good, he did not show relief. When times were bad, he wore the same impassive face. When he was young, his father taught him to remain

146

detached so his clansmen did not worry. On Crusade, among his fellow warriors, he maintained the same emotionless exterior. He didn't know why he couldn't do the same around Isobel.

The wind dropped, and all went quiet.

"A missive arrived from Carlisle," he began. He reached out and took her hands in his own. "King David journeyed there not long after we left. He is...The king is..."

"Dead," she finished, closing her eyes. After a few moments, she opened them but kept her gaze on the sea.

"I am sorry, Isobel. I know what he was to you."

She nodded, releasing his hands.

"What you are doing was important to him. He would have been proud."

She looked back to him. "It is not done yet."

"Nae, but we're nearly there. We'll stay a few days and then journey on to Iona." Alex felt she'd need time to rest after the news of the king's passing.

"Why the delay?"

"I thought you would be distressed..." He did not want to push her.

"The king would want the Rood to be safe, Alex. I will grieve when I have fulfilled my duty to him."

As the days passed, Alex was more and more impressed with Isobel. Nothing could break her spirit. A woman needed that kind of spirit to survive in the Isles. The sea could be cruel and unforgiving. The mistress of the MacKinnon keep would need to be brave and determined. She would need to be a fighter, like Isobel. *Like Isobel...Could she be Isobel?* Alex let the thought sink in. Isobel would make a fine mistress. She'd make a fine wife. *But she cannae rebuild the keep or the crofts. I must think of the clan.* Alex's mind would not let him dream. The needs of his clan came first. But he had to know what she would do when their journey ended.

"Isobel, what will you do after you've given Bethoc the Rood?"

"I am not certain what I will do. When my deed to David is done, I may journey on alone."

Alex looked at her sharply. "What do you mean?"

"You said I should see Ireland for myself. Why not go now?"

"Isobel, I cannae let you go off on your own." She wasn't thinking clearly.

"Your agreement was to see me safely to Iona. From there, I am none of your concern."

"I see," he ground out. He looked back toward the keep. The practicing warriors were starting to disperse.

"The evening meal will be served soon. We should go in," Isobel said.

Alex nodded curtly and followed her back inside the keep.

****

Isobel retreated to her and Alex's guest quarters. She'd told Alex she needed to freshen up for the evening meal and asked that he go to the great hall without her.

She could not believe the king was dead. He'd been ill for so long it almost seemed as though he could go on living as he was forever. *Perhaps the journey to Carlisle was too much for him.*

Now she was entirely alone in the world. She had no one. She felt small and scared, like the child she'd been when David rescued her. How distant those feelings had seemed with the passage of time, and yet that fear of the unknown was as close as ever.

Isobel didn't know why she'd told Alex she might go to Ireland. She didn't wish to travel on alone.

I would not be alone at the nunnery. There she would be surrounded by others. *But I yearn for so much more. Adventure, purpose, friendship, and perhaps even love. These are the things I desire.*

David had believed the journey would show her what she needed from this world. It had done that, but now she didn't know how to take those wants and make them part of her life.

Isobel untied her cloak and laid it gently across the straw bed, letting her hand linger over the relic's case. She would see the Rood safely to Iona, and then she would decide her future.

****

The Maclean chief was eager to hear tales from the Crusade. Alex was less than eager to share them. His mind was preoccupied with his earlier conversation with Isobel. The words "I am none of your concern" weighed on him. He should be relieved she felt that way. He should hold no obligation to her beyond his duty to King David. But knowing that the king had passed, and therefore her only family on this earth was gone, he felt responsible for her. He looked at her now, by his side, picking at her plate of food. She looked pale. Perhaps he should take her to their room to rest.

Before he could act on his thought, the chief asked, "What of Damascus? Were ye there for the siege?"

"Nae, I was part of the Christian army that laid siege to Lisbon," he said, giving his attention to the chief.

"And ye were successful?"

"It took some months, but eventually the city fell."

"Very few Scots have gone on Crusade, MacKinnon, let alone Islanders. Why did ye go? Looking for glory?"

"My mother's people, the Grahams, hail from the Trossachs. I got word from a clansman there about a fleet that was set to leave on Crusade in the spring of 1147 from Dartmouth. My obligations at home were few at the time; if I was to go, it was then or never. We traveled under the command of Saher de Archelle, an English knight."

"I've heard tell of him," the chief said. "I also heard the fleet that departed was over three hundred strong."

"The fleet was a good size, but not that great. We traveled with some one hundred fifty vessels. Our ship carried fifty men alone."

"I am surprised that many went from England and Scotland."

"The men also came from the east—Flanders, Cologne."

"Ye had a strong force then?" Maclean asked, intrigued.

"We were ten thousand strong at Lisbon. The siege began in the spring. Some of the men regretted not going on to the Mediterranean when the siege waged on, but eventually we took the city by autumn. A great success of the campaign." Alex smiled at the eager faces around him. Few men from this area had gone on Crusade, so he understood the interest in hearing the stories. Normally, he'd be happy to tell tales to entertain the clan (as a lad, he'd clung to every word of his uncle's stories of battle as a mercenary), but he was worried over Isobel.

"Did ye have any good kills?" Maclean asked, between taking mouthfuls of roasted venison.

Out of the corner of his eye, Alex could see Isobel's shoulders tense.

"Come now, MacKinnon. What was yer best one? Cut the head clean off anyone?"

Alex grabbed hold of Isobel's hand under the table to calm her.

"Chief Maclean, we are tired from our journey. Forgive us for retiring early," Alex said.

The chief looked insulted, but he quickly recovered and smiled for the onlookers in the great hall.

"Of course, MacKinnon. Of course. Ye and the lass…what's her name again?" The Maclean leaned over to see past Alex to where Isobel sat. She did not turn to acknowledge their host, something Alex knew the chief noticed.

"Isobel," Alex supplied.

"Ye and Isobel should have a good night's rest."

Alex nodded his thanks and took Isobel back to their room.

****

"It must be them," Watkin said to Rolf, as a couple left the dais. The men sat among the crowd; the hall was bursting with over five hundred men and women, easily allowing them to blend in. "She matches the description the bishop gave us."

Rolf agreed. The woman had to be Isobel Campbell, and the man appeared to be a warrior. They would handle him, if needed, and take the woman.

"I'll see what room they're in," Watkin said.

"I'll wait a few minutes and follow you."

Watkin nodded and trailed after the couple; Rolf took a swig from his tankard of ale, biding his time.

Chapter 18

As soon as the door was closed to their small quarters, Alex tried to explain the chief's interest in the Crusades.

Isobel didn't let him get very far. "He was glorifying battle, Alex! It was disgraceful."

"Maclean is a warrior, Isobel. He understands the purpose and cost of battle well enough."

"His words did not show it." Isobel paced back and forth in their room. "You should have said something."

"We are guests, Isobel. We are not here to cause trouble for the chief in front of his clan."

"Perhaps someone needs to tell him battles are not entertainment. Men died fighting for something they believed in. They do not deserve to be talked about as a 'good kill.' "

"Did I discuss them in such a way? Nae. I did not. Nor will I ever."

"I'm glad of it, but Maclean should be put in his place."

"Someday he may be, but it won't be by me, Isobel. He holds the eastern shores of Mull. I cannae go and create conflict with my neighbor—a neighbor my clan appeals to for safe haven on most journeys to the mainland."

"Spoken like a weak man."

Alex stood there briefly stunned, as Isobel lifted

her chin and looked at him like he was nothing more than a scrap of meat.

"Nae, Isobel. Spoken like a man who is to be a chief one day. I understand the necessity of maintaining peace. I will not wage a war with a man over his views on battle. I am many things, but I am no fool and I am not weak."

"If you do not stand up for your beliefs, then what are you, Alex?"

"Alive," he said with sincerity. "Maclean is a powerful chief with powerful allies. I hold my beliefs, but I will not impress them on anyone outside my clan."

"He makes sport of death, Alex. How can you keep silent?"

"Because I must," he said, growing tired of the argument. He understood her anger. He was angry, but she had to understand why he didn't confront Maclean.

She stopped pacing and looked at him. *Perhaps she has finally calmed down enough to see my reasoning,* Alex thought.

"You must do what you must, Alex. And I must do what I must."

"What does that mean?"

"It means that as soon as I have the nunnery in my sights, we will part ways."

"Oh, aye, so you can go off on your own. Is that right?"

"Yes," she said, crossing her arms over her chest.

"How will you travel to Ireland? How will you find food and shelter?" Alex asked, challenging her.

Isobel shrugged. "I do not know, but I'll do what I must to survive."

"What do you know of surviving? You've lived

your life at court."

"I know the struggles of survival. I've done it before, and I will do it again," she said.

"What are you talking of? Your life before you came to live with King David?"

"It's none of your concern."

"That's the right of it, isn't it? Nothing is my concern. I must not give a damn about anything." *Why doesn't she want my protection? Why is she pushing me away?* Alex didn't understand.

"I never said that, but I cannot be your concern. You must let me go."

"You don't need to be on your own, Isobel. You have me." He tried to be gentler. They were on the same side; she just couldn't see it.

"Do I?" she asked.

"Of course. If you dinnae wish to be a nun, I can find a place for you among my clan."

"A place for me?"

"Aye, I'm sure you would fill a niche." He knew his people would welcome her. How could they not?

"I'm grateful to be sure, but I won't be filling any niches for you, Alexander MacKinnon!"

"I didnae mean it in such a way. I would not dishonor you," he explained.

"Then what, pray, would you have me do?"

Alex stood there with his mouth open. She was angry, and he needed to think quickly. *What could she do?* As he stood there trying to conjure a position for Isobel, he took in her appearance. Her cheeks, which had been sad and pale during the evening feast, were full of color. Her eyes were no longer dull. She looked fierce and alive. He then became aware of her deep breathing and their closeness. The room was small. Save for the straw mattress and a solitary chair, there was little space for anything else in the chamber but them. He closed his eyes and tried to clear his mind. After a few deep breaths, he looked at her and found Isobel's eyes were not just fierce and alive—they were on fire, but it wasn't from passion. She was angry.

" 'Tis nice to know you lust after me, but I won't settle for being a poor crusader's whore."

The jab at his reduced circumstances made the lust disappear immediately. "Mary told you, did she?" Alex drew toward her, and Isobel quickly backed against the wall.

Isobel said nothing, but he'd seen Mary's jealousy of Isobel when they'd arrived. The love of his youth was beautiful, but she could be cruel.

"Alex, I did not mean…" She held up her palms, as if to push him away.

"Aye, you did. You meant exactly what you said." Alex pressed against her open palms, crowding her. "I may be poor, but at least I know my place in this world. Can you say the same?"

Now her cheeks were stained crimson with shame. At first, Alex felt satisfied. But then he saw the uncertainty in her eyes, and his anger dissipated. *What am I to do with you?* "What do you want from me, Isobel?"

"I do not know," she whispered.

"I think you do."

He cupped her face with his hands, lifting her chin upwards. He bent his head. Their eyes locked, but Alex hesitated. Then he felt Isobel's hands reach up and wrap around his neck, pulling him down to her.

"Kiss me, Alex," she whispered.

And he did.

Moments ago, Isobel had wanted to scream at him. *He means to find a place for me? Fill a niche? He isn't offering marriage.* The jab at his state of poverty wasn't intentional, but Isobel could not have controlled her anger if she wished it. Then he asked her what she wanted from him, and suddenly her arms were wrapped around his neck and she was asking to be kissed.

The warmth of his breath on her face sent chills of anticipation down her spine. She inhaled slowly to steady herself. Exhaling, she left her mouth parted, waiting for him. But he didn't move.

He was giving her the chance to refuse him. Did she want him to stop? Her blood pounded in her ears, and her throat felt dry. *No, I want him.* She closed her eyes and tilted her face up. In the next instant, his mouth covered hers.

She responded, kissing him back hesitantly at first, then more assuredly when she heard him sigh in pleasure. Alex pressed her up against the wall.

At court, she'd shared a few stolen kisses with the son of one of David's advisors. Those kisses, however, were very different from this one. This was hot and consuming. She never wanted it to end.

Alex knew there was a reason he needed to stop this madness, but with every sigh and moan that escaped Isobel's lips, that reason slipped further away. He'd kept his hands against the wall beside her head—fighting the urge to touch her. The temptation to feel her body eventually won out, and he let his right hand slide down her side to the top of her thigh. He lifted Isobel's leg and fitted himself against her. She wrapped her leg around his hip and moved against him. It was ecstasy.

Until the knock came. At first, Alex dismissed it. Someone was knocking on a room down the hall. But then the knocking became louder—more insistent. As if lifting his head above water, the sound finally rang loud and clear.

Breaking the kiss, he held Isobel against him as he steadied his breathing. "Who is it?" he finally called. They were just a few feet from the door.

"The chief wishes to see ye in his solar," a man said, his voice muffled by the barrier of the door. "He insists that ye come now."

"Tell him I will be there in a moment." After the footsteps retreated, Alex looked down at Isobel. She gazed up at him in bewilderment, as if she too didn't understand what had overcome them.

He tucked a loose strand of hair behind her ear and kissed her on the forehead before stepping away.

"Isobel," he began, unsure of what to say, "I didnae mean—"

"You should go," she cut in. "It could be more news about the king."

Christ. The king. Alex felt sick. Here she was mourning the man she looked up to as a father, and he'd just nearly taken her to bed. *How could you be so callous?*

"Isobel," he said again, trying to take her hands, but she evaded him.

"Truly, Alex, you should see what the chief wants. We can talk when you get back. I'll be here." She smiled, but Alex didn't take much comfort from it. *She thinks I was taking advantage of her. If only I could explain.* But what could he say? He was overcome with need and had to kiss her? Frustrated with his own weakness, he simply nodded and excused himself from the room.

Alex made his way through the great hall, where the evening meal was still underway. A guard directed him to the chief's solar where Alex found the chief and several other Maclean men gathered around a table. There was also one man who had been absent at the evening meal: the chief's son, Ewan. His childhood friend did not greet him though.

"Come," said the chief, pointing to an open chair at his side.

Alex did as he was bid and sat down at the table. Everyone else sat when the chief nodded. All the men, save for Ewan, were older and appeared to be the chief's counsel. He studied each man carefully, but none of the faces looking back at him gave Alex any sense of the meeting's purpose. He took stock of the chief's son. He had not seen Ewan in six long years. Looking at him now, Alex could tell his old friend was exhausted. *Did something weigh on his mind? Perhaps he has been traveling. I probably look the same,* Alex thought, feeling the ache in his arms from the afternoon of rowing.

"I spoke to yer father the summer last about his lands," the chief began. "He was nae amenable to negotiating, but I thought ye might be."

Alex was taken aback. *What does the Maclean want with our lands?* "You claim over half of the isle, Chief, and hold the gateway to the mainland. What land is it that you desire of the MacKinnons?"

"All of it," he said simply.

"All?" Alex repeated in shock.

"Aye," the chief said firmly. "In exchange, none of yer people will die."

Alex felt his jaw tighten. It took everything he had to remain outwardly impassive. Inside, his blood boiled.

"I may want yer people to remain—however many are left—to continue to farm."

However many are left? He didn't understand. *Have my clansman deserted?*

"While they remain on my land, they will have my protection, and they will be allegiant to me."

The chief's offer was an insult, and it made Alex furious, but it also drew concern. *What has happened since I left?*

"My father and I will think on your offer, Chief," Alex said, keeping his voice even and steady.

"I'll expect a decision from ye both by the next full moon." The Maclean reclined in his chair, tapping his fingers together. "Be wise, young MacKinnon. Since ye failed to bring home the wealthy Angus bride, this could be the only way to end yer clan's suffering."

With that, Alex was dismissed.

****

The door creaked open and Isobel's stomach turned to knots. *Alex is back.* She kept her eyes shut, uncertain whether she wanted him to know she was awake. She'd tried to fall asleep after he left to see the chief, but their kissing had left her restless. His reaction to their intimacy also made her angry. *He will call it a mistake, but I feel no regret.* Learning about David's passing had made her emotional, but she knew what she was doing. Alex wasn't taking advantage of her, and she wasn't taking advantage of him. She debated whether she should keep pretending to be asleep or if she should talk to him. She was curious to know what the chief wanted.

Resolved to speak with him, she took a deep breath to steady her nerves, and a foul odor filled her nose. It smelled like sweat and manure. *Where in the heavens has he been?* Feet shuffled on both sides of the bed. *He's not alone.*

"Alex, what on earth?" Isobel opened her eyes and sat up in bed. Then her heart plummeted in her chest, for the man looking back at her was a stranger. Before she could react, she was struck on the back of the head, and her vision narrowed. Then everything went black.

****

Alex needed some fresh air. He ducked out the back entrance of the great hall, where the men still gathered in song and drink, and found a quiet spot in the bailey where the sounds of the keep were distant. He stayed outside for a long time, letting his mind and pulse completely calm. Passing back through the great hall, where now only a few Macleans sat in conversation, Alex overheard two men near the main entrance.

"I need to see the MacKinnon," the man insisted.

"What's this about?" Alex asked, as he approached.

"It's me, MacKinnon. It's MacDonald."

"Robbie?" Alex jogged up to the door, knowing something was wrong. "What is it?"

He stood quiet, giving a pointed look to the guard blocking his entrance.

"Let him in," Alex demanded.

The man moved aside, letting Robbie pass. They walked out of earshot of the guard, then Alex pressed him again. "What's wrong, MacDonald?"

"Men are coming for you and Lady Isobel."

"We expected this, but I thought it would take the bishop more time," Alex said, not understanding.

"Aye, that's what I thought. When I got back to Edinburgh, the bishop told me he'd sent another team after the Rood. I raced as fast as I could to get here, but I fear they have already arrived on Mull. A fisherman in Oban said he'd taken two men, and their horses, by boat to Duart just this afternoon."

"You're certain it's the men the bishop sent?"

"Nae, I can't be. But I have a feeling."

Alex nodded. "Come," he said, and Robbie followed him through the keep. He needed to check on Isobel. When they reached the landing, Alex's heart caught in his chest.

"The door is open," he said, as Robbie reached the final step.

Robbie unsheathed his sword, and Alex took out his knife; he'd left his sword and other weapons in the room when he'd gone down to meet with the chief. They carefully approached the door, which was pushed open a foot or so. Alex signaled to Robbie, preparing him for his next move. Robbie nodded. In the next moment, Alex kicked the door completely open and backed aside, allowing Robbie to charge the room.

Alex followed after him and searched the room for Isobel, but there was no sign of her.

"They've taken her," Alex said. "Christ, how could I let this happen?"

"There's no time for that, MacKinnon," Robbie said. "How long were you gone?"

"A few hours."

"Then they can't be very far away," Robbie said.

Alex searched the room and found Isobel's cloak lying on the floor.

"If they only came for the Rood, why would they take her hostage?" Robbie asked.

"They don't have the Rood," Alex said, reaching down to pick up Isobel's discarded cloak. The Rood was still tucked inside the hidden pocket of the garment. "It's in here. Once they realize they aren't in possession of it, they may kill her."

"Or use her as ransom." Robbie sheathed his sword. "They'll know you still have it. They'll exchange her for the Rood."

"Aye. Perhaps."

"Do you trust the Maclean chief?"

"Not like I did before I knew he wanted my land," Alex said. He gathered up his weapons, which thankfully hadn't been stolen.

"Then I think you should take everything if you aren't planning to return."

Alex agreed and packed up all of his and Isobel's possessions. When everything, including the Rood, was securely packed, the men quietly descended the stairwell. Alex didn't want to deal with any Maclean warriors on the way out, so they kept to the shadows, skirting the great hall. They found the guard, from just minutes ago, already asleep at his post. Alex and Robbie snuck out into the bailey and headed for the stables.

They found Robbie's horse, Coira, tethered just inside the stable doors.

"You'll need a horse too," Robbie said, untying Coira. "The merchant I came over with had that horse aboard his boat." He nodded toward a white horse, near the back corner of the stable. "He was half drunk when our boat landed. I doubt he'll be up too early to come looking for her."

Alex jogged down to the end of the stable, looking around for a guard. Seeing no one in sight, Alex quickly tied his belongings to the horse and led her back toward Robbie.

"The stable lad won't be back for a while. He checked me in, then got called away to help in the kitchens," Robbie said, from his perch on Coira's back.

Alex climbed atop the horse and gently nudged his heel into her side. She didn't budge.

"Come on," he said, nudging the horse again.

"I think her name is Honey," Robbie offered. "Try that."

"Are you serious?" *Who the hell names a horse Honey?*

Robbie just shrugged.

"Come on, Honey," Alex said, and the horse trotted out of the stables. They rode to the wall that surrounded the perimeter. This time, the guards at the gate were wide awake and on patrol.

"What's the play here?" Robbie asked.

"We'll tell them we were following the party that just left a short while ago," Alex said. "Perhaps they'll even give us the direction they went."

When they reached the gate, two guards approached.

"No one leaves until sunrise," the men said in unison.

"We're already behind," Alex said. "My two brothers and sister had to travel ahead. It's important

164

we catch up to them."

"Brothers and sister, aye? Then why'd they sound English?"

Alex and Robbie exchanged looks. The bishop had sent English warriors after Isobel.

"We can all speak English," Alex said, with a perfect English accent. "Now, let us pass. Our father has called us home on urgent business."

"Who are ye?" one guard asked.

Alex didn't see any reason to lie. "I'm Alexander MacKinnon."

The man nodded. "I've heard the chief is unwell, but I didn't know ye had any brothers, MacKinnon."

"Oh, aye," Alex said, deciding not to elaborate. If he added too much, the tale would be harder to spin.

"Then why'd they go north?"

Alex frowned. The Maclean's keep was on a little peninsula that jutted into the Sound of Mull. No matter what direction you needed to go in when you left, unless by boat, you had to go south.

"By boat?" Alex asked, not understanding.

"Nae," the man said. "They left before the curfew, but they were acting strangely, so we had a scout follow them a ways. They cut north, toward Craignure."

"Damn, my brothers have a poor sense of direction and probably took too much drink at the feast." Alex shook his head and laughed. "Well, we best catch up to them." He nudged his horse forward, and Robbie did the same.

"Ye may pass," one guard said, waving for the gates to be opened. "We hope yer father is well, MacKinnon."

"Thank you," Alex said, nodding his head as the

gates opened before them.

Alex and Robbie rode out at a slow canter, again trying not to raise suspicion. Once the keep was in the distance, Alex spoke first.

"We'll ride north, in the direction of Craignure, and hope the Maclean men spoke the truth."

"It's our best chance," Robbie said. "The English are a surprise."

"Aye, I didn't expect that. Perhaps King Stephen is already involved in this," Alex said.

"I heard of King David's passing. I know the bishop is trying hard to win a place in the English king's court."

"Let's make sure he does nae succeed by using the Rood." *And let's get Isobel back alive.*

They hastened their pace as they cleared the peninsula and started the journey northbound. *I'm coming for you, Isobel. Don't give up, lass.*

Chapter 19

Isobel awoke to darkness. She realized immediately she was on top of a horse, riding through the night with two strangers: one at her back and one on a horse ahead of her. The back of her head throbbed. She tried to reach up to touch it, to see if she was bleeding, but her hands were bound and tied to the saddle. She could not move them.

Think, Isobel. She didn't remember much before blacking out, but she heard the men's voices. They sounded English. Alex had anticipated the bishop would send more men. Perhaps they were here to take the Rood. *Do they have it?* She was not wearing her cloak, but that didn't mean they weren't in possession of it.

She inhaled deeply, trying to calm her racing pulse, but the air around her smelled of rot. She took another breath and found the smell's source: the rider seated behind her. Bile rose in her throat, but she fought against it, trying to suck in the fresh air that blew in her face as they rode. She sat in front of her abductor, his arm wrapped around her waist.

She tried to lean forward so she didn't have her backside pressed up against his body, but every time she inched forward, he pulled her back against his chest with a laugh. Isobel gave up protesting, deciding to conserve her energy for a more opportune moment.

When they let their guard down, she'd be ready.

They rode for what seemed like hours in the dark, and then finally dawn filtered into the sky, giving birth to a new day. With the rising sun, Isobel could finally tell they were going northwest, along the coastline.

She wasn't sure what the English fiends had in mind for her, but she needed to prepare for the worst. She was outnumbered and weaponless. Her best chance at survival was keeping her captors busy until Alex could find her. She knew he would come for her, if only to fulfill his obligation to David. The thought of the late king brought a tear to her eye, but she fought to keep more from coming. She would not cry in front of these men. She would show no weakness.

She struggled against the bindings around her wrists, trying to uncover her hands, but her captors had wrapped a plaid tightly over her. No doubt the plaid was used to conceal her bindings so the Maclean guards would not know she was being taken against her will.

"You won't be getting out of those bindings, Lady Isobel," the man behind her said. "I tied the knots myself, and I assure you they are tight."

"Where are you taking me?" she asked. The direction did not make any sense. To get back to England, they needed to go southeast.

"The Rood is going back to England, but your journey will likely be of a shorter duration."

Isobel took his meaning plainly. They would kill her.

"We can do with you as we like, but if you beg, I may let you join us. I am sure the bishop and my master could punish you well enough, but they won't enjoy it as much as I will."

The hair on the back of her neck stood on end. Suddenly, she was back in the forest outside of Stirling being attacked. She played out the scene in her head, remembering every detail of her chase through the woods that night, knowing how very differently that night could have ended if she hadn't carried her *sgian dubh*. If only she had it now.

"You were careless with the Rood. Leaving it sit out on the chair, as though it were of no importance. I cannot see why the Scottish king entrusted it to you."

I didn't leave the Rood sitting out on the chair.

"Made the search easy on us," her abductor continued. He fumbled with something at his side, and then stretched his arm out in front of her. "I knew this was it as soon as I looked at it. The bishop said it would be unmistakable."

There, in the palm of the English fiend, was her jewel-encrusted *sgian dubh*, sheathed in its matching jewel-encrusted case.

He thinks it is the Rood! She could not believe her luck. The Rood, pray, was still safe at Duart Keep. He or his companion would realize the folly at some point, but at least she knew the men had failed in taking the precious relic.

****

Alex and Robbie rode their horses hard, following the coastline northwest. They'd picked up the trail of the English riders just off the peninsula. With the short nights this time of year, it was already dawn, and they were gaining on them.

"They'll need to let the horses rest sometime," Robbie said.

"Aye. You can tell by the tracks their pace has

slowed." Alex knew they were close. *Be strong, Isobel.*

****

After a few more miles, the English fiend yelled to his friend, "Let's rest here." The other man slowed his pace and rounded on them.

"The boat is not much farther," the man said, bringing his horse to stand beside them.

Boat? Who would they be meeting by boat on the northwestern side of the island? Their plan did not seem logical, Isobel thought.

"I need to take a piss, Watkin," her captor said.

Isobel cringed at his crude language, but she was happy to be given a break from riding. The other man, Watkin, dismounted from his horse, and then helped Isobel to the ground. As her captor dismounted, she finally got a good look at him. She was struck by his familiarity. While she did not recognize his voice, she recognized the tall dark-haired Englishman.

He was in David's court. She searched her memory, trying to recount the details. He was the personal guard of someone important, but who?

The man in question strode off to relieve himself, and Watkin took her to rest on a fallen log. He, she noted, was entirely calm and relaxed, as if kidnapping maidens and holy relics was an everyday occurrence for him. He was younger than his partner, perhaps near her own age of four and twenty. His hair was golden, and his mustache was well groomed. He did not appear to perceive her as a threat, for as she sat on the log he gazed up at the sky.

She did not have enough time to act. Fear of the older man returning soon kept her from trying to flee. If her only captor was just the casual Englishman, she would take her chances and run. With the other nearby, she would not get far on foot.

This isn't the right opportunity, Isobel. Be patient, and you'll find the right moment to act.

While the man, Watkin, continued to gaze upward, Isobel looked around her. There, on the ground a few inches from her feet, was a small rock. Though small, it had a sharp jagged side. She could use it to work on the bindings at her wrists.

She glanced up at the Englishman again; he still gazed up at the morning sky. She carefully bent, reaching for the stone. Her hands were bound together with her palms touching, as though in prayer, but she could use her fingertips. Just as she reached the small rock, she heard the Englishman cry out and ask, "What are you doing?"

"Nothing," Isobel said, as she clasped the stone between her fingers. "My shoe was coming off." She carefully wiggled her foot, bringing it partially out of her leather slipper.

"Sit up," he said. "I'll put the shoe back on." Watkin knelt at her feet, and Isobel straightened, quickly concealing the stone between her hands.

The Englishman gingerly held her ankle and pulled the shoe back onto her foot.

"There," he said, setting her foot back on the ground. He then resumed his post, standing a few feet away, and admired the sunrise once more.

A moment later, the English fiend returned, and they all remounted the horses. Watkin helped get her situated in front of his companion. He carefully tucked a plaid around her, covering her hands and bound wrists.

As they rode off once more, Isobel set to work moving the stone down between her hands to the point where the bindings started on her wrists. With the sharp edge of the rock pointed at the cloth, she turned her hands side to side. While her freedom of movement was restrained, it was enough to start wearing down the bindings.

Watkin said they were close to the boat, so she did not have much time. She would work the bindings as much as she could, then hope her strength would be enough to break free.

****

"This is where they stopped," Alex said, noting the fallen log.

"Aye," Robbie said. "There are three sets of footprints and two horses."

"She was able to walk on her own," Alex said, bending down to examine the distinct footprints of a lady. *She is not dead.*

Alex and Robbie remounted their horses and took off.

****

Isobel looked at the boat. The vessel was large enough for them and the horses, but no one else. She felt relief the Englishmen were not meeting up with more soldiers. She was a strong swimmer. Once she broke free of the bindings, she could jump into the sea and swim for shore. One of her captors would likely jump in after her, but not both. Someone would need to stay on the boat with the horses. *That's it. That is how I will make my escape. Or die trying.* The sobering thought of drowning caused Isobel's stomach to plummet. *Do not think that way. Focus on survival.* She took a steadying breath and glanced behind her, down the road she'd just traveled with the men. *How close are you, Alex?*

"Don't look for your man to come for you," the English fiend warned. "Don't look for anyone to rescue you for that matter. The Macleans would not let anyone out after curfew, and when they do, your man will take a boat back to the mainland."

"Is that why you came in this direction?" she asked.

"Of course," he said. "Why else would we go so far out of the way? Did you imagine we were meeting up with some big army? You aren't worth such attention."

I may not be, but the Rood is. Once King Stephen gained possession of the Rood, he could use it to manipulate the young Scottish king, Malcolm. *You have failed again, Bishop.* But how many more attempts would there be?

Perhaps he will send an army. Isobel did not underestimate what greedy men would do to gain power.

She also did not underestimate these men. The English fiend intended her harm. She was certain he planned to kill her and do worse before the life went out of her. His fair-haired companion, though reserved, could have appetites just as dark.

As the men prepared the horses for their journey on the sea, Isobel continued to work at her bindings. She lifted her wrists to check her progress; she was only halfway through the cloth. *It may have to be enough.*

****

As Alex crested the last hill before the sea, he

caught sight of Isobel and her captors. He held his hand up, and Robbie came to a stop beside him.

"There," he said, pointing to the boat and the people below.

"Surprise attack?" Robbie asked.

"Aye, I want to approach when they are away from Isobel. I don't want them to use her as a shield," Alex said.

They backed down the hillside, out of view, and tethered their horses to the remnants of an old croft house. The farm had long been forgotten, but a sturdy stone wall remained. Once the horses were secure, they deftly snaked down the hillside toward the sea, keeping to the tall grasses to stay out of view. They made quick progress down the hill. When they reached the beach, they remained in the high grass not far behind Isobel. She faced the sea, and one of her captors stood at her side, watching his companion tend to the horses. After a few minutes, the Englishman by the horses called to the man beside Isobel. The man joined the other by the water's edge. Isobel was now alone. This was the opening Alex and Robbie needed.

"On three, we attack," Alex whispered to Robbie, who sat crouched at his side.

Robbie nodded in agreement.

In seconds, they were on their feet, charging down the beach. He didn't have time to speak to Isobel, but he looked at her as he ran by and he felt relief in seeing no visible signs of abuse. Her hands were bound, but she looked well. He focused once more on the assailants before him.

With swords drawn, they ran through the surf and attacked the surprised men. The Englishmen reached for their swords, but Alex and Robbie got in the first hits. In nearly perfect coordination, they brought their swords down hard against Isobel's captors.

The sick thud of metal cutting through flesh sounded in Alex's ears. He dislodged his sword from the man's shoulder and stepped back in the knee-deep water. This time he swung low from his side to hit the captor in the thigh.

The man's scream of pain was drowned out by the crashing waves and cry of seabirds overhead. Though in pain and bleeding, the Englishman brought his sword down and deflected Alex's hit. The Englishman then raised his sword and swung for Alex's head, but, with a loud clash, Alex met him—his enemy's blade waved just shy of his cheek. Sunlight broke from behind a cloud and glinted off the metal of Alex's sword, temporarily blinding him. Alex held fast, leveraging himself against the waves in the wet sand. He felt himself sinking. *I need to get out of the water.*

A large wave crashed over Alex and his opponent, with swords still joined in battle. As the wave receded, it took with it the Englishman's footing, and he stumbled backward into the surf. Alex thrust his blade into the sandy bottom and fought the pull of the tide. His opponent rose from the water empty-handed. *He dropped his blade!*

With his bare hands, the man lunged at Alex's throat. Alex did not hesitate. With his sharp reflexes, Alex pulled his blade free from the sea floor in time to see Isobel's abductor run through.

****

Isobel raced up the hillside, away from the men, and crouched in the tall sea grass. She parted the stalks and looked down at the beach, yet she could not stand to watch. She kept her eyes shut after she witnessed Alex and Robbie deliver the first blows against the English. She saw blood and more and nearly heaved. She buried her face in her hands, which she'd freed from the bindings the moment Alex and Robbie took the beach.

The sound of the waves crashing to the shore helped deaden some of the noises, but Isobel still heard every scream and clash of metal. Time hung suspended as she waited for the battle to end. Then, all she heard were the cry of the seabirds and the neigh of the horses as they ran away from the fighting men.

"Isobel," Alex called to her, and she finally opened her eyes. "Were you harmed?"

"I'm fine," she said, but her voice wavered. The sound of the ocean waves crashing on the beach faded and Alex looked blurry, as though she were seeing him through mist. She blinked and looked past Alex, her vision a little clearer. Robbie stood silhouetted in the distance; Watkin's body lay at his feet. In the surf, a short distance from Robbie, the limbs and head of the other Englishman bobbed up and down in the water. She looked away, pressing her hand to her lips, a wave of nausea bubbling up inside of her.

Alex knelt before her and scooped her up in his arms. He faced her away from the scene and sat her across his lap. Isobel felt like a cloth doll. Her arms and hands felt limp, and she made no attempts to move them as Alex situated her across his body.

She laid her head on his chest, noting the rough feel of his aketon beneath her cheek. But there was something else. The padded wool of his war coat felt wet. *Is it from the water?* Isobel lifted her head; her cheek was cool and damp. Finding some strength in her right arm, she wiped the left side of her face, the side that had touched Alex. Her palm was coated in blood.

She pushed away from Alex, her hands sliding over his blood-covered aketon, as she struggled to get away. She screamed as he tried to grab her. She needed to get away from the blood. She reached for the sea grass. The sharp stems cut into her palms, but she didn't care. Her breath grew shallow and labored.

"You are safe, Isobel. It's all over," Alex said in a soothing voice, but Isobel could still see the blood on her hand and feel the blood on her face.

"Let me go!" she cried. His hands instantly released her, and she crawled off Alex's lap and heaved into the grass.

"I don't know what's wrong with her," Alex said. "She's taken ill."

"It's the blood," Robbie said from behind her.

"Christ!" Alex shouted. The grass rustled around him as he ran down to the beach. Alex dove into the waves, splashing water on his chest and arms, trying to clean off the blood.

Isobel collapsed in the sandy grass and passed out.

****

When Isobel woke, she found herself wrapped up in a plaid lying in the grass. The sun was hot, and she had sweated through her dress. She was no longer by the beach, but instead lay against an old fencerow. She sat up, pushing off the plaid, and took in the rest of her surroundings. There was a small earthen hut carved into the hillside nearby, and Alex and Robbie sat atop of it, gazing out at the sea.

Isobel stretched her arms. The movement must have caught Alex's eye, for he jumped off the mound and was by her in an instant.

"How are you feeling?" he asked, cupping her chin. He tilted her head slightly side to side, examining her eyes. "Are you dizzy?" He moved his hand down to her shoulder.

"No, I feel fine," she said. "I think I just panicked. I've never seen—" She trailed off, but Alex nodded his head, seeming to understand her meaning.

"I'm sorry I did not shield you from the sight of it," Alex said, moving his hand gently up and down her arm, as though to comfort her.

"I am well, Alex. Truly," Isobel assured him.

Alex didn't say anything but squeezed her arm lightly.

"Where are the Englishmen?" she asked, looking around.

"We took care of it," Alex said, averting his eyes. He was no longer wearing his war coat. Instead, he was in a plain linen tunic.

Isobel nodded her head. She didn't want to know more.

"Could you eat?" Alex asked, reaching around her for his bag.

She did not want to eat, but even as she shook her head, her stomach growled in hunger. Her throat and mouth also felt dry.

"Try some," Alex said. He handed her a few oatcakes.

Judging by the sun, it was late afternoon. Her abductors had given her no food or drink. She did need to keep her strength up. *The journey isn't over yet.*

Isobel managed to eat two small oatcakes and drank some water. It wasn't much, but it subdued her hunger and thirst. The whole ordeal—from the kidnapping to the scene on the beach—left her aching head to toe. There was also an ache in her heart: a fear for what might have been if Alex and Robbie hadn't arrived in time.

"Rest now," he said. "We'll leave in a while."

Isobel wanted to protest; the sun was too warm, and she didn't need to rest any longer, but it seemed Alex had considered that, for he set to work creating a makeshift tent. Using the fence and some tall sticks, he made a frame and draped a plaid over it. While it couldn't cover her completely, it would shield her face from the sun.

"There," Alex said, helping situate her under the cover. " 'Twill keep you a wee bit cooler."

Isobel lay down on the ground and found the plaid did help cool her, as most of her body was now in the shade. Only her calves and feet were exposed to the sun, but she didn't mind. Soon she was fast asleep.

Chapter 20

"You will nae go on with us to Iona?" Alex asked Robbie, as they prepared to part ways. He'd let Isobel rest as long as he could, but they needed to journey on now.

"I've left my siblings with your friends, Katherine and Thomas. I must be getting back to them. If Agnes is well enough, we'll return to Mull within a week."

"A healer will see to her as soon as you arrive." Alex hoped he could make good on his promise. After his meeting with the Maclean, he feared whether physicians remained at MacKinnon Keep.

"Are you certain you have a place for us?"

"We need strong warriors, MacDonald. Especially now that the Macleans threaten to take our land. If my father's weakened state has made them feel we are ripe for the picking, then the might of our men must prove them differently."

"I'm up for the fight," Robbie said. "My brother, Murdoch, is eager to join the ranks as well. He's just seen his fifteenth summer, but he's good with a blade and even better with a bow and arrow."

"We'll be glad to have him," Alex said. "And my sisters will delight in having new company."

Robbie nodded. "I think Agnes will enjoy being part of a clan again."

Alex could not imagine what Robbie had gone

through to care for his younger siblings, but clearly he regretted what he'd been unable to give them: Murdoch, proper training to be a warrior; and Agnes, a proper home with friends around her. While Alex could offer the MacDonalds very little, he could offer them those things.

Robbie nodded toward Isobel, who sat perched on a boulder looking out over the sea. She'd woken from her second nap a short time ago. "Will she be all right?" he asked.

"She's got more iron in her blood than I've got in my sword," Alex said. "She just needs time."

"You could do worse for a wife," Robbie said.

Alex frowned.

"That's a hell of a scowl, MacKinnon."

"It's complicated," Alex finally said.

"Isn't it always?" Robbie shook his head. "If you still haven't proposed to her by the time I return, I just may have to kick your arse again."

"I was distracted, and you damn well know it."

"As you say," Robbie said. "Well, I'd best be on my way if I'm to catch a boat back to the mainland today. I will see you and Lady Isobel soon."

"Safe travels to you and your kin," Alex said.

Robbie nodded and guided Coira and the merchant's horse away; he would return Honey to Duart Keep before he journeyed back to Oban.

As Robbie galloped away into the distance, Alex approached Isobel. "I know you have been through a rough go of things, but if you can, we should press on."

"Of course," Isobel said. As she turned to face him, the afternoon light illuminated her features. He could look at her face a thousand times, and it would still take his breath away. He wanted to remember her like this forever.

"Ready?" she asked.

"Aye," he said, putting her appearance to memory. "We'll ride the horses through the valley and reach Fionnphort this night. From there, 'tis a short boat ride to Iona." With Isobel's attackers dead, Alex had claimed their horses and their weapons.

"I didn't realize how close we were," Isobel said.

"Aye," Alex said. He reached to his side and pulled Isobel's *sgian dubh* from his belt. "We are fortunate the English were fooled by your knife. I assume they took it thinking it was the Rood." He handed it back to her.

Isobel took the knife and studied the jeweled case. "When David gifted it to me two summers ago, I did not like it. I found it too ornate. But that very thing made the thieves believe it was the Rood." She tucked the knife beneath her belt and concealed it under her cloak.

"That blade has aided you several times on this journey. Let us hope you will nae have to use it again."

Isobel nodded and looked up at him. "Thank you for keeping the Rood safe," she began. "And for saving me."

Alex nodded, though inside he was full of regret. *If I had been in the room, she wouldn't have been in danger.* The meeting with the Maclean chief had been necessary, but afterward, when he'd gone outside…While he was sitting there taking in the fresh air, she'd been kidnapped. *I thought we were safe.* A foolish mistake, and it had almost cost Isobel her life.

"Come," he said. "The sooner the relic is in the hands of Bethoc, the safer you and it will be."

And the sooner I will have to decide my future.
Isobel did not doubt her strength or perseverance. She would find a way to exist in this world, just as she had before her life with David and Mattie.

She looked at the man before her. Though their time together was brief, she felt connected to him in an inexplicable way. It would be hard to part from him, but he was right. It was time to see the Rood safely into Bethoc's hands. Her kidnapping this morning had proved just that.

"Then let us go, Alex, for I am ready for this journey to be at its end."

****

They rode for several hours, the long spring day giving them sun to travel under, before they saw anyone else in the valley. Alex reached out and reined in Isobel's mare, bringing both of their horses to an abrupt halt. He saw two riders in the distance.

"Do you recognize them?"

"I can't be certain," Alex said. "Follow me. Quickly!"

He guided the horses out of the valley and into a thicket of pines. Alex kept them waiting in silence for several minutes after the riders galloped past.

"The road is not safe. I didnae want to go over the mountains, but I think it will be safer."

"And the horses?"

"They will do fine through the mountain passes. It will slow our pace though. We will not make it to Iona this day."

" 'Tis better to be safe," Isobel said.

"Agreed," Alex said. "Come. We will find a place to make camp for the night."

Chapter 21

When they stopped for the evening, Isobel collected water from a nearby spring as Alex laid a campfire beneath a canopy of Caledonian pines and oak trees. Isobel marveled at their size. The trees were striking, especially the ancient pines. They towered above her head, arching over her as though she was standing in the aisle of St. Andrew's Cathedral, the grandest church in all of Scotland. No matter what other lands she saw, Isobel felt nothing could ever compare to the beauty of the Western Isles.

Isobel joined Alex by the campfire, as he sat preparing their meal. She soaked in the heat from the flames. Though the air was cool that spring eve, Alex said they would have to put out the fire when the sky grew dark.

"I do not want to attract any undue attention," Alex explained.

"I worry they will keep coming for it," Isobel said.

"The bishop would not violate the sanctity of the nunnery. No matter how much he craves power."

"He may not, but he is working with someone," Isobel said. "I recognized one of those Englishmen from David's court."

"Who was he?"

Isobel shook her head. "I cannot remember, but I hope it will come to me."

"King Stephen's men have never been to David's court, have they?" he asked.

"No. They were not part of the English king's guard."

"I wonder who the bishop has aligned himself with now," Alex said.

"Do you think he realizes the Rood is being taken to Iona?"

Alex nodded. "Robbie met with the bishop in Edinburgh, and the bishop suspected that the Rood was for Iona."

"Then it won't be safe," Isobel said. "It cannot stay there."

"The Lord of the Isles built the nunnery on Iona. He will protect what is his, Isobel. The bishop will not start a feud with the island king."

Isobel wished she had Alex's confidence. She did not know the Lord of the Isles or if the bishop feared him. Even if he did, they still had another man to worry over.

Think! Who was that English soldier with in David's court? Isobel closed her eyes.

"What are you doing?" Alex asked.

"Give me a moment." Isobel pictured the great hall in Edinburgh Castle. It was a spring day, and many noblemen had gathered to meet with the king. She stood on the outskirts of the room, as she often did, taking in the commotion.

A vision of the English soldier appeared in her mind. He was standing beside another soldier and a finely dressed man, a nobleman. The nobleman waited his turn and was eventually greeted by the king.

"The Duke of Lincoln," the king's man announced,

as the nobleman bowed to the king.

Isobel's eyes snapped open.

"I think the English were sent by the Duke of Lincoln," she said.

"The Duke of Lincoln?" Alex asked. "Why would he help the bishop?"

"I do not know," Isobel said. "But I am certain that is who the English work for."

Alex nodded. "I am not familiar with the duke. What do you know of him?"

"Only what I overheard in court, and who knows what truth is in any of it," Isobel said. "He may be making a move for more power himself."

"Then we must be on alert," Alex said. "I will increase the presence of guards at the crossing to Iona and on the isle itself. I will also speak to the prioress about getting more aid from Somerled."

"Has he a large army?" she asked.

"His warriors are not great in number, but I've heard they are the finest in the Isles."

"Then I will have faith in him, as you do."

She gazed into the fire, marveling at how much her life had changed in the past twelve days. A month ago, she could not imagine facing the challenges this journey had presented. Yet, with the determination she did not know she possessed, she had faced and overcome those challenges. All with the help of Alex.

She glanced at him. He also gazed into the fire. She was anxious for him. Tomorrow would be his homecoming. After six years, he would be reunited with his people. She could not imagine what went through his mind.

They would both face unknowns when daylight

found them, but for the night, they had each other. *Make it count, Isobel. You do not know when life will give you a chance at happiness again.* She blushed as she recalled the night before in Duart Keep. The way he'd kissed her. It made her feel alive in ways she had not imagined. *What would the rest be like?*

Isobel continued to study Alex. He sat with his legs bent, his hands joined in front of his knees. She looked at his muscular arms; they seemed to glow in the firelight. She remembered well what it felt like to be in those arms. *I could be in those arms again.*

She set the mission and her future aside. Tonight, only she and Alex existed.

Alex stared at the fire, watching the flames dance and flicker in the gentle breeze. His stomach was in knots; he did not know what waited for him at MacKinnon Keep. *How sick will Father be? Will my sisters welcome me home? How dire will circumstances be for them and the clan?* Alex shook his head. It was a waste to think on these things. He would find the answers to his questions soon enough. It did no good to worry. No matter what the circumstances were, he would deal with it.

Alex focused on the dusky sky. They'd need to quell the fire's flames soon.

"We should rest," he told Isobel. "I'll lay the plaids."

Alex spread the plaids on each side of the fire.

"It's cool this evening," Isobel said. "Perhaps we can lay our plaids side by side for warmth."

The suggestion set Alex's skin on fire. He was in for a night of torture being so near her, but he nodded in agreement. After he arranged the blankets, placing them side by side, he smothered the flames. The camp was cloaked in hues of gray, and there was a quiet calm around them. It seemed all of nature had bedded down for the evening. Not even the breeze, which had carried the smell of the salty sea but moments ago, reached their camp. The quiet gnawed at Alex. It built his awareness of Isobel's every movement.

She knelt on her plaid and lay down on her side; the silhouette of her hip beckoned him.

Alex didn't move.

"Are you joining me?" Isobel asked.

"Aye." Alex took a deep breath and squared his jaw. *One night. I just need to keep my damn hands to myself for one night, and then I will be free of this need.*

Alex laid down on his plaid, careful to face away from her. After all they'd been through that day, he did not have the strength left in him to resist her. Fear of losing her to the English had nearly driven him mad. If she looked at him with those big violet eyes now, he'd do anything she asked. He yearned to kiss her again. She was so passionate. He'd kissed his fair share of lasses, but he'd never felt such a spark before. He hardened at the memory of her sighs of pleasure. *And that was just from kissing. Imagine how she'd cry out if I made her come.*

"Damn it," he cursed.

"Is something wrong?" Isobel asked.

"It's fine. Go to sleep," he ground out, embarrassed by his weakness. He needed a distraction. He looked out into the woods and tried to count the number of trees in the darkened copse around them. *One, two, three...*

Isobel stretched, and her bottom pressed up against

his own.

"Can you nae get comfortable, lass?"

"The ground is hard," she replied.

"It's been hard most nights, and yet you slept."

"It feels different tonight," she said.

Alex didn't know how to respond, so he continued counting the trees. *Four, five, six...* Isobel slid up against his back, and he immediately tensed. She was pressed against him, head to toe.

"You are warm," she said, snuggling closer to him.

"Do you want another plaid?"

"No. Your warmth is enough."

Alex smiled, savoring the feel of Isobel against his back. If only he could make the night last. *I will miss this. I will miss her.* The admission felt strange. Alex had never missed a woman before. He'd missed his family, his clan, and his home. But never had he missed a woman.

In the next moment, Isobel turned over and touched his arm. She moved her hand up to his shoulder, then over his chest, covering his heart. It stayed there for a few moments, but then her hand glided down his stomach and rested just above the top of his trews.

Alex lay frozen in place as her fingers dived beneath his trews. Remaining above his braies, she outlined his hardened manhood.

She gasped, as if surprised by his state. Alex remained immovable as Isobel slid her hand up and down his length. The pressure of her hand felt good, but it wasn't enough. He needed to remove the barrier between them. Reaching down with both hands, he undid the ties of his trews and braies.

Isobel gasped again as she made contact with his

naked flesh. He bit his lip in ecstasy as she moved up and down his shaft once more, this time without anything between them.

"Is this good?" she asked.

Her hot breath blew in his ear as she spoke, and Alex felt a chill. The heat from her hand—the sound of her voice—the smell of her skin. The heady scent of lavender radiated from her neck.

"Tell me what to do," she whispered.

Alex turned to see her; the sight was intoxicating. There, pressed up against him with her hand wrapped around his cock, was Isobel. In the twilight of the sky, her eyes flickered with passion.

In seconds, he had Isobel on her back, pinned to the ground. Her mouth opened in surprise. He couldn't wait. His lips covered hers, his tongue darting into the warmth of her mouth, seeking out her tongue. His open-mouthed kisses grew in intensity, trying to coax a response from her, until finally—hesitantly—her tongue flicked back. Alex groaned and reached down to pull her legs up, but her skirts were tangled. Frustrated by not being able to feel her, he broke the kiss and pulled back far enough so he could reach down and lift her dress up over her thighs. The motion exposed her delicate smooth skin. He ran his hand from her calf to her hip, savoring the silken texture of her body.

The faint silvery light that filtered through the trees gently illuminated Isobel's face.

"You are so beautiful," he whispered, before seeking her mouth again. He wedged himself snugly between her thighs and moved against her.

You're going too fast, Alex. You need to slow down. But when Isobel reached down and touched his lower back, urging him on as her nails pressed into his tunic, he couldn't remember why he needed to go slow.

He kissed down her neck to her shoulder, pushing away the fabric of her dress to expose the skin there.

"I want you to show me everything, Alex," she whispered.

Her words reminded him of why he needed to take care. *She's a maiden.* Though in the moment, Alex felt like an inexperienced youth himself. He was letting the passion consume him, and he was rushing. He knew why; it had been a year since he'd last been with a woman. *If I keep grinding against her for much longer, I'll spend myself like a sixteen-year-old lad.*

Changing positions, he lifted himself off her and gently closed her legs. Alex leaned onto his side, using his right arm for support, while letting his left hand drift over Isobel's stomach, then breasts. He wished he could feel her flesh in his palm, but their circumstances made it impractical to fully undress her. Not when danger still sought them.

In the next instant, Isobel reached up, capturing his face in both of her hands.

"Kiss me again," she said.

Alex did as she bade, but while he still had the clarity to do so, he leaned over her, feeling along the ground for his gallowglass sword. He grasped its handle and brought it closer to them, tucking it beneath the plaid. He always kept it within arm's reach.

Isobel broke the kiss. "What are you doing, Alex?" she asked.

"Just keeping us safe," he whispered, then captured her lips again.

Isobel sighed between kisses as his hand skimmed

over her breasts, feeling across the exposed skin of her cleavage. With a final kiss on the lips, Alex bent his head and kissed his way down her neck, then to the valley between her breasts.

If only I could take off the damn gown. He knew her breasts would be perfect, like every other part of her. He licked across the top of each breast, and then flicked his tongue beneath the fabric. The action made her cry out.

"Alex, please," she said. He could tell she grew restless, as did he. She reached for him, urging him back to her. He obliged, lifting his head to kiss her. He thrust his tongue into her mouth, and she met him, driving him mad with every touch of her tongue.

Without breaking the kiss, Alex found Isobel turning into him, hooking her leg over his hip. He was grinding up against her again; his hand glided under her skirts to touch her thigh. Her skin was so smooth, like the surface of polished sea glass. *This feels perfect.*

But it's wrong. The thought forced itself from the back of his mind. *She is a maid, and she is in mourning, and she saw me kill a man today. Stop being a selfish bastard.* Finally, he broke the kiss.

"Isobel, we cannae do this," he said, between labored breaths.

"Why not?" Her lips were red and swollen from kissing. " 'Tis clear you want to." She ground up against his hard length; Alex knew she was proving her point.

"I desire you more than anything. But you must see that this isn't right."

Isobel pulled away from him, giving Alex the space to regain more of his sanity.

"Alex, I do not know what the future will bring, but I know what I—what we—can have right now. I'm not asking for anything beyond what this night holds."

She sounded sincere, but Alex felt a tingling in his spine. *She isn't asking anything of me.* It is what most men would desire of a woman. And, yet, it wasn't what he desired. He wanted her—all of her. But Alex could offer her nothing, and she could not save his clan. What he wanted was impossible.

"I care for you too much, Isobel. I will nae use you in such a way." If he could not marry her, he would not take her innocence.

"You are not using me, Alex. I want this. I want to feel some joy and pleasure with someone who cares for me."

"But I cannae marry you."

"I'm not asking for that. I just want you. Tonight." With that, she pressed her lips to his neck, just like she had done outside Katy and Tom's cottage days ago, and drew away from him.

He closed his eyes, trying to see what was right. When he opened them, he took in Isobel's appearance. She lay on her back, her hair spread out and flowing over the plaid, onto the forest floor. For the rest of his days, he knew he would never behold anything as lovely as she.

Alex climbed on top of her then, taking care to keep his weight off her. As he looked into her brilliant violet eyes, he pushed inside her in a single thrust.

****

Isobel awoke before dawn. She was blissfully warm, wrapped in Alex's strong arms. She nuzzled against his chest, savoring the solid feel of him beneath her cheek. She could hear his beating heart—calm and steady. *Did it race last night, as mine did?* The memory of their lovemaking made Isobel dizzy with happiness.

She'd nearly died yesterday. Knowing that she could have left this world had given her the courage to reach out to him last night. Whether she stayed at the nunnery or somehow managed to travel on to Ireland on her own, she wanted the memory of being with Alex to stay with her. And what a memory he'd given her, though the experience had been nothing like she'd imagined. Alex was so strong, and yet, his touch could be feathery light. He was passionate but gentle.

Isobel sighed and snuggled closer to him. She could stay like this forever, but dawn was fast approaching.

"How do you feel this morn?" Alex asked.

Isobel wondered how long he'd been awake; she never heard him stir. She tilted her head back so she could see his face. "I am well."

"I'm glad." He kissed the top of her head.

She could not help but smile. "And you, Crusader? How do you feel this morn?"

"Your crusader is verra happy, lass." He smiled then too, and Isobel's heart fluttered.

My crusader. There, on the forest floor, it was just her and Alex, and nothing else at all mattered in the world.

I love him. The words felt so distant, but as she looked into his eyes they grew closer and closer. *I love him.* The realization felt overwhelming, for what if he did not love her?

Isobel broke free of his arms and sat up, trying to hide her worry.

"We should talk," Alex said, as he sat up beside her.

"There is nothing to discuss." She did not want to hear him speak of his regret.

"There is much to discuss, Isobel," he said. "As you know, my clan is impoverished. In truth, I do not know how severe the circumstances are."

"Alex, you don't have to—" she began, but he raised his hand to silence her.

"Isobel, please, let me explain," he said, reaching out to take hold of her hand. "The marriage to the Angus bride was supposed to save my clan. While I did not see her, I did meet an Angus clansman in Kirkcaldy the night I received the missive from the king. The contract was dissolved during that meeting."

"Then why did you make it seem as though she was still your intended?" Isobel was confused. *If the agreement was dissolved, why did he pretend otherwise?* She was also struck by her own selfishness. She never gave one thought to his betrothed last night. The Angus woman may be his betrothed no more, but Isobel had not known that when she'd acted.

"Because I felt something for you, and I knew I should not," Alex said quietly.

It wasn't "I love you," but with his hushed tone, she could tell he struggled to speak of his feelings. But why did he believe he should not care for her?

"Because I told you I was intended for the church?" she asked.

Alex nodded, but said, "Aye, that was part of it. The rest doesn't matter now." He squeezed her hand. "Isobel, I know I have little to offer you, but will you marry me?"

When this journey began nearly two weeks ago, she could not have fathomed the struggles she would face. She'd killed a man in self-defense, stabbed Robbie MacDonald, and was abducted by two English soldiers. She'd also fought her own mind, finding easily how isolation could damage one's soul, and how the physical world could punish and challenge when the comforts of civilization were removed. Yet, she had not complained, for she was on an adventure, something she had secretly craved in the luxurious confines of her life in David's court. She was getting what she desired, if only for the briefest of times, and she would not decry it for anything.

This experience was now giving her something she had not expected: the chance at a happy marriage. She loved him, and in time, his care for her could become love. This was not a marriage offer based on what he could gain from her, for he did not know that he could gain anything. Even if he assumed David would have set aside a dowry to be gifted to the church upon her taking the vows, it wasn't likely he could have imagined the king's generosity in that regard. David had endowed her with the same sum he had provided for his own flesh and blood. Isobel could help Alex's clan.

But what if his offer is only rooted in duty for taking my innocence? What if he can never love me? She could imagine nothing crueler than marriage to a man she loved but who did not love her in return.

"Isobel?" Alex asked.

"I will give you my answer when our mission to the king is done."

He frowned at her words, but said, "I think that is

fair."

Isobel felt relief. He was not rushing her to commit to anything. She needed time to clear her head, and he needed to return to his family.

"I will see you to the crossing at Fionnphort. MacKinnon soldiers are stationed there, and they will escort you to the prioress. When the Rood is safe, we will speak of what is between us."

Isobel agreed. After breaking their fast, Isobel and Alex gathered their belongings. Mounting their horses, they rode through the pink and yellow light of dawn to their journey's end.

Chapter 22

Once Alex saw Isobel safely onto a boat with two
MacKinnon soldiers for protection, he headed north, up
the coastline of Mull, the short distance to his home. He
coaxed his and Isobel's horses into a gallop. She would
have no use for the horse on Iona, so the mare was
destined for the MacKinnons' small stables. As he
galloped away, he thought on what had passed between
him and Isobel. Once he took her innocence, he knew
what had to be done. While Alex was certain about
precious few things, he knew he was a man of honor.
He only wished he had something to offer her, besides
uncertainty. *Perhaps that is why she withheld her
answer.* He could not fault her for wanting time to think
on his proposal. His clan's circumstances did not leave
him feeling ashamed, but he was anxious to see the true
state of things for himself. His preview came at
Fionnphort in meeting with the MacKinnon soldiers.
The men said nothing of the clan's situation, but their
worn armor and weapons spoke clearly. Circumstances
had not improved in his absence.

As he rode along the rocky coastline, the wooden
keep came into view. There, above the jagged red
granite peaks, stood the dilapidated structure. It was as
if time had stood still in his absence, preserving the
keep just as it had been the day he left on Crusade.

He approached the keep at midmorning where two

soldiers met him at the gates.

"I am Alexander MacKinnon," Alex declared. "Open the gates."

The men exchanged surprised looks but did as he commanded. When the gates parted, he was greeted with an empty bailey. *Where are the men? 'Tis midmorning. The men should be practicing their swordsmanship in the yard.* Yet, no one was about. He walked the horses over to the stables, finding only one stable boy on hand.

"Where is everyone?" he asked the lad, climbing down from the horse.

"In the great hall, *ridire*."

"What is going on in the great hall?" he asked. The morning meal should have been well over by now.

"They are in mourning. Our chief died yesterday."

The weight of the lad's words crashed against him. He felt stunned, like he'd just had the wind knocked out of him. *My father is dead.*

"Where are my sisters?"

"Sisters?" The lad seemed confused. Realizing how young the boy was, Alex knew the lad had no idea he was the chief's son. He introduced himself, then inquired about his sisters once more.

"They might still be at the chief's deathbed, *ridire*," the boy said. "I mean, Chief." He blushed and bowed his head, showing his embarrassment over how to address Alex.

Alex then heard the boy's stomach growl.

"Have you eaten this morn?" he asked.

The lad shook his head. "Nae, Chief."

Alex reached for his leather bag and sorted out a few biscuits and cheese. "Here lad. Eat, then tend to the horses."

"Thank ye, Chief." The boy's eyes lit up as he took the food.

Alex felt angry with himself. *I stayed away too long.*

He made his way into the keep, avoiding the great hall so he could speak with his sisters before announcing his return. He quietly walked up the back stairwell to the family's quarters. He found two guards stationed outside his father's room; he recognized one of them.

"Alexander, 'tis ye!" the old man exclaimed, reaching out to clasp hands with him. His father's most trusted servant and the head of the MacKinnon guard, Donald, was a welcome sight.

"Aye, I am returned home."

"We are glad of it, laddie, but I fear ye are too late," Donald said, solemnly. "The chief died yesterday afternoon."

Alex nodded. "Are my sisters with him?"

"Aye. They wouldn't let us take away the body until ye came back to see him."

"I'm sure that was Joan's decision," Alex said.

"Oh, aye. She's taken charge better than most men, I think. She'll give ye hell, but yer other sisters will welcome ye."

It was as he expected. Joan was much like him. She would be the hardest to reconcile with.

"I want to speak with you and the rest of my father's council at midday."

"Things have gotten worse here in the last year," Donald said. "I'm sorry for what ye have come home to, lad."

Alex nodded, though he felt like he should have been the one to apologize. *How much have they all suffered in my absence?*

Donald and the other guard opened the door to his father's chamber. There, kneeling around his father's bed, were his three sisters: Joan, Anna, and Flora. Their heads were each bowed in prayer as his father, the chief, lay lifeless on the bed. Alex quietly approached them. He reached Flora, the youngest, first. When he'd left, she'd just seen her ninth summer. Now she was a young woman. She lifted her head as he rested his hand on her shoulder.

"Alex!" she exclaimed, launching herself into his arms.

His other sisters rose immediately, with Anna reaching for him too.

"Alex, you're home!" Anna wrapped her arms around him and Flora.

As they all embraced, Alex looked to Joan. She stood still, at their father's side, her face as expressive as uncut granite. *Be patient with her, Alex. She has more reasons to be upset with you than most.*

"It is good to see all of you," Alex said, still hugging Anna and Flora. "I am sorry I was not here when he passed."

" 'Tis all right, Alex. You are here now. That is all that matters," Anna said.

"Aye, Brother. We are grateful you have returned to us," Flora added.

"We sent word of Father's health months ago," Joan said. "Why did it take you so long to return home?"

"I could not obtain passage home sooner, Joan. I

am sorry for it." He broke the hug with his sisters and approached her.

"But you sent word when you reached Edinburgh over a fortnight ago," Joan said, rubbing her emerald pendant necklace. Alex recognized the jewelry. It had belonged to their mother.

"I had business in Kirkcaldy," he explained.

"Oh, aye, and have you brought home the wealthy bride that is to save us all?"

"Nae. That contract with the Angus is broken."

"If you weren't making a marriage alliance, then pray tell us, brother, why did it take you so long to get home from Kirkcaldy?"

"The late King David put me on a mission, which I just finished this morn."

"The late king?" Joan asked. "He is dead?"

"Aye."

All of his sisters bowed their heads in respect. Joan was the first to speak again.

"If you finished it this morn, did the mission have something to do with us?" Joan asked.

"Nae," Alex said. He could not tell them of the relic, and he did not want to lie. " 'Tis naught for any of you to worry over."

He knew Joan was displeased with his response, but his sisters and the Rood were safer if he kept the true meaning of his mission a secret. Once he spoke to Isobel again, he would tell them of her and, he prayed, his impending marriage. If Isobel didn't reject him because of his poverty, then he could see no reason for her to decline him.

Anna and Flora would welcome Isobel, but he was less certain of Joan's response.

Alex looked back to his father's deathbed. There was more white than brown in his beard, and the chief's warrior build had been lost to the illness.

"Sisters, will you give me a moment with him?"

"Of course," said Anna. She and Flora exited the chamber. Joan remained.

"Before the day is through, I would speak to you, Brother," Joan said.

"We will speak soon, Joan. I promise."

She strode from the room, leaving him alone with their father. Alex sat at a chair that had been placed by the bedside.

"Father, I am returned," he began. Though he knew his soul was gone from this world, Alex had to say his piece. "I know what you had hoped of me, but I have brought home no wealthy bride nor spoils of war. But I will make this clan strong again. I will rebuild the keep and fortifications, and I will defend our land from the Macleans."

He did not know how, but Alex would make good on his promises.

"We did not part on good terms, and for that I am sorry. I wanted you to be a better man; your failures angered me, but you always had my love."

No matter what the past held, Alex needed to look to the future. He would not carry the burden of anger with him.

"Be at peace, Father, for I am at peace with you."

With that, Alex stood and with one final look at his father—his chief—he left the room.

****

Around midday, Alex stood in his father's solar, now his solar, and spoke with the council members.

"We are hopeful of a better farming season," Old John said. John had been in charge of the farming since Alex was a lad. "Last year, we faced a blight. Lost over half the crops. 'Tis why the stores are so low, Chief."

It felt strange to be called "chief," but that was his title now. He needed to get used to it.

"Have the fields been sown for the summer?" Alex asked.

"Aye, we did it a few weeks back." Old John looked to his son, Ian. "Planted dozens of fields, plus there are the crofts." Ian nodded in agreement.

"Have many croft tenants do we have?"

"I am nae certain, Chief," Old John said.

"There is no record?" Alex asked in surprise.

"Nae," Old John and Ian said in unison.

"I want a record of all the tenants. I also want a list of crops planted and the expected yield," he told Old John and Ian. "Use the scribe to help prepare it." If the men hadn't thought to keep records, perhaps they could not read and write. Even so, the lack of organization was problematic. *Had they never kept records?* Perhaps this is why his clan had struggled so. Things were not being done as they should be.

Next, he turned to Fergus. He was in charge of the fishing and hunting. One by one, each man gave the account of what they supervised. By the end, Alex was fully aware of just how dire the circumstances were.

In addition to the poor record keeping of the crops, the fishermen had but two boats to fish from, because there were no craftsmen left in the clan and the soldiers didn't know how to build fishing boats or larger *birlinns*. The hunters were ill trained and ill equipped.

He had respected the men his father put in charge,

but now he no longer did. Such incompetence would kill them all.

Alex would address one problem at a time. First, he would send a messenger to his uncle in Ireland. He needed skilled warriors, and he needed supplies. Then, Alex planned to meet with the fishermen. Once the food stores were restocked, he would address the bounty of other problems that lay before him.

Before the men dispersed, he wanted to glean what they knew of the Maclean chief's plans.

"The Maclean said he propositioned my father. Do you all know of this?"

The men nodded.

"The chief has made it clear to me he will take our lands by force, if the MacKinnons dinnae freely submit to him."

"We are nae prepared for battle, Chief." The comment came from Donald, the head of the guard. "I know ye have yet to take stock of the men, but ye will find they are in nae shape to go up against the Macleans."

"I trust you are right, Donald. But no MacKinnon will submit to a Maclean. Not while I live," he said. "We will speak on it more later. Now, bring me a messenger and prepare a boat."

"Yes, Chief," Donald said, and the men dispersed.

When the door closed, Alex dropped into his father's chair and sighed heavily. He raked his fingers through his hair, bowing his head over the desk. He gave himself a few moments to compose himself. With his frustration temporarily set aside, he took out a fresh piece of parchment and set to work writing a letter to his uncle. He prayed men would come. He prayed it would be enough.

Chapter 23

Isobel sat before the prioress, taking in the serene calmness the woman displayed. The stories of her were true. The Lord of the Isles's daughter, Bethoc, was all purity and light. The woman's peaceful nature seemed to fill the room, surrounding Isobel with a stillness and sureness she had not felt in some time. The prioress held a letter from David, the one attesting to the authenticity of the relic.

When she'd arrived at the nunnery the morning before, the prioress had been in the midst of a day of prayer. Since Isobel could not meet with her, the nuns offered her shelter for the night, promising she would have an audience with the prioress the next morning. Isobel agreed and, though she was anxious to hand over the Rood, the exhaustion of the journey finally caught up to her. Intending to take a brief nap, she slept the whole day and night away, awaking just after dawn.

The nuns brought her a meal and took her on a tour of the nunnery. The buildings were modest but well built. All the buildings were connected to the square cloister at the center, including the humble chapel where Isobel spent the morning waiting to meet with the prioress.

Eventually, a nun presented herself and bid Isobel to follow her to the quarters of the prioress. She was seated across from Bethoc, and after exchanging a few pleasantries, Isobel presented her with the Rood.

After reading the letter from David, the prioress lifted the Rood case, which Isobel had placed on the table between them.

"I will keep it safe, Lady Isobel. David was wise in many things, and he was wise in sending you to us," Bethoc said.

"Thank you, my lady. I am happy I have completed David's last work."

The prioress took the case and carefully wrapped it in a fine wool cloth. "We have a place to house such treasures. The relic will have a home here, along the sea, and it will not be lost."

"I fear more men will come for it," Isobel said. She explained the attempts made on it during her journey to Iona.

"Danger follows all treasures of this world, especially one as important as this. But with the MacKinnons and with the help of my father, I am certain it will be kept safe."

Isobel nodded. She was confident in the prioress and at peace with giving the relic over to her. Now Bethoc would be its steward, as David was before her.

"And what of you, Lady Isobel? Will you make your home here as well?"

"I confess I am not entirely certain, my lady."

The prioress nodded and reached for a piece of folded parchment that lay on the table in front of her. "I think you should read this before you decide."

"What is it?" Isobel asked, taking the parchment from her.

"A letter from King David. It arrived from Carlisle a few days ago. An accompanying letter told me to anticipate your arrival."

"Truly? He sent me a letter?" Isobel could not have hoped to hear from him again.

"Lady Isobel, I want you to know Iona can be your home, whether you choose to take the vows or not. You are welcome here."

Isobel had not anticipated this. She assumed to stay on Iona meant taking her place in the church.

"Your offer is most generous, my lady."

Isobel could no longer contain her interest. The prioress appeared to hold great admiration for the late king, but the Maclean woman had said Somerled claimed Iona and Mull.

"I am curious about something," Isobel began.

"Yes?"

" 'Tis just that rule of the Isles confuses me. I always understood that King David laid claim to these lands, yet I hear your father claims them for himself. Still, you respect King David's last wishes."

The prioress nodded in understanding of Isobel's confusion. "The king was a good man," Bethoc said. "As to the rest, I have no easy answer to explain control of these lands, though I can tell you my father would have a definitive one."

Rule of the Inner Hebrides was more complicated than Isobel imagined if even Somerled's daughter would not say who controlled them, though it was clear the Lord of Isles claimed them.

"I can tell you my father values the MacKinnons' stewardship of these lands, and he will protect the Rood," Bethoc said. "You need only worry over your own future now."

My future, Isobel thought.

The prioress smiled. "I understand Alexander MacKinnon escorted you here."

"Aye, my lady," she said, unable to meet Bethoc's eyes.

"I imagine it would be easy to get close to someone under such circumstances."

Isobel felt her cheeks grow warm. She knew exactly what the prioress was implying. What could she say? *Oh, yes. I fell madly in love with him, but I do not know if he loves me.*

The prioress stood and walked the short space around the table to reach Isobel. She took one of her hands and folded it between her own. "Love is not simple, is it?"

"No, my lady. It is not," Isobel admitted.

"I will pray for you, Isobel. I will pray that your path to happiness will be shown to you."

Isobel thanked the prioress again and excused herself. She wandered out into the nunnery's kitchen garden, admiring the wildflowers that bloomed in the late June sunshine. She found a spot on the low garden wall to sit and unfolded the letter from David. It read:

My dear Isobel,

When we parted, I fear I may have left you feeling as though you would disappoint me if you did not choose the church. This is not true. I never found the right mate for you at court, so I wanted you to have a home, should you never find the love you sought. But, in truth, I knew the church was not for you. There is a light in you that should be shared with the world.

I do not know what you have come to think of the crusader, Alexander MacKinnon, but in my brief meeting with him, I could tell he was a man of honor. I know he would respect you and value you, though love is a more complicated thing to predict.

If you do not come to hold him in that regard, then you can still make Iona your home, even without the vows. The prioress will welcome you as an indefinite guest, as I hope she has already made clear to you. Your land and coin will be yours to do with as you see fit. Whatever path you choose, Isobel, know that you have my full blessing.

Be brave. Be kind. Be a light.

Love,

Your father

Isobel hugged the letter to her heart. David was giving her the freedom she sought. *No, not David. My father.* The decision of what to do was entirely her own, free from any limitations. Her father had made certain of that.

Feeling lighter than she had ever felt, Isobel took a turn around the garden. As she walked past a bed of lavender, she caught sight of men walking toward the abbey, just up the path from the nunnery. They carried a bier between them.

"The chief has died," a voice said from behind her.

Isobel turned to see a nun covered in flour appear, presumably from the kitchens. The nun dusted some of the flour off her gown and came to stand by Isobel.

"The MacKinnon chief?" Isobel asked.

The nun nodded. "The day before last."

Alex never got to say goodbye to his father.

She looked on as the men continued their progress from the boat. "They are taking him to Columba's Church?"

"They are walking the body up *Sráid nam Marbh*

to *Reilig Odhráin*," the nun said.

"Forgive me. I am not familiar with those words."

" 'Sráid nam Marbh' means 'Street of the Dead,' and 'Reilig Odhráin' is 'Oran's burial ground,' " the nun explained. "Many great kings and chiefs are buried there: Kenneth, son of Alpin, Macbeth, and Donald Ban are interred there."

"It is a great honor to be buried there then," Isobel said.

"Oh, aye, my lady." The nun looked over her shoulder. "I should return to the kitchen."

After the young nun disappeared into the building behind her, Isobel walked to the road and observed the MacKinnons once more. Surely Alex was among them. He would see to his father's burial. She slowly approached, keeping a respectful distance. She watched from behind the stone wall surrounding the cemetery as the men dispersed. Eventually, only one remained: Alex. After a few moments, she found herself standing by his side.

"He rests among the greatest men in the Isles now," Alex said.

Isobel reached for him. Without looking, he captured her hand in his.

"The situation for my people is worse than I imagined," Alex said, after several moments of silence. "I can see now why Maclean thinks our land is ripe for the picking."

"Does he?" This must have been what the Maclean chief summoned him for at Duart Keep.

"He wants our lands and our allegiance."

"Are you afraid he will attack?"

"Aye. Perhaps by the full moon. When we last

spoke, I said I would consider his offer. I did so to buy time."

"What preparations have you made?" Isobel asked.

"I sent a messenger to my uncle, William, yesterday. With his counsel and men, I will make a plan."

Isobel nodded. She could not fathom what he faced. He was the new chief, and with it he had inherited a complex set of problems. The clan's ability to survive depended on him.

And I can help him. Her father's words came back to her. *My lands and coin are mine to do with as I please.*

"Ah, lass. I didnae even ask you if the Rood is safe. Did Bethoc accept it?"

"Yes, she is happy to protect it."

"I'm concerned about the bishop and the duke," Alex said. "I sent more men here this morning and stationed extra guards at the crossing. I hope the Lord of the Isles will also help keep the relic safe."

"The prioress expressed as much to me when we spoke. She expects his help," Isobel said.

"I will visit with her soon, but not today."

"She is enchanting, as you said she would be."

Alex nodded and looked down at his father's grave. "Can you give me a moment?" he asked.

"Of course." She went and stood at the gate to the burial ground, as Alex paid his final respects to his father.

Isobel looked around her. Beyond the tombstones stood Columba's church. The gray and red stone structure was simple with little ornamentation. However, in the churchyard, towering at least twenty feet into the sky, stood three stone crosses. From her distance, she could not see all the details of their designs, but she recognized the Celtic scrollwork carved into the center cross. There were examples of such craftsmanship in Edinburgh. Isobel's tutors had told her the pieces came from Ireland and the Western Isles.

"Aren't they remarkable?" Alex asked, joining her.

Isobel hadn't heard him approach. "They are extraordinary," she said.

"Come. There is much to see. I'll show you the island." Alex took her hand, and they left the cemetery.

They walked down a lane that led to the dunes. They strolled along the sandy beach, and Isobel took in the beauty of the noonday sun glistening off the blue water. She'd lived near the North Sea most of her life, yet she had never been mesmerized by it in the way she was with the inner seas of the Western Isles.

She couldn't imagine living in such a place with anyone other than Alex. Whatever path lay before her, she knew she wanted to share it with him.

"Alex, I've made my decision." She stopped their progress up the beach and reached for his other hand. She stood before him, looking up into his gray-blue eyes.

"Will you be my wife?" he asked. Lines of worry traced his brow.

"Aye, Alexander MacKinnon. I will be your wife."

"Do you mean it?"

"Yes." Isobel smiled, and Alex swept her up in his arms. She laughed at his exuberance and wrapped her arms around him. He twirled her around in a circle as a gentle sea breeze blew past them.

Suddenly, Alex stopped spinning and set her on the ground. "Lass, you cannae marry me."

"What are you talking about?" She didn't understand.

"I've no money, the Macleans will be bearing down on us any day, we've no army, no food, and the damn keep is falling apart." He spoke like a man possessed. "What was I thinking making an offer to you? I have nothing to offer, Isobel. Nothing!"

He looked defeated, and Isobel could not stand it.

"All I want is you, Alex." Isobel reached up to touch his face; he leaned his cheek into her palm, then took it in his hands and laid a kiss on it.

"Isobel, ye deserve a proper home. I don't even know if my home will be standing next week." His voice was calm but full of regret.

"Then we'll rebuild it."

"I've no coin for that right now," Alex said. "But maybe once I handle the Macleans and replenish the food stores, I'll find a way to make some coin. It could take years, but would you wait for me?"

"No," Isobel said. "I will not."

"You won't wait for me?" He looked stunned.

"No. There is no need to," Isobel said. "My dowry will be enough to rebuild the keep and restock the stores."

"Your dowry?"

"Did you not think I had one?" Now Isobel was surprised. "The king provided for me. It is a good sum. I should even be able to provide dowries for your sisters as well. They are not yet married, are they?"

"Nae," he said. "But Isobel, are you certain?"

"I would not jest about such a thing." She took his

hands in her own again, squeezing gently to emphasize her sincerity. "Let me help. Let me be of use to your clan."

"They will be your clan too, if you will still have me."

"I will have you, Alex."

"It will not be an easy life, even with the coin to rebuild," he warned.

"I do not want my life to be easy. I want it to be full."

"That, I think, I can give you, Isobel," he said, wrapping his arms around her.

Isobel held onto him tightly. *And, just perhaps, you can also give me love, Alexander MacKinnon.*

Chapter 24

The next morning, Alex returned to Iona to bring Isobel back to MacKinnon Keep. He gathered his sisters in the great hall after the noonday meal and made the introductions.

"Lady Isobel, I'd like you to meet my sisters. This is Flora," he said, pointing to his youngest sibling. She stepped forward and bowed, just as he'd asked her to do. He then introduced Anna and Joan, who also stepped forward and bowed.

"It is a pleasure to meet you all," Isobel said.

Alex took Isobel's hand in his and looked at his sisters. "I have some news for you," he said. "Isobel has agreed to marry me."

Flora and Anna cried out in joy.

"That's wonderful!" Flora exclaimed.

"How exciting!" Anna said. "Congratulations to you both!"

Joan remained quiet.

"Are you not happy, Joan?" he asked.

"Can I speak with you privately, Brother?" Joan asked.

"Aye," he said. He kissed Isobel on the cheek and left her to speak with Flora and Anna. At least they were happy about the marriage. Joan, it seemed, was not. He followed her outside into the bailey. The soldiers were taking a break from their training, so they were able to speak without an audience.

"Why did you not congratulate us?" Alex asked.

"Why should I?" Joan countered. "We know nothing of this woman. Could you have nae prepared us for your announcement yesterday?"

"I thought it would be a nice surprise," Alex said.

"Alex, I am two and twenty. I dinnae want any damn surprises. I want to know what is going on," she said.

"Since when do you curse?" he asked.

"Since I became the interim chief and chatelaine of this keep," she said, with her head held high. "Now answer me. What is this marriage about?"

Alex sighed. Since their father took ill, and perhaps even before that, Joan had stepped up and taken charge. It would be hard for her to relinquish that role, now he was returned home. He should have prepared his sisters for the announcement, but for some foolish reason, he thought they'd enjoy the surprise. At least Anna and Flora didn't seem to mind.

"Forgive me, Joan. I should have explained things before," Alex began. "Isobel is King David's daughter. My mission was to escort her to Iona."

"For what purpose?" Joan asked.

"Well, she was originally destined to take her vows at the nunnery, but things changed." Alex felt strangely embarrassed explaining the situation. "We care for each other."

"Wooed her with your heroic tales of battle, did you?" Joan asked.

Alex frowned. "I didnae woo her."

"What is the real reason you are marrying her?"

"I've just told you. I care for her, and she cares for

me."

" 'Tis not why people marry," Joan countered.

Pray to the kings of Alba, she sounds just like me. Alex had to grin. " 'Tis why we're marrying."

"Alex, I'm happy for you if you truly care for this woman, but does she understand our circumstances? You have little to offer her," Joan said.

"I know. She understands our situation."

"Then she must really care for you," Joan said, and smiled. It was the first time he'd seen her smile since he'd returned home.

"Let's go back inside. There is more to discuss, and I want Anna and Flora to hear it."

"Alex, I still want to talk about some things," Joan said. Her eyes were tired, not fierce and determined, as he remembered them being. He'd promised to speak with her, but there hadn't been time yet.

"I know I've been busy since I returned, but we will talk."

They went back into the great hall. Alex found Anna and Flora sitting around Isobel at one of the hall's long tables. They seemed completely enamored by her. As he and Joan approached, he overhead their conversation.

"And you would teach us how to read and write?" Flora asked.

"Yes," Isobel said. "Your brother has said you would enjoy learning." Isobel looked at him and smiled as he joined them at the table.

"But we have nae books. Do we, Alex?" Flora asked. Her lower lip trembled, and her face was pale.

"Nae," Alex said. He did not like to see Flora distressed, but they had no books and no means to acquire any.

"I've sent for my trunks," Isobel said. "There will be a dozen books here within a few days' time."

Alex was surprised to hear she'd sent for her belongings. He assumed her location needed to be kept secret. Though, if the bishop already knew of the Rood's location, it probably didn't matter if he learned Isobel was set to marry Alex. Still, he would ask her about it later.

"There are two more things to discuss," Alex said, interrupting the lasses' talk of Isobel's book collection. He asked Joan to take a seat as well.

"First, a man by the name of Robbie MacDonald will be arriving within the next few days. He brings with him his sister, Agnes, and brother, Murdoch. Agnes is unwell and will be treated by the clan's physician."

"Why are they coming here?" Anna asked.

"MacDonald is a strong warrior, and we need his help."

"For what?" Flora asked.

"That is the second thing I want to talk about." Alex straightened his spine and looked around the table at each of his sisters. "The Macleans want the MacKinnons to submit to them. They also want our lands. I believe it is the chief's design to lay claim to the whole of the island."

"He spoke to Father last summer, but Father said he wanted to buy some of our lands. Not take them all or force us to submit to him," Joan said.

"Things have changed," he said. "I am preparing the men to fight, but I wanted you all to be aware."

"We lost many strong fighters when Father took

ill," Joan said. "What if we lose?"

"I've sent word to our uncle, and it is my hope he will bring a contingent of warriors with him. I am also working with the remaining soldiers, and I have seen some promising skill."

"There are always the terms to negotiate as well," Isobel said. "Should the Macleans even try to attack, they will still present terms."

"I cannae see that we have anything to negotiate, Isobel," Alex said.

Isobel simply smiled, but he suspected she would have more to say on it later. Since he'd relayed all the news he needed to share with his sisters, he excused himself to take Isobel on a tour of the keep. He showed her the kitchens and, with pride, the growing store of food supplies. His few hunting and fishing trips had been successful, and the cooks were curing the meats in the cellar. He then took her upstairs, showing her the guest quarters, and finally, his room. Soon to be their room.

"It's plain," Alex said, as they stepped into the room.

"You may miss the days of it being plain," Isobel said. "A woman's touch is not always light."

"You are welcome to change anything you like," Alex said, finding he meant it. He was actually curious to see how she would put her touch on things, how she would make the keep her home.

"My trunks should be well stocked with tapestries," Isobel said.

"You sent for them quickly."

"Yes, yesterday after you left." Isobel frowned. "Was I being hasty?"

"Nae. Of course not," Alex said. "I was just concerned for your safety, but the bishop already assumes your location. It matters not if he knows we are to wed."

"David's closest adviser, James, is in charge of dispatching my dowry. It is my understanding, from the correspondence the prioress has received, that he has gone back to Stirling, which is in fact where my possessions are being kept," Isobel explained. "I was only meant to send for them if I married. I do not think the bishop is a threat to me without the Rood, though it is unlikely for him to have knowledge of our marriage as a result of my trunks being returned to me."

Alex nodded. It never occurred to him Isobel would have a dowry or trunks of treasures to bring to Mull. It showed how little he understood her relationship to the late king, though he knew she viewed him as a father figure.

"But about my dowry..." Isobel began. "When I spoke of the terms between you and the Macleans..."

"Aye?"

"Does the Maclean have a son?"

"Aye. Ewan. What of him?" Ewan would not negotiate on his father's behalf, even though he was a reasonable man or, rather, he'd been fair-minded in his youth.

"A peaceful way to resolve this conflict could be through marriage," Isobel said.

"Who would marry Ewan?" Alex was confused.

"Perhaps Joan or Anna," Isobel said. "Both are of age."

"Even if I wasn't completely against marrying off one of my sisters to those bastards," Alex said. "What incentive would they have to take her anyway?"

"I told you I could provide your sisters with dowries. I think the right sum could be enough to subdue Maclean's ambition."

Alex had been so busy, he'd forgotten of Isobel's offer to supply the dowries. *How much she offers me and my family and how little I can give her in return.* "Isobel, I dinnae think—"

"I do not mean to imply I wish to force your sisters' hands," Isobel interrupted. "But if this Ewan is a kind sort, perhaps one of your sisters could find happiness with him."

"Ewan is kind," Alex said. "At least, I remember him being so." He would not force one of his sisters to marry a man who was anything like the Maclean chief. He hoped the son did not take after the father.

"Then perhaps it could work?" Isobel asked, coming to stand beside him.

"Aye, perhaps," Alex said. "But it would only work if Anna agreed. Ewan and Joan would not suit."

"We should speak to her about it tomorrow, after I start their lessons."

"Lessons?"

"Yes, I promised to teach the girls about geography. Anna said your father has a collection of maps. I thought it would be a good place to start," Isobel said.

Her eyes sparkled with such excitement; she was beaming with joy. Her words to him a few days ago came back. She wanted to use her knowledge and gifts, and she was finally getting to do so. He had no doubt she'd be an excellent tutor.

"Aye, he does have some fine maps," Alex said.

"And you are welcome to them."

"Thank you, Alex."

" 'Tis I who should give thanks," Alex said. "You are willing to give so much. I cannae say how grateful I am."

Isobel reached out to him and took his hands in her own.

"You are giving me a home, Alex. The exchange is equal. We both gain much with this marriage," Isobel said. "I only hope that with time—"

"What, lass?" Alex said.

Isobel shook her head. " 'Tis nothing."

Alex did not press her, but he wanted to know what else she desired. Whatever was in his power to give would be hers.

A knock sounded at the door, and Isobel released his hands.

Alex answered the door. A man said, "Forgive the interruption, Chief, but the supplies have been gathered, and the men are ready."

"Thank you, Fergus. I will be down in a moment." Alex closed the door.

"Who was that?" she asked, as he turned back to face her.

"Fergus. He was, still is for the time, in charge of hunting and fishing," Alex said.

"Are you planning to go out with the men to fish?" Isobel asked. Being so close to the ocean, she imagined the clan all but lived off the sea.

"Nae. Today I am showing them how to build boats," Alex said. "We only have two seaworthy crafts, and we are shy one since I sent men to Ireland in search of my uncle. Fergus says a half-finished fishing boat is sitting near the bay. If the wood hasn't rotted, I aim to complete it today."

"It will be good for you to build something with the men," Isobel said. Though she grew up near the North Sea, she knew little about fishing. The talk of the boat reminded her that she also knew very little about Alex and his past. "Did you fish as a child?"

Alex shook his head. "Surprisingly, nae, but I learned how on Crusade. That is also where I learned to build boats."

Now wasn't the time to focus on his past. She wanted him to feel confident about the task before him.

"Your clan is fortunate then," Isobel said. "Your experiences give you invaluable knowledge and skills."

"I dinnae know that the men see it that way," Alex said.

"They will. In time," Isobel said. *He needs to be patient. The chief just died, and the new chief has been gone for six years.* Alex had not endured what his people had suffered during his absence. The clan's people would naturally have strong feelings about everything, but such feelings would fade with time.

"Why are you so certain of things?" Alex asked, wrapping his arms her.

Isobel leaned her head against his chest. "I'm not certain of everything," she said. *I'm not certain if you love me.*

Chapter 25

Alex stood atop a small wooden podium in the bailey. Before him were all the clan's soldiers, farmers, hunters, and fishermen. The men selected represented not only the strongest of the MacKinnons, but also every man and lad able to lift an axe or a bow. It did not matter what their skill might be, for in the fight against the Macleans they were all needed. He'd already worked with the soldiers and evaluated their skill, but today, he would begin training all the men and start to reestablish the clan's small fleet of boats.

"Why are we all training for battle?" a man from the crowd shouted. "We are nae soldiers!"

"You will train to be one," Alex said. "We need every able-bodied man to ready themselves for a fight."

"Just submit to the Macleans!" another man shouted. "Or we will all be dead!"

"No MacKinnon will ever kneel before a Maclean. Not so long as I am chief," he shouted at the crowd.

"What about our women and children?" the clansman who originally challenged him demanded.

Alex understood their concerns. There was much to lose if the Maclean army attacked. His sisters and Isobel were among those who could die in enemy hands if he didn't defend the keep. Surely his people knew that, but as he looked around at the faces staring back at him he saw only one thing—downtrodden men. They had lived through dark times that Alex could only imagine. But he knew their fate would be worse serving a tyrant like the Maclean chief. Alex understood the necessity of maintaining relationships with the neighboring clans. No one wanted bloodshed, though it often came to that. His clan had been fortunate to experience a long time of peace, especially given their reduced circumstances. But that peace was threatened now, and it was time for the MacKinnons to stand up. They needed to give all they had for the welfare of the clan.

"Maclean is concerned with domination," Alex said. "Once he controls these lands, your daily lives will be controlled by him. Your women and children will be his to do with as he wills. He can discard you as though your life is meaningless."

"Ye dinnae ken that!" The man that last spoke challenged him again.

"What is your name?" Alex asked.

The man looked around the crowd before answering. "I am Neil."

"Neil, I just broke bread with the Maclean chief a few days ago," Alex began. "You must trust me when I say he is nae a man you want to rule over your children."

And yet I ask my sister to wed the bastard's son. The thought wore on Alex's conscience. The only hope was that Ewan was different from his father and that the old chief would not be in power for much longer.

"More men will be joining us," Alex said. "We will have help, and God willing, no man here will have to draw a weapon against a single Maclean. But we must be prepared. And we all must be willing to step up and help wherever it be needed. That is the only way we nae only survive, but thrive again."

He looked back to Neil, finding the man's sun-worn face in the crowd. "Neil, I know I ask much, but I ask no more than I myself am willing to give. Will you help me protect our people and our home?"

The man looked around again; all eyes in the crowd were on him. He didn't respond, so Alex continued.

"I am your new chief," Alex said, looking out over the faces of all the men that gathered around him. He took note of their tattered clothes. Many were far too thin. *This is why they dinnae trust me.* He could not change the past though—no man could.

"I cannae take away the last six years, but together we will build a better future."

He took his time, looking each and every man in the eye. He wanted to give them hope, but he also had a warning.

"For those of you who are nae willing to give me your full allegiance, I bid you a safe journey for you are nae welcome here."

Alex waited; not one man budged.

"Then let us get started," he said. "Today, we build a new fishing boat. Tomorrow, we train to fight."

****

The next morning Alex and half a dozen of the MacKinnon men carried the finished boat down to the water. They were fortunate the frame was strong, with the wood showing no signs of rot. The task was simple to complete, with the logs cut, dried, and waiting in storage to be used. The builders in the clan had left for Ireland long ago, when Alex's father took ill, and so, like the keep, projects were left unfinished. That was finally changing.

"Nearly there," Alex said, as they carried the boat beyond the stables, where they could access the sea.

A band of red granite snaked out into the water like a crescent moon, providing a natural barrier from the rough waters that storms created. The clan used the shallow inlet there as a natural harbor. Alex recalled the days when the harbor was brimming with activity of fishermen departing and returning. Now, only one boat was being prepared to go fishing in the sea.

As they neared the water, ships appeared on the horizon.

"Who do ye think it is?" Fergus asked, coming to stand beside him. "We've nae seen a fleet that size in these parts since the Viking raids."

"With any luck, it is my uncle," Alex said. "Let us get the boat in the water."

Alex and the men lowered the boat into the harbor. To his relief, it stayed afloat.

Fergus slapped him on the back. "Look at that! She floats!"

"She's a fine craft," said Neil, the man that had challenged him yesterday.

"We'll fish on her together," Alex said, grasping the man's shoulder.

"I'll be happy to join ye, Chief," Neil said, returning the gesture.

It had only taken one day and a new fishing boat to win the respect of some of his men. Only a few hundred men remained under his charge, but they were all loyal MacKinnons. They would fight to protect the clan. He was confident of that now.

Fergus explained how many of the men lost faith when Alex's father took ill. Circumstances were already dire, and they feared there was no end in sight. Alex could understand it, but he would never abandon his people—no matter how impossible the situation seemed. He would prove that to the men, but it would take time. He'd gained a lot of ground with the men today; it was enough for now.

Alex joined everyone by the water and studied the mass of ships sailing toward them. *Should I alert the soldiers?* When he saw the MacKinnon banner flying on the leading ship, the *birlinn* he'd dispatched the day of his return, he knew the force was friendly. Alex let out a triumphant whistle.

"Men, let's give these Irish a warm welcome!" he shouted. "My uncle brings skilled warriors to help us fight!"

The men cheered and clapped.

Alex took in the sight of warriors approaching on the *birlinns*. There were at least twelve vessels. Alex guessed there to be over a hundred men.

"Is this all of them?" one of the MacKinnon men asked.

"I believe so," Alex said.

"But there is only a hundred or so men on these boats," the man said.

"A hundred skilled warriors are worth a great deal," Alex said.

"He's right," Neil agreed. "Just look at them."

There were few greater sights to behold. Alex hadn't seen anything comparable since he'd left on Crusade. Though the contingent was much smaller than the one he had sailed with to Lisbon, it was no less impressive to him now. As the boats drew near, he could discern more details of the group. Alex spotted his uncle; he led the convoy in the MacKinnon *birlinn* with twelve other men. Most were over six feet tall, muscular, and well-equipped with weaponry and armor. There was no mistaking them for anything other than warriors.

Alex and a few men gathered the ropes that his uncle and the Irish tossed over to them. They pulled the boat in, allowing the men to come ashore. His uncle was the first off the *birlinn*.

"Uncle William," Alex said, clasping hands with his father's younger brother.

"Alexander," he said, as they embraced.

"I thank you for coming with haste." Alex looked around as the warriors unloaded the boats. The men looked battle ready, and Alex could not have been more grateful. *We can fight now. If we must go to battle, we stand a chance.*

"Aye, nephew. I brought ye as many men as I could gather. They'd be keen for some food and drink, though we brought our own rations. I didnae ken how dire circumstances were."

"Things are nae good, Uncle."

"I should've checked in on my brother more often," Uncle William said. "We've been distant for many years, but 'twas nae an excuse for staying away from ye and my nieces."

"That is the past. You were not responsible for Father's choices." As far back as Alex's memory could take him, there was always conflict between his father and uncle, though Alex never knew the cause of it. When Alex went to foster on Skye, his uncle left for

Ireland to make a life for himself. Since he'd become a gallowglass warrior, Alex's uncle made few visits home. Alex could not fault him for it; his uncle needed to live his own life. "I am grateful for you coming now. The Macleans are a strong force, and the MacKinnons that remain are ill prepared to meet them."

"How much time do we have?"

"A fortnight," Alex said. "Assuming he attacks when I decline his offer to submit."

"I've trained warriors in less time," Uncle William said.

"What about croft farmers and fishermen?" Alex asked.

Uncle William frowned but said, "When it comes to protecting the clan, everyone is a warrior."

Alex nodded. "Come. We shall speak inside while you and your men enjoy refreshments."

****

A few days later, Isobel's trunks arrived and with them enough food, wine, and ale for a grand feast. The food and drink were taken to the kitchens, and Isobel's trunks were taken to Alex's chamber. Isobel could not contain her excitement at the reunion with some of her treasured possessions, things she thought would be lost to her forever if she took her vows to the church. Her fine gowns and shoes were not what elicited her joy—it was her collection of books. Isobel knelt beside the trunk and carefully removed each volume, laying them out on the floor before her.

A knock sounded at the door.

"Isobel, are you in there?" It was Alex.

"Yes," she called. " 'Tis unlocked."

Alex came in and knelt on the floor in front of her.

"Are they not magnificent?" She carefully lined the books up in front of Alex. "They cover history, art, medicine, and literature."

Alex picked up one of the volumes between two fingers. The weight of the tome caused his fingers to turn red with the pressure he exerted to keep hold of it.

What on earth? Isobel's brows furrowed at the peculiar way he held the book. Then she realized, *He's never held a book.*

"Gently," she said, cupping her hands under his, showing him the way to hold it. "Use both hands." Alex did as she said, cradling the tome in his palms. Isobel opened to the first hand-written page to show him.

"This is *Beowulf*," Isobel said. "Have you heard of the epic poem?"

"Nae," Alex said.

"It's wonderful!" Isobel exclaimed. "We can read it together sometime. If you like."

"I would enjoy that," Alex said, gently handing the book to her. "These are more books than I have ever seen. My sisters will be overjoyed when you teach them to read."

"And I am overjoyed to be able to share my gifts with them," Isobel said, carefully placing *Beowulf* back on the floor with the other books. "Did you see the feast David's man sent?"

"Aye," Alex said. "I've just come from the kitchens. The cook was in tears." He moved so he could lean against the wall at Isobel's side.

"With the coin I have, the food stores will always be full. So long as we manage the funds well."

"I agree," Alex said. "I never want my people—our people—to suffer again."

Isobel felt her heart flutter when he said "our people." Soon she would be one of them. She understood his concern; the clan's impoverished state was evident everywhere she looked. Alex's sisters' gowns were worn nearly as thin as parchment. She'd also seen many men, women, and children who were underweight. Isobel knew hunger. No matter how much time passed, the memory of her childhood pain never faded. Her heart ached for anyone who had ever gone hungry.

"Why is it like this, Alex? What happened?"

"I dinnae know the whole of it," Alex began. "I know Father mismanaged my mother's fortune. Things were difficult when I left, but I did not imagine they would grow worse in my absence. Naive thinking, aye?"

"Did your father write to the king when things turned dire?"

"Nae," Alex said. "Not so far as I know."

"David would have helped. I am sure of it."

"That may be true, but it does nae matter now," Alex said. He slid away from the wall to sit cross-legged by Isobel. "I would love to stay, but I best get back to the solar."

"What are you working on?"

"The records." He sighed and ran his fingers through his hair, leaving his locks disheveled. The sight of him looking unkempt made Isobel's pulse quicken.

"I'm having a hell of a time making sense of everything," Alex said. "Joan tried her best, but with her limited ability to read and write and do figures, much has been confused."

Isobel nodded, trying to focus on his worries and

not his lips. *It's shameful to be thinking of him kissing me when he's clearly concerned about the records.* Then it occurred to her. "I could help," Isobel offered. "If you will permit me." She had not considered what role Alex would expect of her. Most women were not involved in the record keeping, but she was the practical choice.

"Would you want to?" Alex seemed intrigued by her suggestion.

"Yes, I would," Isobel said. "I can read and write in Scots Gaelic, though I will admit I am not familiar with all the words yet. And I can do my figures. I had a mathematics tutor in Edinburgh."

"I welcome your many talents, Isobel," Alex said. "We can work on it together."

"I'll come to your solar after the midday meal."

Alex agreed.

Already, Isobel felt purposeful, and it made her happier than she ever imagined. She'd had no firm purpose in her father's court, and she'd never established a kinship with his children. They were not mean to her, of course. They were just indifferent to her. She loved David and Mattie, but she felt if they had tried to create a connection between her and their children, things could have been different. Perhaps she would have felt like she belonged.

Now, as Alex's soon-to-be wife, she would be more than just the chatelaine of the keep. She would help manage the bookkeeping and tutor his sisters. She could belong here, though she needed to take care as she assumed Joan's role. Isobel could only imagine how she would feel if all her duties were taken away and given to someone else.

"We should talk about the wedding," Alex said.

They did need to think on the wedding, though Isobel was hesitant to move forward.

"Perhaps we should wait until the Maclean threat is dealt with," she said.

"There is still time before he expects my answer," Alex said. "Besides, a celebration would be good for the clan. They've had little cause to celebrate over the years."

"It would lift everyone's spirits," Isobel agreed.

"Besides, I am eager to have you here with me." Alex leaned forward, placing his hands on the floor beside him, and kissed Isobel on the lips. He pulled back and whispered, "I want to be able to do that any time of the day."

"You have no patience, Crusader," Isobel said, climbing onto his lap. She adjusted her skirts so she could wrap her legs around his waist.

"Nae, I do not," he said, kissing his way down her neck.

The playfulness of the moment quickly dissolved, and Isobel grabbed his shoulders, digging her nails into his tunic as he licked across the exposed skin above her bodice. After a few moments of tortured bliss, she bent her head in search of his lips. When her mouth made contact with his, she melted against him. His lips were warm and sure as they pressed against hers.

Alex wrapped one arm around her; Isobel savored the feel of being close to him.

"Hold on to me," he whispered, after breaking the kiss.

Isobel was already holding on but crossed her ankles at his back and tightened her hold on his shoulders. He lowered her carefully to the floor. They just fit in between her trunk and collection of books.

Isobel sighed in pleasure when he moved his hardness against her core. She reached down between them, trying to untie his trews. Alex lifted off her, giving her the access she needed. When her hand came in contact with his shaft, he moaned. He felt hot, and Isobel was cool from lying on the floor. The contrast gave her chills.

"I want you so much," Alex murmured.

"And I you," Isobel whispered against his ear as he kissed her shoulder. Isobel sought his lips again, and he captured her mouth in an open kiss, flicking his tongue against hers. *This feels so good.* She never wanted it to end.

But the desires of two lovers did not outweigh the pressing needs of the clan, and a knock on the door reminded Isobel of that.

"Chief?" a man called. "Are you in there?"

Alex groaned as he detached himself from Isobel's lips and called, "Aye."

"Yer uncle and the men are waiting fer ye," the man called through the door.

"I'll be down," Alex called back but made no move to get up.

Isobel caressed his upper arms, squeezing his muscles and delighting as he flexed them under her hands. Her mind drifted back to their very first night together, at Fort Doune, when she'd seen him half naked. The memory of his chest and stomach, banded with muscle, made her ache for him even more.

Then she heard the grunts of men engaged in swordsmanship outside, and the lust cleared from her mind.

"You should go, shouldn't you?" she asked, relishing the warmth and feel of him for as long as possible.

"Aye," he said. "But I will see you later."

He planted one more kiss on her neck and jumped up. The passionate man was replaced with a serious warrior. After helping Isobel to her feet, he left.

When Alex closed the door, Isobel resumed sorting her belongings. She was so happy, and yet, she knew she needed to be wary. The sound of ringing metal brought her to the room's window, which overlooked the bailey. Her betrothed clashed swords with his uncle, showing his men the techniques of battle.

The scene below reminded of her of the morning Alex and Robbie had killed her kidnappers. Gruesome images flashed through her mind, and she had to look away. *Please let there be a peaceful end to this conflict,* she prayed.

****

After their demonstration, Alex and his uncle supervised the men's practice in the bailey.

"I see ye still use my gallowglass blade," his uncle said. "Did it serve ye well on Crusade?"

"Aye," Alex said, holding the sword outstretched in his hand. "God willing, it will serve me for many years to come."

"Yer clansmen have spirit, Alex. They will give everything they have to protect their home."

"I know it," Alex said, sheathing his sword across his back. "But will it be enough?"

"Doubt before battle is a dangerous foe," Uncle William warned.

"It's a new feeling," Alex admitted.

"I was the same when I was betrothed."

"You were married?" Alex asked in surprise. He studied his uncle, who had seen less than forty-five years on this earth. His hair was black and streaked with gray. His sun-tanned face showed some wrinkles around his green eyes, but his smile was still youthful. With his way of life, Alex always assumed he had never taken a wife.

"Nae." Uncle William shook his head. "I came close to marrying a lass once, but it wasn't to be. Though I loved her enough to worry about what would happen if I ever lost in battle."

"How did you overcome it?"

"Never did," he said. "I just learned to live with the worry."

"I need to learn to do the same," Alex said. *She's been a distraction to me before,* Alex thought, recalling the night he was bested by Robbie. Yet he'd done what was necessary the morning he and Robbie cut down Isobel's kidnappers, so he'd proven he could fight without losing focus in her presence. *And I probably gave her nightmares for life.* Alex still cursed himself for not being able to hide her from the savagery of his blade.

"Even when we are apart, I'll worry for her still."

"That's part of being in love," Uncle William said.

Love? He looked at his uncle. "I don't—" But he couldn't say it. He couldn't deny it.

Uncle William slapped him on the back. "Sorry to be the one to break to ye, Alex, but that is exactly what ye are—a man in love." Uncle William chuckled and walked off toward the practicing men.

Love? Is that what this is?

"Let's work on yer form, lad," his uncle said to Ian, Old John's son. The man, nearly Alex's age of six and twenty, was too old to be called a lad, but if he took offense, he did not show it.

Alex continued surveying his soldiers. Uncle William's men were well trained, and their skill was well beyond the MacKinnons. Even with the might of the Irish mercenaries, it could not compensate for how unprepared his men were. If it came to hand-to-hand combat, he feared how well his own men would fare. But there was hope.

Alex and his uncle had devised ways to make the MacKinnon force appear mightier to their opponents. They only needed to guard the front entrance to the keep. Being situated on a small peninsula, the sides and back of their fortifications bordered the sea and jagged granite cliffs. They had enough archers to stand atop the keep's walls and to be the first line of men in the formation they would dispatch onto the hillside adjacent to the keep. If they arranged the men just so, the Macleans would see an illusion of more men. The geography made it possible to imply a greater force than was truly there.

It will have to be enough. If the Macleans agree to the terms, then no blood need be shed by either side. And my clan, family, and Isobel will be safe. His mind couldn't seem to stray far from her. *Perhaps Uncle William is right. Perhaps I do—*

"There is a MacDonald of Skye at the gate, Chief," a guard said, interrupting Alex's thoughts. Alex hadn't even noticed the man approach his side.

"Show him in," Alex said, grateful for the

distraction. He jogged up to the gate and reached it just as Robbie and his brother and sister entered. Robbie was carrying his sister; the brown-haired girl did not look well.

"She took a turn last night," Robbie explained.

"Come, we'll get her inside," Alex said, guiding him into the keep. "Send for the physician at once!" he ordered, yelling at the nearest guard.

Alex took Robbie and his siblings to a guest chamber and helped Robbie lay his sister down on the bed.

"She had difficulty breathing all morning," Robbie said. "I've used all the medicine Katherine gave me; I didnae know what else to do."

"She'll pull through," Alex assured his friend as Isobel entered the room.

"Robbie," she said, and smiled, but her lips formed a straight line as she approached the bed. "Is this your sister?"

"Aye, this is Agnes. And this is my brother, Murdoch," he said, nodding toward his brother. The boy looked like a younger version of Robbie; Alex put him close in age to Flora. Agnes appeared to be a few years older.

Isobel approached the girl and felt her face, then hands.

"She is cold," Isobel said. "I'll bring furs."

She returned a few moments later with Joan in foot. They immediately set to work, laying the furs and tucking them in around Agnes. The physician arrived shortly after and asked the men to leave. Alex took Robbie and his brother to the great hall.

"The physician is talented. I am confident he will

help Agnes," Alex said. He was grateful one of his father's physicians had agreed to stay on after his passing.

Alex took Robbie and Murdoch to a table near the fireplace. Despite the warm daytime temperature outdoors, the inside of the keep was still cool. The warmth of summer had not yet penetrated the walls, so a fire was still lit daily in the great hall.

"Are you hungry?" Alex asked, looking at the brothers.

"Nae," Robbie said. "What about you, Murdoch?"

The young man shrugged, but his stomach growled, giving him away.

"Perhaps I could eat," he said, as Anna and Flora came into the great hall.

"Where are Joan and Isobel?" Anna asked, as she and Flora approached the table. "We've looked everywhere for them."

"They are tending to our guests' sister, Agnes," Alex said. He introduced Robbie and Murdoch to his sisters. "Lasses, would you do me a favor? Could you take Murdoch to the kitchens and get him something to eat?"

"Of course," Flora said. She smiled brightly at Murdoch, and the boy blushed.

"Perhaps after he's eaten you could give him a tour of the grounds, but keep clear of Uncle William's practice with the men."

Anna and Flora nodded and ushered Murdoch from the room.

"Much has happened since last I saw you, MacDonald," Alex said, looking at Robbie. "Isobel is to be my wife."

"Then I won't be kicking your arse after all," Robbie said with a laugh. "Congratulations to you both."

"Thank you."

"And the relic? Is it safe?" Robbie asked.

"Safe for the time being," Alex said. "Right now, my most pressing concern is the Macleans."

"You anticipate a battle?"

"Aye," Alex said. "I am preparing my men now, and my uncle, William, has brought mercenaries from Ireland. We have been planning for an impending attack. I am to send word of my decision to Maclean in ten days' time."

"Do you think he suspects your refusal of his terms?"

"Does any clan ever submit willing?" Alex asked.

"Fair enough," Robbie said. "Will you present your own terms?"

"I'm still working on that," Alex said. He and Isobel needed to talk to Anna. He would not force a marriage alliance on her, even if it meant going to battle with the Macleans. Even if she was agreeable, the Maclean chief might not accept the alliance. But the dowry from Isobel might just be enough to subdue Maclean's greed.

Alex looked away from Robbie when he saw Isobel appear at the bottom of the steps. Robbie followed Alex's gaze and immediately stood up. Alex joined him.

"How is she, Lady Isobel?"

"She is resting comfortably, Robbie," Isobel said. "She'll need to keep to her room for a few days, but the physician feels confident he will be able to manage her condition."

"Thank you," he said to Isobel. He then turned to Alex. "Thank you as well, MacKinnon. I owe you more than I can possibly repay."

"You owe me nothing, MacDonald." Before the man could argue with him, Alex said, "Come. You need to eat." Robbie did not argue as Alex and Isobel led him from the great hall.

****

Castlelaw Fort, south of Edinburgh, that evening.

The Duke of Lincoln and the Bishop of Edinburgh stood on the ramparts, overlooking the ancient settlement of Castlelaw Fort. Sprawling hills stretched out around them, touching the golden orange hue of the setting sun. Such a tranquil place to discuss each man's failings.

"I've had no word from my men," the duke said.

"Then neither of us has been successful," the bishop responded.

"This was never my mission. I only offered to help," the duke said in defense. "The king will not be disappointed with me, Bishop."

"Perhaps," the bishop said. "The matter is no longer of interest to me anyway. I must return to Edinburgh to be of assistance to young King Malcolm."

"You do not expect me to believe you have given up on this."

The bishop shrugged. He knew there were other treasures the king would find of value in Edinburgh. They would be easier to obtain now that the watchful eye of King David was no more.

"You are welcome to pursue the Rood," the bishop said. "If it is on Iona, then it will be protected by

Somerled, Lord of the Isles. You will have to negotiate with him."

"Everyone has a price. I am certain this 'Lord of the Isles' could be swayed."

"We shall see," the bishop said. "But as I said, it is no longer my concern."

"Then I am afraid your efforts to join the king's council are for naught. Without the Rood, you have nothing to offer him."

"And you have nothing to use to gain more power and influence," the bishop countered.

The duke shrugged off the bishop's words. "Everyone has a price."

"Then I wish you luck in your negotiations with the self-proclaimed island king." The bishop waved to his attendants, who stood down below in the earthen ruins of the old fort.

"Until our paths cross again then, Bishop," the duke said, with a nod of his head.

The bishop returned the gesture and departed. The alliance with the duke had not been productive—yet. The bishop would keep an eye on things from a distance and see what developed with Somerled. Should an advantage arise, he would be ready.

Chapter 26

That night, after the evening meal, Alex asked Anna to join him and Isobel in his solar. He knew Anna had grown much during his six-year absence, but when he looked at her, he still saw a good-natured, compassionate, yet naive lass. *Is she even ready for marriage? Had Father discussed such things with her?*

Alex straightened his spine then leaned forward, folding his hands on the table. Isobel and Anna sat opposite him.

"Anna, what are your thoughts on marriage?"

"What do you mean?" she asked.

"Have you ever thought of marrying?"

"Well, of course," she said, averting her eyes. "But Father said it was unlikely any of us would make acceptable matches. We have nae dowries, Alex. You know this."

"Well, that has changed," Alex said, looking at Isobel.

"My own dowry is generous enough that I can give you, Joan, and Flora all your own dowries," Isobel said.

"Truly?" Anna asked. Her eyes grew large in shock.

"Yes," Isobel said, taking Anna's hand in her own. "But there is more."

"What is it?" Anna looked between Isobel and Alex.

"You know we are preparing for battle with the Macleans?" Alex asked, looking at his sister.

"Aye. What does that have to do with marriage?" Her face scrunched up in confusion.

Alex could have laughed, if the matter was not so serious. The lass could never keep anything a secret. She had the most expressive face. It gave away her every thought and feeling. "Remember Ewan?"

"Of course, Brother," Anna said. "He came here with his father last year, though I didnae speak to him."

Alex looked at her expectantly.

After a few moments, she asked, "You want me to marry Ewan?"

"Aye," Alex said.

"It is part of the terms your brother would like to propose to the Macleans," Isobel explained. "But if you are not agreeable, then we shall speak of it no more."

"I dinnae know if I am," Anna said, reclining back in her chair. She pulled her hand free from Isobel and looked at Alex. "What do you know of him?"

"He and I were friends before I left on Crusade. I remember him as kind and fair," Alex began. "But, I confess, I dinnae know if he has changed."

"Would I be able to speak with him before I make my decision?"

"Mayhap," Alex said, considering how it could be done without Chief Maclean knowing. He could not send one of his own men. The chief would expect his answer if a MacKinnon showed up at his gates. Alex would have to think on it.

"Is that all you wished to discuss?" Anna asked.

"Aye, you may go," Alex said. "Dinnae let yourself worry. The training with the men goes well, and with our uncle's force, we are formidable. I dinnae want you to feel as though the clan's livelihood rests on your shoulders."

Anna nodded and gave a weak smile before she left the room. Alex knew his words had not convinced her of their clan's ability to defend against the Macleans. Perhaps because he himself was not entirely convinced. *Doubt is dangerous.* His uncle's words came back to him.

"How will you reach out to Ewan?" Isobel asked, coming over to stand beside him.

"I'm not yet certain," he said. "Come. I haven't touched you in ages." He pushed back from the table to make space for Isobel on his lap.

"You had your hand on my thigh through half of the evening meal," Isobel said, arching her eyebrows.

"As I said—ages."

Isobel laughed, and he grinned. There was no sweeter sound on earth than her laugh. It instantly calmed him, and the weight of his troubles felt lighter.

Isobel sat on his lap and leaned into him, laying her head on his shoulder. Alex wrapped his arms around her and sighed in contentment.

"You could send Robbie to Duart," Isobel suggested.

"He would go," Alex said, considering it. "He would also be less likely to draw attention than any of the MacKinnon men."

"You could invite Ewan to the wedding."

"Have you chosen a date?" he asked.

"I spoke with your sisters this afternoon," Isobel began. "We thought five days from now would be best."

"Five days' time?" Alex asked. That meant four more nights without her.

"I did not want it any closer to the potential arrival of the Macleans," Isobel explained. "And it will take the cook a few days to prepare food suitable for a celebratory feast."

"Everyone will be excited to see such grandeur inside the great hall again," Alex said. He couldn't recall the last time there had been such an occasion at the keep. It would boost the morale of the men before battle. *If there is to be a battle.* He kissed Isobel on the forehead and held her close. He had much to lose. He could not fail Isobel and his people.

****

The next morning, Isobel returned to MacKinnon Keep from the nunnery on Iona, where she had stayed every night since she arrived. She sat in Joan's room with Anna and Flora. The women were admiring Isobel's wardrobe. She had every last one of her gowns laid out on the bed (save for her wedding gown).

"Please choose one," Isobel said, looking at the women. "You are welcome to any of them. I assure you I hold no attachments to them. Pick the one you like best, and then we can begin making the necessary alterations."

"But then they will nae fit you," Flora said.

"Which is precisely the point," Isobel said. "These will be gowns for you to keep."

"I cannae choose. They are all so lovely," Anna said, reaching out to touch a few of the dresses.

After a few more moments of awkward silence, Isobel stood and approached the heap of gowns. She eyed the girls carefully. They were all lovely with unique features. Joan had dark brown hair, nearly black, and sharp green eyes. Isobel sorted through the gowns and reached for a mossy green velvet gown that had gold embroidery along the bust line.

"Try this," Isobel said, handing Joan the gown. "I think the color will bring out your eyes."

Joan hesitantly took the gown and held it up in front of the polished silver mirror, another luxury that had arrived with Isobel's trunks.

"She's right," Anna said, coming to stand beside her sister. "It does bring out the color of your eyes."

" 'Tis beautiful," Flora said. The girl's face glowed in delight.

Isobel noted Flora's pale blonde hair. She too had green eyes, but she thought something more youthful and light would complement her hair color and age. She surveyed the gowns and searched through them; a bright pink damask gown caught her eye. The cut was simple, but there was lovely silver detailing around the bodice and down the sleeves.

"This should work nicely for you, Flora. We'll just need to address the length."

Flora took the gown and ran to the mirror and held it up in front of her. " 'Tis the loveliest dress I have ever seen!" she exclaimed.

"I am happy you are pleased with it." Isobel smiled at the girl's joy. She had forgotten being excited for such things, but there was a time when the sight of a fine gown would have made her equally as happy. She was grateful to be sharing her good fortune with Alex's sisters.

She then looked to Anna. Anna could be meeting her own betrothed on Isobel's wedding day, so she wanted Anna to feel comfortable and confident in her gown. Anna was similar in height to Isobel, which meant alterations would be minimal. She studied her features—brown eyes and long, wavy brown hair. Any of Isobel's gowns would suit her.

She sorted through the gowns but could not make a choice.

"I think you will have to select one," Isobel said. "All of them will look beautiful on you."

Isobel stepped aside, giving Anna access to the gowns. Joan and Flora were admiring each other's dresses and noting the places where adjustments would need to be made. Anna sorted through the gowns, carefully examining each as she went. Her face was a rainbow of emotions as she reacted to each one. She pouted when she appeared to think one was unattractive. Then, she would smile when she touched the lush fabrics and ornamented beadwork on Isobel's finest gowns. Suddenly, Anna's eyes lit up.

"What do you think of the yellow?" Anna asked, holding up a bright yellow damask gown. The fine dress came from France as a gift from David last autumn. It had no ornamentation of any kind, but the shimmering fabric did not need it. The bodice was low cut, but still more modest than many of the current fashions.

"I think it is perfect," Isobel said. "I have a matching ribbon for it as well. We can weave it through your hair."

"That sounds lovely," Anna said. She joined her sisters at the mirror.

"You will turn every head at the feast, and none of you will want for a dance partner."

That drew an instant frown from all the women.

"What is wrong?" she asked.

"Dance partners?" Joan asked. "What do you mean, dance partners?"

"There will be dancing," Isobel said. "A few of your uncle's men brought instruments. They are very skilled and know a bounty of songs to perform."

"But we cannae dance!" cried Flora.

"What?" Isobel asked. *Surely the girls have been exposed to dancing. All the clans welcomed traveling musicians.* She'd heard of the performances when the clan chiefs came to pledge allegiance to King David at court.

" 'Tis true," Anna said. She looked miserable at the admission.

"Father never liked musicians in the great hall and without music…" Joan began. "Sad, isn't it?"

"No. It's fine. We'll have lessons." The men were in the bailey, which meant the inside of the keep would be empty. "Let's go down to the great hall."

"But what if someone sees us?" Flora asked.

"The men are all in the yard practicing. No one will see," Isobel said.

The women put down their dresses and followed Isobel to the great hall. Isobel chose Joan as her partner and paired Anna with Flora. After showing the sisters the basic steps, they took turns around the hall. Flora kept stepping on Anna's feet, and Joan was determined to lead, which put her at odds with Isobel trying to teach her the role of the lady in the dance. They muddled through a few more spins before they were interrupted.

All the women halted as Robbie, Alex, and

Murdoch entered the hall.

"Perfect timing!" Isobel said, stepping away from Joan. "Alex, can you dance?"

"Of course I can," he said.

His sisters all frowned.

"When did you learn?" demanded Flora.

"When I was your age," Alex said. "It was part of our training on Skye."

Isobel was surprised. "You mean, they trained you to fight and how to dance?"

Alex shrugged.

"Does that mean you can dance too?" Isobel asked Robbie.

"Aye," Robbie said, his cheeks turning the slightest shade of pink. "So can Murdoch."

"Why did you say that!" Murdoch scowled at the prospect of dancing.

"Then you can all be of help," Isobel said. "Murdoch, would you kindly pair up with Flora? And Robbie, you can partner with Joan."

Joan and Robbie both blushed at the suggestion. *Interesting.* Isobel made a mental note of that for later. "Alex, pair up with Anna."

Isobel instructed everyone on what to do. Then she clapped a beat and sang a tune. She did not have a beautiful voice, but her songs were pleasing enough never to make the wolfhounds cry at court. Anna was a quick learner, and she was able to follow Alex around the great hall with perfection. Flora was a bit overexcited and stumbled through some of the steps; poor Murdoch followed along, trying to lead, but Flora would have none of it. Joan fumbled some of the steps, but Isobel wasn't certain if that was the cause for the color in her cheeks or if it stemmed from interest in her dance partner. *Perhaps the embarrassment is a combination of the two.*

Shortly after Isobel's observation, Joan broke free of Robbie's embrace and dashed from the room. Isobel stopped singing but continued clapping a rhythm the remaining couples could still dance to.

"Did you step on her foot?" Alex asked Robbie with a laugh.

How could Alex miss her reaction? Robbie looked equally as affected. *That could be a good match.* While not her intention to go sorting partners for Alex's sisters, it was hard to ignore the signs that they were both interested in one another.

Robbie walked from the hall, going in the opposite direction of Joan.

"That's good," Isobel called. "I think everyone's had enough practice."

"Come on, Murdoch," Alex said. "Time to get back out to the practice yard."

Murdoch awkwardly detached himself from Flora, who stood looking after him with starry eyes. *Oh, goodness. Are all the MacKinnon sisters lovesick?*

Anna took Flora by the hand and headed for the stairwell to their rooms; Alex came to stand beside Isobel and grinned.

"I'll wager you did not think I could dance," he said.

"Indeed, I was surprised. You are good." Isobel wrapped her arms around his neck, looking around to make sure they were alone in the hall.

" 'Tis not the only thing I'm good at," Alex whispered.

"I recall, though the memory is becoming distant," Isobel teased.

"I will remind you soon enough, lass," he promised, then captured her lips in a hot kiss.

When he finally released her, Isobel felt dizzy. She looked up into Alex's eyes, and the flame in those gray-blue eyes sent a shiver down her spine. *Is all that intensity from passion or something more?* Time would tell, she supposed, but not knowing left a bittersweet feeling in her heart.

Chapter 27

The next day, Alex found Robbie outside the keep sitting on a granite outcropping overlooking the sea. It was time to speak with him about Ewan Maclean. It would be dangerous, and he did not want to ask it of his friend, especially with Agnes still recovering, but he reasoned the marriage alliance could save them all and, therefore, was worth the risk.

"Robbie," Alex said, as he approached him. "May I join you?"

"Of course," Robbie said, moving his sword so Alex could sit beside him on the boulder.

"A fine day," Alex commented, looking out over the calm inner seas. The sun was bright, and the blue waters shimmered like the scales of the silvery butterfish.

"I assume you didnae come to comment on the weather," Robbie said.

"I have a favor to ask," Alex admitted.

Robbie looked at him, waiting.

"I need you to bring me Ewan Maclean," Alex said.

"Dead or alive?" Robbie asked.

"Alive."

"You want me to sneak into Duart Keep to find him?"

"Aye," Alex said. "I want to propose a marriage

alliance between him and my sister."

Robbie tensed and looked away. *I should nae ask this of him,* Alex thought. *'Tis clear he is still worried for his sister and does nae want to part from her.*

"It was wrong of me to ask," Alex explained. "You should be with your sister now. Forgive me for not thinking."

Robbie finally turned to look at him. His expression was unreadable, but the islander said, "I will do it."

"Are you certain?"

"Aye," Robbie said. "Joan marrying Ewan could keep your clan from being attacked. I will go."

"That is my hope," Alex said, relieved he'd agreed. "But the alliance would be formed between Ewan and Anna. Not Joan." *Strange that he assumed Joan,* Alex thought. *But then Joan is the oldest.*

"Bringing him here the day of the wedding would be ideal," Alex said. "With the feast Isobel is preparing, it will make us look as though we are coming from a position of power. Not begging."

"Agreed," Robbie said. "Consider it done."

****

After Alex left Robbie, he joined his uncle in the stables where they mounted horses and departed for Iona. Alex was due to meet with Bethoc to discuss the Rood.

"The men are coming along in their practice," Uncle William said, as they cantered down the path to Fionnphort. "Especially Robbie MacDonald's younger brother."

"Aye," Alex said. "He's a fine archer."

"I thought of offering the lad an opportunity to

257

train with my men back in Ireland."

Alex glanced at his uncle and then looked ahead. It was a generous offer to foster the young man. Murdoch could learn a great deal from the gallowglass warrior and his men. "I am confident he would be agreeable."

"And Robbie?"

"That I cannae tell you, Uncle," Alex said. "Though I don't see how he could turn down such an offer for his brother."

"He would learn much from me," Uncle William said. He tapped a finger to his chin, as though considering something. "I'd make sure he was fed too and keep him away from the lasses."

"Robbie will be glad to hear it," Alex said, with a laugh. His uncle never had children, but the idea of fostering Murdoch showed a fatherly side to the old warrior.

They rode on in silence to Fionnphort. After leaving their horses with the MacKinnon guards, Alex and his uncle boarded a small watercraft, sailing the short distance to the isle. From the bay, they walked up *Sráid nam Marbh*. The last time Alex walked this stone path, he was taking his father to the chief's final resting place, which was why Uncle William had asked to join him. He wanted to pay his respects to his late brother.

They took their time up the path, passing by a drove of sheep guided by a young monk. Alex also studied the new nunnery, which had just been completed within the past year under the order of the Island King, Somerled. The red granite structure was familiar to Alex, for he'd encountered similar Augustinian nunneries on his travels.

"I hear they brought some of the nuns over from

Ireland," Uncle William said, as they passed the nunnery.

Alex nodded. "I heard the same, though it seems the prioress grew up in England—away from her father."

"Have ye met him yet?" Uncle William asked.

"Nae," Alex said. "You?"

"Nae."

Alex was curious about the Lord of the Isles. He was a warlord with Viking blood. His older clansmen said Somerled saw an opportunity to control the Hebrides, as it was beyond the reach of both the Norwegian crown and the King of Scots. He'd come to power around the time of Alex's birth, though he'd flexed little muscle on places like Mull and Skye. Somerled was invested in Iona and the holy life here, which gave Alex hope the Lord of the Isles would protect the Rood.

Alex parted ways with his uncle at the burial ground and continued on to the abbey church. He passed the grand high crosses, ornately carved with Celtic symbols, and made his way inside. He stood in the nave, noting the sections rebuilt in his absence. He walked down the length of it, past the marble font, and down to the choir. The sun was generous, but the east-facing windows cast little light inside the stone church during this time of day. It was midafternoon, but the candles were lit in the aisles. The light flickered off the rough stone walls, where ferns grew. The fragile green leaves cascaded down over the arches and columns around the church. Alex took a seat on a bench and admired the stonemason's work as he waited for the prioress.

A short time later, Bethoc joined him in the choir. She took a seat beside him and folded her hands neatly in her lap. She wore the traditional garb of a nun, concealing her hair, ears, and neck. Her face was pleasing, and sincere kindness warmed her pale blue eyes. Though hard to judge her age, he sensed she was older than he.

" 'Tis a pleasure to meet you, Chief MacKinnon."

"The pleasure is mine, my lady," Alex said.

The prioress smiled like a fairy, captivating and welcoming. He understood the rumors now and why Isobel agreed with them: the prioress did have an enchanting way about her.

"I wish to offer my congratulations to you and Lady Isobel on your upcoming marriage," Bethoc said.

"Thank you," Alex said.

"You have chosen your equal. She will challenge you and support you. Such things are rare," she said. "You are fortunate."

"She makes me happy, and I hope to bring her the same measure of happiness."

"You will," the prioress said. A confident statement, spoken like someone who had seen the future.

I hope you are right, Alex thought, wanting nothing more than to bring Isobel joy.

"You have much that occupies your mind, Chief. Let us speak on what worries you."

The time for pleasantries was over. "I am here to discuss the protection of the Rood."

The prioress nodded. "It is safe."

"There seems to be an alliance between the Duke of Lincoln and the Bishop of Edinburgh. Two attempts were made on the Rood on its journey here. I am confident more will be made," Alex said. "As I believe you aware, the MacKinnon forces are nae what they once were. I question my clan's ability to protect it."

"I am aware of your clan's situation," she began. "When I spoke with Lady Isobel, I told her my father would offer protection as well. I wrote and got word from my brother, Ranald, that our father is in Normandy. My brother, however, assures me arrangements will be made to guarantee protection of the relic."

"You are confident in this?"

"I am," Bethoc said. "In the meantime, I have hidden the relic. Only I know its exact location. I feel this is best until my father makes arrangements."

"I agree," Alex said. The fewer people who knew of the location, the safer it would be. "In the meantime, promise you will come to me if you feel the relic is in danger."

"I will," Bethoc said, standing. "Now I must leave you, Chief, for it is time for my prayers."

"Of course, my lady." Alex stood as well. "You have taken on a great burden. I know David was grateful, as we all are."

"There is no burden in the care of a relic, Chief MacKinnon," the prioress said, as she walked out of the choir and into the nave aisle. Alex joined her. She turned to face him; the light from the west-facing windows cast a glow around her. "It is the great honor of my life."

With that, she bowed her head and disappeared behind a wooden door off the nave. Alex took a moment in the abbey church, then walked back out into the afternoon sunshine, the high crosses covering him in shadow as he walked through the yard. He crossed into the royal burial ground, passing by St. Oran's Chapel, which was built by Queen Margaret. Beyond the humble chapel lay the burial place of the great kings. Alex paused in front of Kenneth mac Alpin's grave. *The unifier of the Scots and Picts.* The grave was weathered and aged by the centuries. The great king's reign had ended in the 800s, but his history lived on.

Soon, Alex was joined by his uncle.

"Did you make peace with him?" Alex asked, as Uncle William came to stand alongside him.

"In my own way," he said. "He belongs here."

"Uncle?" Alex did not take his meaning.

"Nae matter what was between us, yer father was chief. He had his failings, but he loved his people. He loved ye and yer sisters. And he loved yer mother." Uncle William's eyes welled up, and he shed a single tear. The tanned warrior brushed it away and turned to face the sea.

"We are both at peace with him," Alex said. He lightly patted his uncle on the back. "We will toast him tonight at the evening meal."

Uncle William nodded and cleared his throat. "Ah, that is enough of that. Tell me, did ye have a nice meeting with the prioress?"

"Aye," Alex said. He had not told his uncle the purpose of his visit. Few knew of the Rood and that was how he planned to keep it, for everyone's safety and the safety of the relic.

Speaking with the prioress had made him confident of one thing: she was the right person to care for the Rood. As to what help they could rely on from

Somerled himself…he would have to wait and see. For now, he would continue to rely on his own men to guard Iona.

"Come, Uncle. Let us return home."

They walked down the stone path once more and set sail in their boat. As the wind blew them across the water, Alex looked back to Columba's church. There, standing by the sea, stood the prioress. Her head was bowed in prayer. With the sun at her back, she looked ethereal. Her words came back to him. *You have chosen your equal. She will challenge you and support you.*

Alex smiled. *Such things are rare and yet, I have found them in Isobel.*

****

Isobel surveyed the records before her. She and Alex had made some progress earlier in the week, but the accounts were still in shambles. She could understand why the clan was in such dire circumstances and why Alex had been frustrated with his father's care of the clan. The old chief's mismanagement had cost his people and children much, but Isobel was determined to set everything to rights. It just wouldn't all be done in a day, and right now she needed a break.

Isobel decided to go check on Alex's sisters and see how the gown alterations were coming along. She looked in Joan's room, then Flora's and Anna's, but they were nowhere to be found. Then she heard laughter coming from the guest quarters, where Agnes was staying. She knocked on the door and entered, finding the girls gathered around Agnes, who was sitting up in bed.

"How are you feeling?" Isobel asked, taking in the scene. Agnes was working on one of the gowns. She was still pale, but there was brightness in the young woman's eyes.

"Very well, my lady," Agnes said.

"Please call me Isobel."

"Agnes is helping us with the gowns," Flora said. "She's a wonder with a needle."

"It's true. She is much more talented than the three of us combined," Anna said, pointing out some of Agnes's work.

Isobel approached the bed and studied the garments. "This is exceptional." And it truly was. "You are very gifted."

" 'Tis kind of you to say so," Agnes said. Pink color filled her cheeks; she was embarrassed by the praise, but the compliments were well deserved.

"Are you self-taught?" Isobel asked. She pulled up another stool so she could sit with everyone.

"Aye," Agnes said. "With my illness, there is little else for me to do. I started sewing here and there and found I had skill at it. Things progressed from there."

"If you are feeling up to it, perhaps you could do some wall hangings for the keep," Isobel said. The rooms in the old keep were plain, and her limited collection of tapestries would only do so much.

"I would love to," Agnes said. "I have so many ideas in my head; it would be wonderful to start some of them."

"I will acquire the supplies you need," Isobel said. "But you mustn't overtire yourself. Robbie would not be pleased."

"He has a temper?" Joan asked, speaking for the first time since Isobel entered the room. Joan continued working on the hem of her gown, trying to show disinterest, but Isobel knew the islander intrigued her.

"Nae, of course not." Agnes laughed. "He may look like a brute, but you will find no one kinder than my brother."

"Truly?" Joan asked, looking up from her work.

Agnes nodded. "You should talk to him. I am sure you'd get along."

"Nae, I couldn't." Joan looked flustered, which was not a look Isobel imagined was common for the fierce green-eyed woman. She was usually so serious and determined. At least, that was Isobel's view of her from the limited amount of time they'd spent together.

"Why not?" Flora asked.

"I just mean that he is busy," Joan stammered out. "I should go. I've things to do before the evening meal."

Joan quickly left the room, leaving her gown, needle, and thread lying on the bed.

"What's wrong with her?" Flora asked.

"I'm sure she's fine," Isobel said. "I will take these things to her room." She gathered up Joan's dress and sewing supplies and made for the door but suddenly stopped.

"You are all doing lovely work, but I wonder..." Isobel spun on her heel to face the women. "You are missing a dress."

"Nae," Anna said. "Agnes has Flora's, and I've got mine."

"Agnes has no gown," Isobel said.

"I dinnae know if I can attend the feast," Agnes said. She looked down at her plain wool gown, then to Flora's fine damask dress, and Isobel could see how much the girl would love a gown of her own.

"Even if you are not well enough to attend the ceremony, you shall have a dress of your own, Agnes MacDonald."

"Are you certain?"

"Best not argue with her," Flora said. " 'Tis pointless."

Isobel smiled. "I will bring some choices by later, and you can pick."

"They are all so lovely," Anna said. "You are sure to find one that suits you perfectly."

"You must show her your books too, Isobel," Flora said.

"Books?" Agnes asked.

"She's got twelve of them!" Flora exclaimed.

"I have never seen a book," Agnes said.

"Would you like to learn to read?" Anna asked. "Isobel is teaching us."

"Oh, I would love that!"

"Then we shall do the lessons in here tomorrow," Isobel said. "We're reading *Beowulf*."

" 'Tis very dark."

"Dinnae spoil it for her, Flora." Anna frowned at her sister.

"She probably guessed from the name it was nae a love story," Flora said. She then wistfully looked at Isobel. "Do you have any love stories?"

"I'm afraid not."

Flora pouted, then shrugged and continued sewing. The girls carried on in conversation, and Isobel excused herself. Smiling all the way down the corridor, she made her way to Joan's room. After depositing her things, Isobel went back to the solar and resumed her work. After all, the records would not improve on their own.

The sound of the men in the bailey and the laughter of children playing echoed through the open doors and windows. Isobel reclined in her chair and hugged the parchment to her chest. It reminded her of being back in Edinburgh Castle. Only this time, when all went quiet she did not feel empty inside.

"My life is full." The realization brought her peace. How many years had she searched for a sense of belonging, and here, in the Isles, she'd finally found home.

Chapter 28

An early July wedding in the Isles could be stormy or bright. Alex was thankful today was the latter, with abundant sunshine and calm winds blowing in off the inner seas. Isobel wanted the ceremony to be held outside along the coast in view of Columba's church, so it was. She stood before him looking so certain of the choice she made. He felt the same certainty about her.

Isobel was bringing renewal to his clan, ensuring his sisters could each make a good match and even helping make sense of the clan's record keeping. There was no end to her talents and generosity. She was passionate and courageous. He had never met her like, and he was awed she had accepted him to be her partner. He recognized how lucky he was and hoped to be a man deserving of such good fortune.

The softness in Isobel's violet eyes made his chest ache as she recited her vows. Today, she wore a gold velvet gown with fine gold-thread needlework embroidered across the bodice. Adorning her hair was a gold circlet, and she wore a delicate gold necklace with a ruby pendant. With the sun shining on her, she possessed a graceful radiance. In that moment, it was easy to imagine her as a princess standing proudly beside King David in the great hall at Edinburgh Castle. At the same time, he also saw that this radiant woman fit perfectly into his life. Isobel made his world complete.

Isobel studied Alex's expression as he repeated his vows. His face was like granite—the crusader's façade she'd seen in place countless times over the last few weeks. *Why wear such a mask on our wedding day?* She had a sickening thought for a moment that Alex could not love her, but she dismissed it. Even though the words had not yet been spoken between them, he cared for her just as she cared for him. His love could be seen in his actions, from his thoughtfulness in gifting her a new cloak and gingerbread on their journey, to his treatment of her as his equal with the record keeping, and, of course, his passion and care of her the night in the forest when they made love. The memory of it heated her skin, for tonight she knew they would be together once more.

She hoped her appearance pleased him, for his appearance pleased her. Alex had taken particular care with his grooming today. His hair was combed back, and his face was clean shaven. He wore a fine navy tunic that deepened the blue of his eyes. His leather trews were also fine; Isobel could tell they were not ones he wore in battle. She inhaled deeply, savoring his scent. The heady smell of rosewater radiated from him. She'd only smelled it on Alex a few times, so she knew he used it sparingly. Strange how such a floral scent could be so masculine.

The outside was perfect; she just needed to be patient for what lay within. His crusader's heart would not easily allow love in. She could not rush him, nor did she want to.

As he finished reciting his vows, Isobel studied his gray-blue eyes. Unlike his face, they were alive with emotion. She could only hope he was thinking what she was: *I love you.*

Alex's people cheered after the exchange of vows. As the clan funneled into the great hall for the wedding feast, Alex caught sight of two riders approaching—Robbie with Ewan Maclean. Alex gave Isobel a kiss on the cheek, and she nodded for him to go on to meet the two men. Alex greeted them at the stables.

"Robbie," Alex said. He turned to the other man. "Maclean." He eyed his old friend sharply. The first time they'd spoken in six years. Alex was anxious to see what sort of man he had become.

"MacKinnon," Ewan said, as he and Robbie both dismounted their horses.

Alex reached out and shook his hand.

"Thank you for coming," he said. "Why don't you come inside for food and drink? We are celebrating."

"I am happy for you, Alex, but I am guessing by the way I was…" He paused and looked at Robbie. "Shall we say, encouraged?"

"Aye, that is a good word for it," Robbie said.

"By the way I was *encouraged* to follow MacDonald here, that this is not a social visit."

Alex could only imagine how Robbie convinced Ewan to come with him. He was certain that'd be a story to share over a tankard later. Right now, it was time to talk peace.

"Aye, it is not. I have a proposition for you," Alex said.

"I am not the chief, Alex," Ewan said. "You know I cannae negotiate with you on behalf of my father."

"I know it, but listen to what I have to offer."

His old friend nodded for him to continue. In the

years since Alex had seen him, Ewan's appearance had changed. While he was no longer a lanky youth, his muscular frame was lean—he hadn't bulked up in size like Alex. *He never was a fighter,* Alex thought. Perhaps Chief Maclean's obsession with battle had turned his son from it. Ewan had trained, of course, and his skill with a bow and arrow was exceptional, but he was not a warrior by heart.

"I think I can offer something you and your father will value," Alex began.

"And what is that?"

"A marriage alliance with my sister, Anna, which comes with a handsome dowry," Alex said.

****

Inside the keep, the drinking and frivolity was under way. Hundreds of people were squeezed inside the great hall; the sound of all those voices talking and laughing was so loud, Isobel could hardly hear a word Joan said to her. They were the only ones seated on the dais; everyone else was off in conversation with the clansmen and women or the Irish warriors. Isobel wanted to laugh when she saw a group of MacKinnons scowling as a handful of women carried on with some of the Irish. She knew the men would be happy when their guests left; the competition for attention was not welcome, even if their skill with the sword was.

Flora was engaged in conversation with Murdoch while Anna was talking with Robbie, who had just arrived in the hall. Joan, it seemed, had taken notice.

"After we eat, you should ask him to dance," Isobel suggested, leaning closer to Joan so she could be heard.

"Did you see me practicing the other day?" Joan asked. "I was terrible."

"You were just nervous."

"And I won't be tonight?" Joan sighed and toyed with the emerald pendant that hung from her necklace. "He is interested in Anna." Joan's eyes went wide with realization, and she looked at Isobel. "Listen to me," she cried. "I sound like a lovesick fool."

This was clearly a position Joan had never found herself in before. Isobel could relate. She'd never experienced such feelings until she met Alex just a few weeks ago. It meant she probably wasn't the best person to give advice, but she'd do her best.

"He is interested in you. He only avoids you because he likes you." The few times she'd seem them cross paths around the keep, it had been painfully awkward. Yet, when Robbie interacted with any of the other women, including Anna, he did so with ease. At least with as much ease as a mercenary could muster. Isobel knew what that meant—Robbie had feelings for Joan.

"You really think so?" She stopped toying with the necklace and looked back to Robbie and Anna.

"I do," Isobel said. "Now have some wine to calm your nerves." Isobel filled a glass and handed it to Joan.

Joan took it and cautiously sniffed the liquid.

"You've never had wine before, have you?" Isobel asked.

Joan shook her head. "Is it like ale?"

"In a way. Just be careful. A little will calm you; too much and you will act a fool and have a terrible pain in your head come the morning."

"So it is like ale," Joan said and took a sip. "But better tasting."

Isobel poured herself a glass and toasted Joan. "To

you and your sisters," Isobel said.

"And to you, Isobel, for coming here to help us."

After taking a drink, Isobel decided now was as good a time as any to talk to Joan about taking over her duties in the keep.

"I should have spoken with you sooner, so forgive me. I do not want there to be any bad feelings about my new position here," Isobel began.

"Nae, of course there are none. 'Tis the way of things. I knew Alex would take a wife and she would take over the duty of managing the keep," Joan said. "If Alex said I am displeased with you, it is not true. I just needed time."

Alex hadn't spoken of it, though she assumed that meant he was unaware of Joan's feelings.

"You have done a wonderful job with Flora and Anna. I have no doubt they have grown into the women they are now because of your guidance and care."

Joan didn't say anything but nodded. Isobel sensed that Joan was not used to taking compliments. Isobel would make sure that she, and her sisters, received praise more often. She had been fortunate in her own life to receive the accolades of David, Mattie, and her tutors. While it did not do to rely on others for one's own self-worth, praise helped build one's confidence. Isobel wanted all of Alex's sisters to feel confident in their own talents and abilities.

"You have done so much with limited resources," Isobel continued. "That takes creativity and determination." She could not imagine what Joan needed to do to keep things going in Alex's absence. Isobel had walked in and taken note of everything that was wrong; she failed to see what was working. Anna's and Flora's positivity was proof that not all was broken here. And Isobel knew that had a great deal to do with Joan.

"There is much I have yet to learn. I hope you will help me so I may serve the MacKinnons as well as you have," Isobel finished.

Joan set down her wine glass and looked Isobel in the eye. "I will be glad to help you."

Isobel smiled in relief. This was an important step in building a relationship with her new sister.

"Now tell me what I should say to the islander when the dancing starts," Joan said. Her glass was half empty; the wine had indeed had an effect. She just hoped the woman paced herself; it would be a long night.

****

Once Alex explained his plan regarding the alliance and gave the details of Anna's dowry, Ewan agreed to it. Alex made it clear that nothing would be final until Anna also agreed, but, for now, terms were tentatively set.

"Then let us go in for the feast," Alex said, when they'd finished discussing the plans. They made their way up from the stables into the entry hall of the keep. Alex could barely fit inside the doors; the room was shoulder to shoulder with people.

"Do you want to meet her?" Alex asked. He cringed as a reveler elbowed him in the side.

"Forgive me, Chief," the man said.

Alex smiled and nodded at the man, and looked behind him at Ewan. "Well?"

"Aye," Ewan said, pushing his way through the crowd.

"She wants to meet you," Alex said, dodging a woman carrying two tankards of ale. "I thought you two could sit together during the evening feast."

"Aye, that is fine," Ewan said, stepping aside to avoid getting hit by the woman carrying the ale. "What does she like to talk about?"

They'd reached the great hall where Alex found Isobel and Joan seated together on the dais. Then he saw Anna. "Ask her yourself. She is the one in the yellow dress standing next to Robbie." Alex pointed to her and turned to see Ewan's expression.

Ewan's mouth dropped open, and his eyes widened. Alex's fists reflexively tightened at his sides. Isobel had insisted all his sisters have new gowns for the wedding. It was a great kindness, for it upset Alex to see his sisters in rags; however, the fashions from Edinburgh were a bit more revealing than he cared for. Clearly, the dress was having an effect on Ewan.

"You haven't married her yet, Maclean," Alex reminded him, unclenching his fists.

Ewan's face hardened, but his cheeks colored over in pink. Alex knew he was embarrassed for showing his interest so freely.

"I will be keeping an eye on you. Remember that my sister has the final say in this agreement." With that, Alex made his way up to the dais.

"Let us tell the cook to bring everything up," Alex said, taking his seat beside Isobel. "The clan is already half drunk. Best get some food in them."

"I sent word to the kitchens as soon as you entered the hall," she said. She then leaned in to him and whispered, "Did he agree?"

"Aye, he did." Alex took her hand in his and kissed

it. "Now we wait and see if Anna agrees to it."

"How did he seem?"

"As I remember him," Alex said. "If my judgment has not failed, I think he would be a fair husband to Anna."

"Then let us hope the alliance works."

"Aye," he said, turning to see Ewan introduce himself to Anna. Alex looked on, trying to study Anna's facial expressions to gauge her interest in Ewan. Anna was known for wearing her feelings on her face, but to his surprise he could discern nothing from her face. *Is that good or bad? Is she disinterested? Is that what her disinterested face is like?*

"Alex, stop staring," Isobel whispered in his ear.

"I should have introduced them," Alex said. "Then I could have stayed to listen."

"If you keep looking on in such a way, you are sure to make them nervous. Just leave it be," Isobel said. "Besides, Robbie approaches. He must want to speak with you."

A few moments later, Robbie stood before him and Isobel.

"May I have a word with Lady Isobel?" he asked, to Alex's surprise.

"Of course," Isobel said. "Shall we step into the solar? It is quite noisy in here."

As Isobel and Robbie left the dais, Alex glanced over at his sister, Joan. She was scowling, and her face was bright red.

"Sister, are you well?"

"Hand me that wine," she instructed, as she stretched out her hand.

Alex looked around the table and found a carafe of

wine sitting to his right. He picked it up and handed it to Joan, who nearly dropped it into Isobel's chair.

"Have a care," Alex said. He frowned as Joan attempted to fill her glass, spilling half the wine on the table. "Joan—"

"Not a word, Brother." She held up her right hand to silence him and picked up the drink with her left. "I am two and twenty, and I have to dance."

Alex did not begin to understand what the wine had to do with her age or dancing, so he simply shrugged and let his watchful eye fall once more on Ewan and Anna.

****

When they were both inside, Isobel closed the door to Alex's solar and invited Robbie to sit at the table. He took a seat and Isobel joined him, rather curious to know what he wanted.

"What can I do for you, Robbie?" she asked.

"I have no favor to ask," he said. "I want to apologize."

"Apologize?" Isobel was confused.

"I never apologized for the way I treated you and for stealing the Rood," he said. He cleared his throat, showing his discomfort in speaking this way to her, but he kept his eyes on hers—never wavering. "Though my motivation was only to save my sister, it does not excuse my behavior. I am truly sorry."

Isobel had never expected an apology. He'd proven himself over and over again since their first meeting.

"I can only accept your apology if you will accept mine." She thought often of how she had wounded him. "I am sorry for stabbing you."

"Nae. You had to."

277

"I believe we were both doing what we thought we had to," she said.

Robbie nodded.

"I think then we are even." Isobel stood and reached out her hand in peace.

Robbie accepted it, and they shook. "I also appreciate your care of Agnes," he said. "She is the happiest I have ever seen her."

"She is dear to me and to all of Alex's sisters," Isobel said.

"The MacKinnons are fortunate to have you, my lady."

"And we are lucky to have you and your kin, Robbie."

They left the solar and returned to the celebration in the great hall. Isobel found Alex still watching Ewan and Anna, who were deep in conversation at a table near the dais, and Joan was half falling out of her seat. Isobel rushed to her, but Robbie was by Joan's side in an instant, helping settle her in the chair. He righted her and immediately stepped away.

"I need to fetch Agnes," he said, looking at Isobel. "Murdoch told me the healer will permit her to come down to eat with us. She will be waiting."

"I am glad she can join us," Isobel said, noting how flustered the usually composed islander looked.

Isobel took her seat by Alex, and Donald, head of the guard, offered the first toast of the night.

****

After the meal, and a nearly endless line of wedding toasts, the music began. Alex's uncle, William, and a handful of his men played a lively tune on their pipes and strings. Some of the crowd dispersed outside, leaving open space for dancing in the hall. Soon the clan was whistling, clapping, and dancing along with the music. *It's the perfect time to leave,* Alex thought. He was about to steal Isobel away to their room when Flora rushed up to the dais with a wide grin on her face. "I have a surprise for you both!" she exclaimed.

"What sort of surprise?" Alex frowned. Flora's surprises usually began or ended with a catastrophe, so he had good reason to be wary.

"I made a banner to celebrate your wedding!"

"How thoughtful," Isobel said.

"Oh?" Alex looked cautiously around the hall for it. "Where is it?"

"Look up," she said. She waved her arms, as though signaling to someone in the crowd, and moments later a banner reading "Alex and Isobel Forever" unfurled from the rafters.

"It's wonderful," Isobel said, to a beaming Flora.

"Aye," Alex agreed. "It is verra nice, lass."

"I am so glad you like it! I had Murdoch help me hang it this afternoon."

Alex peered into the crowd and found Murdoch standing beneath the banner, holding onto the rope that kept it up.

Suddenly, a man in the crowd bumped into Murdoch, causing him to lose hold of the rope. The banner dropped, falling into the crowd and onto two torches, where it promptly went up in flames.

"Fire!" Alex shouted above the music. "Fire!"

He leapt from the table and raced into the crowd. Fortunately, everyone had moved clear of the flames, but the fire still posed a risk to the wooden keep.

"Bring water! Quickly!" he ordered the nearest two guards. He found in such cases that orders needed to be given to specific people. If he just shouted out for anyone to help, everyone assumed someone else was managing it.

"Use the banner to smother it," Ewan suggested, coming to Alex's side.

Alex grabbed the banner, but the cloth was nearly covered in flames. "There is no time," he said, letting it go. He stomped on it, but the flames grew by the second.

"Here!" Robbie shouted. He rushed to Alex's side, handing him a bucket of water.

Alex took it and doused half the flames. "One more and it should be under control." The fire was contained now, but smoke was filling the great hall.

"Open the doors, Murdoch," Alex instructed the lad. He looked ill, but obeyed.

The two guards brought in more buckets of water, and Alex and Robbie dumped them on the flames, putting out the fire completely.

Within minutes, all the doors were open and the furs were pulled back from the windows allowing the smoke to escape.

"Let us continue the celebration outside!" Alex shouted, and the men and women cheered in response. The musicians resumed playing their instruments, and the melody mingled with the laughter and conversation of the clansmen and women. Everyone filtered out of the smoky hall and into the summer night.

When the hall had cleared, Alex took stock of the damage.

"These boards will need replacing," Alex said, as

Isobel came to stand beside him.

"You wanted to rebuild in stone anyway, did you not?" Isobel asked.

"I do," Alex replied, rubbing the back of his neck as he studied the wall and floor.

"Then no harm done," she said.

"No harm done?" Alex asked in disbelief. "The keep could have burnt down."

"But it did not," Isobel said. "Your sister meant well, and it was not Murdoch's fault. Someone bumped into him."

Isobel was right, of course, but she didn't understand that this happened every time Flora essayed any of her projects. He'd witnessed all manner of mischief from the girl before she was even old enough to say her own name.

"It does not matter if her intentions were good. She could have injured someone."

"I understand," Isobel said. "But today is a celebration. Go to her now, and tell her all is well. Otherwise, she will fret all night."

"Very well," Alex said, glancing out into the crowded bailey then back to her. "Are you coming?"

"I am going to our room," Isobel said. "Will I see you up there soon?"

"Aye." Alex felt his blood heat as his wife sashayed out of the hall. The sooner he found Flora, the sooner he could join Isobel. He made his way out into the bailey.

Already, a series of bonfires had been lit. The flames flickered in the summer sky as the clan's people danced to the Celtic tunes of their Irish guests. He searched out Flora and found her and Murdoch standing near the stables. The young MacDonald was trying to console her.

"Everything is fine," Murdoch said. "The keep still stands."

"Alex hates me," Flora cried.

"Not true," Alex said, making himself known. He came to stand beside his sobbing sister. Her face was buried in her hands.

"Come now, Flora," he said. He wrapped his arms around her. "Isobel and I loved the banner."

She dropped her hands and looked up at him. "Do you mean it?"

"Aye."

"But what about the keep wall?" Her eyes welled with tears.

"In truth, I think it looks better with the soot stains," Alex said, causing Flora and even Murdoch to laugh. "There now. No more tears."

She nodded her head and wiped her face with her hands.

"It is a beautiful night. Why don't you and Murdoch join the group for a dance?" Alex looked to Murdoch, waiting for the young man to object.

"I would love a dance," Murdoch said. Alex released Flora and clapped Murdoch on the back.

"You hear that?" Alex gently nudged Flora's chin up with his finger. "There are too few nights in life like this one, Flora. Go enjoy yourself."

His young sister looked up at him with her big green eyes and smiled. "I have not danced yet," she said.

Alex waved his hands at Murdoch, as though presenting him to her for the first time. "I believe this young man offered to be your partner."

Murdoch looked uncertain, and Alex knew he was as upset as Flora had been. "No harm done," he told him. "I won't have you think on it a moment longer. That is a direct command from the chief."

Murdoch nodded. "Aye, Chief."

Flora tugged on Murdoch's hand. "I love this tune! Come on, Murdoch!"

She was already dragging him away, but Murdoch leaned back and whispered to Alex, "She won't let me lead."

"Best get used to it." Alex patted him on the shoulder and sent them off into the crowd.

One sister happy. Just one more to see. Since Isobel had forbade him from talking to them during the feast, he wanted to find Anna and see where the marriage alliance stood. He searched through the crowd but did not see them gathered by any of the bonfires, so he checked the front gate, where four guardsmen stood on watch.

"Have you seen my sister, Anna?"

"She and a man just walked up to the ramparts," one of the guards said, pointing to the steps just inside the gates.

Alex jogged up the steps to the top of the gate wall. The wooden walkway was narrow but allowed enough room for two rows of archers to take positions on the wall. He'd fortified the walkway after his return home, knowing men would need to line the walls if the Macleans attacked.

He found Anna and Ewan facing the sea, looking up at the sky. The heavens had gifted the clan with a clear night, and the stars were plentiful.

"I wanted a word with Anna," Alex interrupted. They both turned at the sound of his voice.

"Of course," Anna said.

"A fine feast, Alex," Ewan said.

Alex nodded in thanks.

"I will be over here," Ewan told Anna, pointing to the end of the walkway before he left. Alex waited until Ewan was out of earshot before he spoke. "Well?"

"He is nice," Anna said.

"And?"

"I could marry him."

Alex hugged his sister in relief. "Are you certain?"

"Aye."

"Because if not, just tell me." He released her and held her at arm's length, trying to discern her usually readable face.

"Alex, you just hugged me to near death. I do not think you could have been any more relieved by my choice."

"Anna, I will not see you married against your will. Forget everything else. Forget me. Is this what you want?"

"From what I can garner, he seems a fine man and should make a respectable husband." She shrugged and added, "Honestly, Alex. I do not know what you expect me to say after just meeting the man a few hours ago. All I can tell you is I am at peace with my decision."

It was wrong of Alex to expect more from her. Selfishly, he wanted peace of mind. He needed to believe that this decision benefited Anna, not just the rest of the clan. He would not be able to live with himself if she were unhappy. He bid her good night, resisting the temptation to have the guards keep an eye on them as he passed by the gates on his way back up to the keep.

One sister happy. One sister at peace. Alex could live with that. *Should I check on Joan? She drank so much wine at dinner, she's probably fast asleep in her room.* Deciding he'd managed as much as he could for the night, Alex returned to the keep and made his way up to his chamber.

Chapter 29

Isobel carefully removed her fine gold-velvet gown, circlet, and necklace. With all her finery carefully put away, she dressed in a simple linen shift. She then lit a fire in the grate and sat down. Though it had been a warm day, the cool winds off the inner sea brought a chill to the night air. Tending the fire also gave Isobel a distraction from her mind. As did the noise outside, with laughter and pipe music filtering in through the narrow window in the chamber. By the sound of it, the clan planned to celebrate well into the night.

The cook had done a fine job with the feast. The MacKinnons and the Irish ate their fill and enjoyed the bounty of wine, ale, and mead. A lavish offering, but Isobel knew the evening's festivities were a much-needed luxury. Judging by the way everyone continued to carry on down in the bailey, the feast had served its main purpose—to boost morale. The men would be better prepared, in mind and body, to go to battle now.

But there may be no battle. From a distance, it seemed Ewan and Anna got on well enough. Their marriage could bring peace, but even if Anna agreed to take Ewan as a husband, it did not mean the Maclean chief would agree to the arrangement. Though, the dowry Isobel proposed for Anna was handsome; it should tempt any chief, even one with means.

A light knock sounded at the door.

"Isobel, it's me," Alex called.

Her pulse instantly quickened, and she licked her lips. She bade him enter and stood as he walked into the room. The firelight cast a romantic glow over him, and her knees weakened in anticipation of what was to come. Their first night together in the forest had been uncomfortable at first, but with time, the experience had been pleasurable. *Very pleasurable,* she recalled.

"Anna has agreed to marry Ewan," he said, pulling off his boots. He hadn't really looked at her yet and seemed preoccupied. "I also spoke to Flora and Murdoch. All is good."

"Good," Isobel said, coming to stand before him.

"Though I did not see Joan after the fire in the keep. Did you?" Alex asked.

Isobel shook her head. "I am certain she is fine." Isobel did not want to talk about anyone else right now. She wanted to be with Alex without any interruptions.

"Aye, I'm sure you are right." Alex pulled off his belt and laid his weapons out on the stand beside the door. He paused in his ministrations, finally looking at her.

"You're ready," he said, in a throaty voice.

"Yes," she whispered, inching closer to him. Alex stood still, watching her.

She lifted the bottom of his blue tunic up over his hips. Alex's arms hung at his sides, but his eyes were locked on her. She pulled the fabric higher up, exposing the bands of muscle over his stomach. When she reached his chest, he pulled the tunic off and tossed it on the floor.

Isobel was standing close enough to feel the heat

radiating from his skin. He smelled smoky, but there was still a hint of rose and his natural male scent. The combination was intoxicating, so was his body. Her memories of him had stayed true. He was just as strong as she recalled, though she didn't remember the hair on his chest. She reached out and flattened her palms over his stomach then glided her hands up over his hair-covered chest and onto his shoulders. Moving down his arms, she felt him flex under her inspection. She traced the lines of a scar on his wrist.

"What is this from?"

"A whip," Alex said.

Isobel nodded but did not ask for more details. She continued her perusal of his form, finding a star-shaped scar on his upper arm.

"And this?"

He glanced down to where she pointed. "An arrow."

Isobel traced a few more scars on his chest and arms. His body was a testament to his strength and reflected a history of warfare. She wondered if that history had hurt him on the inside too. He'd spoken of how he was suited for battle, how he did not let himself be haunted by his actions, but there still had to be a toll. Perhaps the cost was on his heart.

She did not want to think about that now. She wanted to be with him.

Isobel touched his waist, and the muscles on his stomach tightened as her fingers worked to untie his trews and braies. Looking him straight in the eye, she slid her hand beneath the fabric and touched his manhood. He was already hard. She grasped him in her palm and gently squeezed up, from hilt to tip. He moaned and teetered forward as she continued to stroke him. His hands fell onto her shoulders and gripped gently.

She stroked him harder, and he abruptly pulled away and grabbed her hand.

"Did I hurt you?"

"Nae," he said. "It felt too good, and I want this night to last." He released her hand and pushed down his trews and braies.

He stood before her completely naked. She took it all in. From his chiseled torso, Alex's hips narrowed. A line of hair on his stomach led south to his prominent shaft, which now stood proudly outside its confines. She looked from his muscular thighs to his knees and on down to his toes. Isobel could find nothing lacking; every part of him was perfect in her eyes.

Isobel stepped away from him toward the bed and lifted the hem of her shift. Alex watched her like a wildcat about to devour its prey. She'd seen that intensity in his eyes before, and it excited her as much as it had the first time. His desire for her left her feeling breathless.

She hiked her shift higher, exposing her thighs. She'd never shown her naked body to a man before, unless she counted what Alex had seen of her when she was bathing at Doune. Finding courage in his gaze, she lifted the shift the rest of the way and pulled it up over her head. She tossed it on the floor beside his clothes and looked back at Alex with her head held high.

The firelight flickered, casting shadows and light across his body as he approached her. Isobel's heart pounded in her ears; she had never felt this kind of nervous excitement before. As thrilling as it was maddening.

Finally, he reached out and touched her. Isobel sighed in pleasure as his hands cupped her breasts, lifting them gently, before his exploration of her body continued. He touched her hips and the fronts of her thighs, then his hand pressed inward, between her legs. She parted them further, giving him access, as his fingers played across her sensitive skin.

Then he dipped two fingers inside of her. Isobel trembled in response. She rolled her head back and arched as his fingers worked in and out.

She reached for him then, wrapping her arms around his neck as she fell against him, too weak to stand on her own anymore.

"I'm going to make you come apart," Alex whispered in her ear.

In the next instant, he lifted her in his arms and placed her on the bed. He lay down beside her and pressed his fingers back inside her passage, only this time he used his thumb to touch her on the outside. Isobel sighed as he rubbed her there.

She closed her eyes, focusing on the sensation building inside of her. In the next moment, she felt his tongue on her neck. She reached for him, burying her fingers in his long hair, holding him to her as he bent his head and kissed her breast. He flicked his tongue out, and Isobel arched into him.

"Your breasts are perfect," he whispered.

Isobel just murmured in response. She was too focused on his hand. She was rising—higher and higher—only she did not know where the sensation was taking her. The sensation was unlike anything she had ever experienced before. Even when she and Alex had coupled in the forest, she hadn't felt anything like this. It just kept building inside of her.

She had to move. Her hands grasped at the bed linens, twisting the fabric as her legs shifted involuntarily.

And then it happened.

She came apart, just as Alex said. Wave after wave kept crashing down on her, and the sensation seemed to fill her entire body. She cried out as the feeling exploded within her.

When it finally faded, her body went limp. She opened her eyes and looked down, finding Alex resting his head over her heart.

"That was wonderful," she heard herself say. He smiled against her breast, and then he lifted his head.

"It is just the beginning," he said. He gently parted her legs and climbed on top of her. She felt him nudge at her entrance, and she relaxed against him, ready to take in his length.

Alex had to fight for composure. He was no longer the selfish lover he'd been as a young man. Over the years, he had learned control. He'd become skilled in making the experience as satisfying for his partner as it was for him. Of course, he'd failed in that the first night he and Isobel made love. He'd taken her and spent himself, but he hadn't brought her the same measure of pleasure. She hadn't been aware of that at the time, but he would make it up to her. *Now she knows what passion should be like.*

She'd found her release, and Alex had never been so aroused. He couldn't wait to be inside her. Then he could make her come again.

She welcomed him, relaxing as her body took in

his length. When he was buried as far as he could go, he looked down at her, taking in the appearance of his beautiful wife. Her eyes were bright with passion, her cheeks were pink, and her hair was spread out over his hands on either side of her head.

Careful to keep his weight off her, he rolled his hips back, then forward, setting a slow easy rhythm. She moaned in response, and Alex had to kiss those sea-pink-colored lips. He bent his head and claimed her mouth.

Soon the kiss grew hot. Isobel's mouth opened, and Alex took the invitation, flicking his tongue against hers.

He continued the rhythm but reached down to lift Isobel's right leg up. She hitched it over his bottom. The motion gave him a deeper angle. He did the same with her other leg, angling her to receive him more fully.

Isobel broke the kiss. "Faster," she whispered. She urged him on with her hands, grabbing his flanks.

Alex increased the rhythm, his breath becoming more labored as he bent his head to kiss Isobel's neck.

"Right there," she said with a sigh.

Alex had found her spot. *Thank the kings of Alba.* He did not know how much longer he would last, but he wanted them to reach that peak together.

He maintained the same rhythm and angle; Isobel's moans assured him she was close. He felt the pressure building—so acute, so close.

He closed his eyes and focused on the rhythm. *Wait for her.*

Then he heard her cry out and stopped holding back. A moment later, he found his release.

****

Afterward, Alex lay on his side and Isobel lay on her stomach. He gently caressed her back as she slept. Alex could not put into words what had just happened, but he knew he'd never experienced the like of it before. The intensity was beyond compare. Isobel was beautiful—her body, her face, everything was exquisite. But he knew the experience had been about more than her physical form.

What they shared went beyond the physical to a place where he'd never treaded with his partners in the past. He felt it deep inside himself, but he never let it come to the surface. Until now.

I love her.

He felt something for Isobel the first time he'd laid eyes on her at Stirling Castle, but Alex had dismissed it. He had pushed the feeling aside dozens of times on their journey here, but it kept coming back. Somehow, they seemed destined for one another, though Alex still felt guilt for how little he offered her. *I've given her a home, but look at all she has given me.* Alex did not want to think of the threat from the Macleans, but if the worst came to pass, then even the home he gave Isobel would be no more.

Alex thought over their conversations on the way to Mull. Isobel spoke of Ireland and traveling there. *This could be what I offer her.*

"That's it," he said.

"What?" Isobel murmured. She turned on her side to face him, bending her arm beneath the side of her head for support. She blinked before opening her eyes completely.

"I was just thinking aloud," he whispered,

continuing to rub her. "Go back to sleep."

" 'Tis all right," she said. "I'm awake now. What are you thinking on?"

"Well," Alex began. "I know you yearn to see new places. I thought we could travel to Ireland to see about recruiting some craftsmen for rebuilding the keep."

"Do you mean it?" she asked. She looked up at him in shock.

"It is your coin, so I'll leave you to decide how it is spent," he said.

"It is our coin now," Isobel said. "And I'd love to bring in craftsmen to do the Celtic ornamentation like I saw on Iona's stone crosses. The masons could do stonework in the great hall."

"We could tour the countryside until you find workmanship that you like," Alex offered.

"I'm sure I will like it all," Isobel exclaimed. "It will be hard to choose."

Alex smiled down at her. She looked so happy. He could not wait until the business with the Macleans was settled so they could start building their new home together.

Isobel raised herself up and kissed him on the lips. With a smile, she lay back down on her side, and Alex caressed her once more.

"David and Mattie traveled to Ireland when I was young," Isobel said. "I was too little to go along with them."

"Was it right after they took you in?"

Isobel nodded her head.

"I was frightened to be at Edinburgh Castle without them. I feared someone would turn me back out on the streets. No one did, of course, but I feared it every day until they returned."

"Isobel, will you tell me about it? About what happened before you came to live with the king and queen?"

Isobel closed her eyes. Alex was afraid he'd asked too much too soon, but then she opened her eyes and started talking.

"I truly have no memory of my parents, but I remember the relatives who took me in," she said. "They were my father's cousins—exiles from the Campbell clan. They lived as thieves, never trying to find an honest way of life."

Alex just listened and continued to gently rub her side and hip as she spoke.

"They taught me about thieving too," she said. "But I was old enough to know sin, so I refused. They beat me for being disobedient. One time the beating was so bad I passed out and did not wake for over a day."

Alex reflexively tightened his fist. Isobel must have noticed his reaction, for she reclined on her back and looked up at him. She took his hand in her own and kissed his knuckles.

She is the one telling me of her painful past and here she is comforting me, Alex thought as she held his hand with care.

"I am ashamed that I did not run away, but I was so young at the time. I did not know how to survive," she said. "But then one day, while we were living on the streets in Edinburgh, they took me to a part of the city I had never seen before. They led me up the street to the castle and told me to wait; then they left. I waited all day and night, but they never returned. The next day, I was still waiting. But by that evening, I knew they'd abandoned me."

Isobel's voice waivered as she spoke. It broke his heart to know her past.

"I survived for a few months, living off scraps and pocketing fruit and bread from the market. I was so little, few noticed me. But then the weather began to turn. Winter was coming and I knew, even as small as I was, that I would die," Isobel said. "But then, just as the snow began to fall in the city, a man on a steed appeared before me. I remember his polished black boots and then his face as he peered down at me. He commanded a nearby guard to give me his cloak. Within seconds, I was bundled up and riding up to the castle. He truly saved my life," she finished.

Suddenly, Alex understood so much. *This is why she risked everything to take the Rood to safety. She owed David her life.*

Alex wrapped his arms around her, holding her close to his chest. He could not take away her past, but he would give her every happiness within his power. He had to tell her how he felt. He did not want to live another moment without her knowing where his heart was.

"Isobel, I—"

But he never got to finish, for the chilling sound of the MacKinnon battle horn thundered in the air.

Chapter 30

The horn sounded again; Alex jumped off the bed and searched for his leather trews and war coat.

"You must get dressed!" he shouted, when he realized Isobel was still in bed.

"What's going on?"

"That was the alarm for an impending attack," Alex said. "The Macleans must be approaching our border."

"But I thought we had more time," Isobel said. She quickly dressed as Alex donned his armor. "Do you think Ewan said something to his father?"

"Nae," Alex said. "But I think he knows more than he shared."

After Alex had strapped on all his weapons, he led Isobel from their room and down the corridor, checking on each of his sisters and Agnes along the way. Alex instructed Anna, who was still in her fine gown, to come down to the great hall; he then instructed Joan, Flora, and Agnes to stay in their rooms and await further instruction from the guards.

By the time Alex and Isobel reached the great hall, Robbie and Murdoch were already waiting by the main doors to the bailey.

"Is it the Macleans?" Alex asked, approaching Robbie with Isobel at his side. His friend looked exhausted; no doubt Alex looked the same. He feared half the men were still drunk but prayed the battle horn helped to sober them.

"Aye," Robbie said. "A rider spotted them; they'll be here within the hour. Your uncle is preparing his men while Donald prepares the MacKinnons."

"Where is Ewan?" Alex demanded, looking around the hall.

"I'll go in search of him," Robbie offered.

"I'm here," Ewan called, approaching from the bailey.

Alex squeezed Isobel's hand. "Wait here."

He, Robbie, and Murdoch met Ewan outside. "What are you doing?" Alex asked.

"I went to see what was going on," Ewan said. "My father is on his way."

"You wouldn't have a hand in that, would you?" Alex drew himself up against Ewan, staring the man in the eye. They were almost equally matched in height, but Alex had more muscle on him. "Your father said I had until the full moon."

"He did," Ewan agreed.

"Does he know of my father's passing?" His motivation for moving up the timeline could mean he suspected the MacKinnon forces were even weaker because of the loss of the chief.

"Aye," Ewan said. "Two riders brought news of his death from Fionnphort the day you departed Duart."

Those were the men Isobel and I saw in the valley on our way to Iona, Alex thought.

"But that is not why he moves against you."

"Then why?" Alex demanded.

"He is concerned you are strengthening your defenses. He is no longer convinced you will submit to him."

"No clan ever willingly submits to another, Ewan. You know this. Your father knows this too."

"In truth, I convinced him you would agree to submission."

"What?!" It did not make sense. "Why?"

"My father's cruelty has grown." Ewan's eyes clouded over.

What has the chief done? Alex's face remained impassive, but a chill ran down his spine at Ewan's words.

"I wanted to protect you and your clan for as long as I could," Ewan continued. "I was searching for ways to change the chief's fixation on expanding his lands. When you saw me that night at Duart Keep, I'd come from the Isle of Man. I was seeking a marriage alliance in hopes of appeasing the chief's desire for more connections and control."

"You were unsuccessful?"

"I am free to form a contract with your sister, MacKinnon, if that is what you are suggesting. I am bound to no one else."

Alex nodded. "I do not think the dowry we offer will tempt your father alone."

Worry passed over his friend's face. Ewan had the same concern. "I will do everything I can to convince him," he began.

"Nae. I will meet him first. When I whistle twice, ride out to join us."

Ewan nodded.

"I must know, Ewan, why do you do this for me and my people?" Alex and his clan gained much from this alliance, and Ewan gained a wife and a fair dowry.

He did not want to diminish Anna's value, but he wanted to make certain his old friend would not come to regret the match or hurt Anna in any way. He needed to know his true intent before he went out to negotiate with the chief.

"We were friends once, Alexander. You know I desire peace. If this brings peace between our clans, then I will be happy," Ewan said, then frowned and studied Alex's face. "I will be a good husband to Anna. I promise you this."

"If we survive this morn, I'll hold you to that, Ewan."

Alex tasked Robbie and Murdoch with keeping an eye on Ewan while he went to the armory to check on the progress there. He found his uncle handing out the last of the *clogadan* and shields to soldiers who would be on the front line. The *clogadan*, strong iron helmets, offered extra protection for the men who would be most vulnerable. The rest of the soldiers were armed with axes and bows and arrows, and a select few had swords like Alex and Robbie.

"The men are ready," his uncle told him.

"You remember the signals?" Alex asked.

"Aye," he said. "We'll be in position and ready for battle before the Maclean shows himself."

The men reached out and grasped each other's shoulders. "For the MacKinnons," they said in unison.

They parted, and Alex went back into the keep in search of Isobel. He found her standing with Anna near the hearth where a fresh fire had been lit. The great hall was still strewn with platters of food and empty ale tankards from the night's festivities.

He drew her away, out of earshot of Anna, and

whispered, "Everything will be all right. But if something should happen…if the negotiations fail…"

"Alex, you don't have to say anything," Isobel whispered back. "We will get through this."

"Nae. Listen," he said. "If the keep falls, take my sisters and as many of the women and children as you can gather and make the crossing to Iona. There are over a dozen boats in the harbor. Seek sanctuary at the nunnery. Maclean will not harm you there."

Isobel nodded, her face solemn.

The battle horn sounded again. *The Macleans are within view.*

"Stay with Anna." Alex reached out and touched the side of Isobel's face. She placed her hand over his and leaned into his palm. "Remember what I said."

"I will."

With one final look into her violet eyes, Alex dropped his hand and strode from the great hall. He went directly to the stables and mounted one of the horses he'd taken from the English. Alex's uncle had wrapped the horse in protective chainmail, a grandeur that was not afforded to any of the other horses in his small contingent.

Alex rode through the gates with Robbie and Donald. They rode out some fifty paces in front of the gates and waited. To their right was the sea. To their left was a steep hill. The Macleans could only attack from one direction—the grasslands before them. A short time later, the Maclean soldiers came into view. As they marched on, line after line of Maclean soldiers filled the southern horizon.

God help us. There had to be a thousand men.

"They are too great in number!" Donald cried.

"We'll all be slaughtered within the hour."

"Hold your damn tongue!" Alex warned.

"Chief, ye must surrender," Donald begged. "Death is certain."

Alex had heard enough. He spun on his horse and faced Donald. "I am the chief! You will do as I command! Hold your ground, Donald, or I will throw you into the sea myself!"

Wisely, Donald stayed silent. Alex spun around again and faced the approaching army.

Soon, the Maclean army stopped. It looked as though the sea had swallowed the land for the dark figures of the Maclean men stood so close together that Alex could not see the ground beneath them.

Within moments of halting the army, the Maclean chief rode forward with his top men at his side. When he came within ten paces of Alex, he held up his hand, and the Maclean men fell back. Only the chief approached.

Alex instructed Robbie and Donald to wait and went out to meet the chief on his own.

"Maclean," Alex said, nodding at the old chief.

"MacKinnon," he said. "A fine morning for battle, but let us hope it does not come to that, aye?"

Alex said nothing. Best to let the Maclean talk first to gauge the situation.

"Many MacKinnons deserted your clan when the old chief took ill," Maclean said. "I know you've less than two hundred men behind those walls. Submit to me now, and no one will die."

"My force is much greater, Maclean."

"Expect me to believe ye have amassed a thousand men from thin air?" He laughed.

"Aye." Alex whistled over his shoulder and from behind the hill, next to the keep, came the sound of soldiers marching. Feet pounded over the granite earth as soldiers crested the hill. The Irish mercenaries wore their black leather war coats, the whites of their eyes visible in the predawn light. Because the hill was flanked by the keep and a steep granite face, the men were squeezed into a narrow area, giving the appearance of a greater force. The Irish mercenaries let out a war cry.

"Do you doubt me still?" Alex asked the old chief.

"There may only be a few hundred men on that hill," Maclean said.

Alex whistled again, and MacKinnon archers appeared above the keep walls, arrows nocked and bows raised. The Maclean frowned at the growing display of force before him.

"Are you willing to take that chance when you could still leave with a fine prize?" Alex asked.

"What prize?" The old man's gray brows knitted together.

Alex whistled twice, signaling Ewan to ride out.

"What the hell are ye doing here?" the chief demanded of Ewan when he rode up to join them.

"I am here seeking a marriage alliance."

"What?" he shouted. "The MacKinnons are impoverished. They've nothing to offer us."

"That is nae true, Father."

"I have just married Isobel Campbell, King David's daughter," Alex said.

"The lass ye brought to Duart is King David's daughter?" the Maclean chief asked, seeming confused.

"Aye," Alex replied. "I am now able to give each

of my sisters a fine dowry."

"Chief, think on this," Ewan urged him. "We could lose many men to the MacKinnons, or we could gain coin and strengthen our alliance with our neighbors."

The old chief's expression transformed from anger to thoughtful contemplation. *He's considering it!*

The Maclean gazed up behind Alex and Ewan, taking in the sight of the MacKinnon force. The Irish wore impressive armor, and the archers had finely crafted bows. By all appearances, they were unmistakably warriors. Alex knew Maclean was smart; he could not risk the loss, especially if what Ewan said was true about Maclean's plan to extend his reach beyond Mull. He would need a large force. *He knows he cannot risk it.* Alex felt confident, but his face remained expressionless. He could not show concern. He had to hold his bluff.

Alex's horse snorted and stomped. The animal was restless. Maclean was taking a long time to consider.

"What are yer terms, MacKinnon?"

"Accept a marriage alliance between my sister, Anna, and Ewan, with a handsome dowry, and let us resume our alliance."

"If your army is a thousand strong, then why offer the marriage alliance?"

"I want peace," Alex said. "My sister also needs a good match. The Macleans are revered in the Isles."

The chief's eyes narrowed on Alex.

Hold your bluff, Alex reminded himself, taking care to keep his face still.

Maclean turned to look at his son. "Ye are agreeable to this?"

"Aye," Ewan said.

After a few moments, Maclean finally spoke again. "I accept yer terms, MacKinnon."

He nodded to Alex, then rode back to his men. Briefly, he exchanged some words with them. As the Maclean chief disappeared into the sea of men, one of his seconds rode up to speak with Ewan and Alex.

"Ye are to put everything in writing and get a date for the wedding, then return home," the man said to Ewan.

Ewan agreed, and the man galloped off.

Alex remained firmly in place until the Maclean contingent turned around. He and Ewan sat atop their horses in silence until the thundering sound of a thousand men marching into the distance became a faint rumble.

Once they were out of sight, Alex turned to Ewan and asked, "Will he keep his word?"

"Aye."

"Then it is done," Alex said. He and Ewan were joined by Robbie and Donald as they rode through the keep's gates.

Alex approached a group of riders he had on the ready.

"Follow the Macleans until they clear our borders," Alex instructed them.

"Aye, Chief," the lead rider said, and the men left. The gate closed firmly behind them.

Alex instructed the soldiers to remain atop the ramparts for the morning but gave the signal for the Irish to stand down. He finally dismounted his horse and took it back to the stables where he confronted Donald.

"You are no longer in charge of my guard," he told

the man.

"But Chief, I have served as the head of the guard since before ye were even born."

"No longer," Alex replied. "You are a weak man and unfit to serve me."

"Weak?" Donald shouted. "Ye almost killed us all!"

He shoved the man against the stable door. "Nae. I saved us all!" Alex turned to leave, but Donald wouldn't be silenced yet.

"Yer father would have listened to me."

Alex sighed and turned to face Donald once more. Their disagreement was drawing a crowd. Ready to be done with it, Alex decided there was only one course of action. Alex looked at the two guardsmen posted by the stables, then fixed his gaze on Donald.

"Take him to the dungeon," he ordered the guards, and then turned to leave once more.

Donald shouted curses and damned him to hell as the guardsmen led him away, but Alex did not care. He would not tolerate weakness in his guard.

In the commotion, Alex managed to find Robbie, Murdoch, and Ewan.

"Come," he told the men. "Let's share the good news with the others."

Chapter 31

Alex walked with purpose into the great hall. He found Isobel and Anna seated where he'd left them, but they had company. Joan, Flora, and Agnes were sitting with them as well. Isobel stood as he approached.

"We heard the Macleans leave. Did he accept your terms?" she asked.

"Aye," he said, coming to stand before all the women. He looked from Isobel to Anna.

"I am glad he accepted the alliance," Anna said. She looked past Alex to Ewan and smiled. "You stayed," she said, talking to Ewan.

"I'll be returning home after we speak," Ewan said. "The sun is coming up. Would you like to take a turn with me in the bailey?"

"That would be nice," Anna replied. His sister took Ewan's arm and left the great hall.

Her face lit up, Alex thought with relief.

"He seems a good man," Isobel said.

"Aye, but I am still distrustful of his father," Alex said. "We will delay the wedding until the new year. I want to watch the Macleans."

"Do you think he will break the agreement?" Isobel asked.

There was concern in her voice, and he did not want to alarm her. He didn't know what the Maclean chief was up to, if anything, but he would not worry

Isobel without cause. Right now, there was no cause. "Nae. He'll keep to the agreement."

"Good," she said with a yawn. She blushed and covered her mouth with her hand. Alex drew her away from the others, so they could speak privately.

"You should go back to bed. You haven't had any rest." She had to be tired. Hell, he was exhausted. *I could crawl back in bed with her. Perhaps no one would miss me for a few hours.* "I'll join you," he whispered in her ear.

"I thought the idea was for me to get some rest," Isobel said. She smiled coyly and wrapped her arms around his neck.

"You can rest later," Alex said, bending his head to kiss her. Just as his lips touched hers, they were interrupted.

"Alex, can I speak with you now?" Joan called.

Alex sighed as he touched his forehead to Isobel's and closed his eyes for a moment.

"On second thought, you can rest now," he whispered. He planted a kiss on her forehead, and then turned to answer Joan.

"Of course," he said. "Come, let's talk in my solar."

"I want Isobel to be there too," Joan said, walking toward them.

"You wish to speak with me?" Isobel asked.

"Aye," Joan said.

Moments later, they were all situated in Alex's solar. Isobel stood by Alex's side and Joan sat across the table from them.

"Go ahead," Alex said.

"I did what needed to be done while you were off

touring the Mediterranean," Joan began, fiddling with the pendant on her chain. "But now that you and Isobel are home, there's no need for me to be here anymore."

Alex looked from Joan up to Isobel. She knitted her brows, showing that she was equally as perplexed by Joan's words. "What are you saying?" Alex asked, eyeing his sister once more.

"I'm saying I want my own adventure." She let go of her pendant.

"But that's not possible, Joan. You cannae go off on your own."

"I've written to Mother's family in the Trossachs. They are happy for me to visit."

"You wish to live with the Grahams?"

"For a time," Joan said. "I want to get away, Alex. Surely you of all people can understand that desire."

He did understand. Alex saw much of himself in his oldest sister. He looked to Isobel. She had not yet spoken, but her eyes were filled with understanding. *She's just finished her own adventure. Of course she understands.*

After taking a moment, he finally spoke. "You can go to the Grahams, but you will go with an escort."

"Very well," Joan said.

"I'll assign four guards," Alex said.

"Four?" Isobel and Joan said in unison.

"Surely that is excessive, Brother."

"Excessive?" Alex laughed. "Did you not see the army gathered outside our gates?"

"You mean our allies?" Joan asked.

"They could still be a threat." Alex didn't have to explain it. She was his kin, and he'd be damned if he let anything happen to her.

"Why not send Robbie?" Isobel asked. "He'd be the perfect escort."

"Aye, I suppose," Alex said. Robbie was a strong fighter. He would be able to protect Joan from harm.

"Any of the guards would do," Joan said, looking down at the table.

"Nae," Alex said. "Robbie will go with you to the Grahams."

"But surely he is needed here," Joan said.

"Robbie is my best soldier. He will keep you safe, Joan. Have no fear." Alex did not like the idea of Joan leaving, but he felt better knowing she'd be safely escorted to the Grahams, assuming Robbie agreed to it. He couldn't imagine why Robbie would turn down the request. *It'll probably be the least demanding assignment he's had in years.*

"We should wait a few weeks then, until Agnes is recovered. I'm sure he would not want to leave his sister until she is feeling well," Joan said.

"That is thoughtful of you," Isobel said. "I think you are right."

"I should tell Anna and Flora. I haven't spoken a word about this to anyone."

"They'll understand, Sister. Do not worry."

"They aren't like us, but they will be happy I'm getting what I desire," she said, standing. The action seemed to cause her pain, for she pressed her palm to her forehead.

"It's the wine," Isobel said. "You had too much last night."

Joan nodded. "I did, but I cannae regret it. I danced all night."

"You enjoyed yourself then, Sister?"

"Aye, Alex," Joan said. "We all did. Flora will be talking of it for weeks." She suddenly laughed, then pressed a hand to her lips and shook her head.

Alex had never seen his serious sister in such a state. "What is it?"

"I shouldn't laugh, but poor Murdoch will be hiding from Flora for weeks; I think she may have broken his toe."

Alex chuckled and looked up at his new wife. She was not amused.

"That is not something to laugh over," Isobel said. "I should have given Flora more dancing lessons." She frowned and added, "She did stomp a lot when we practiced." She bit her lip, trying to keep from laughing herself.

"Ah, the lad's toe will heal, if it is indeed broken," Alex said.

"I'll remind Flora of that when I talk to her," Joan said. She reached for her emerald pendant. A common habit, Alex noticed. But instead of taking the pendant between her fingers, her hand dropped away. With a nod to Alex and Isobel, Joan left.

Alex reclined in his seat and sighed. "One sister is going off on her own, one is to be wed to a Maclean, and I can only wonder what mischief awaits us where Flora is concerned."

Isobel leaned against him, wrapping her arm around his shoulders. Alex laid his head against her stomach, enjoying the feel of her velvet dress on his cheek.

"I am sure you did not anticipate all this would come to pass when you returned to Scotland," Isobel said, combing her fingers through his hair with her free hand.

"Nae, I did not. I also did not know that I would find you," Alex said. *I need to tell her. There may never be a better moment.* He glanced at the door, hoping no one would interrupt them. "I want to say something."

"What is it?" she asked, framing his face with her hands.

Alex looked up into her violet eyes and placed his hands on top of hers. "I love you, Isobel."

Isobel's eyes welled with tears. She pulled her hands away, covering her face as she sobbed.

"Are you well, my love?" he asked. "What's wrong?" He stood, uncertain of how to comfort her.

Suddenly she laughed, perplexing Alex further, and kissed him quickly on the lips. "Of course, I am well." She laughed again. "I am more than well."

She took a deep breath and wiped away her tears. "I have longed to hear those words from you."

"Then you feel the same?" he asked, reaching for her. Alex grasped her hips gently, pulling her to him.

Isobel leaned into his chest and wrapped her arms around his neck, her violet eyes twinkled from the tears.

"Aye, Alex. I love you too."

Chapter 32

The bay at MacKinnon Keep, three weeks later

Isobel looked on as Alex and his men loaded up the small boat with supplies. They planned to be gone for only one month, but Alex wanted to ensure Isobel had everything she could want on their trip to Ireland. With an alliance agreed upon with the Macleans and no new threats against the Rood, Alex felt now was a safe time to travel. Still, Isobel worried about those they left behind.

"You'll be all right while we're gone?" Isobel asked Anna, who stood at her side. "Joan and Robbie depart in a few days' time. It will just be you and Flora."

"We'll be fine," Anna said, squeezing Isobel's hand. "Besides, we've got Agnes and Murdoch for company, and Uncle William is staying on with a dozen or so men."

"I'm thankful for that," Isobel said.

"I think my betrothed intends to visit as well," Anna added shyly.

"It is nice for you to get to know each other before you marry," Isobel said.

Joan, Robbie, Flora, and Murdoch approached.

"We wanted to give you this," Flora said, handing Isobel a scarf. The stitch work on it was very fine, and the fabric was a beautiful shade of rose, like the sea pink flowers Alex had shown her on Iona the day she'd agreed to wed him.

"It is beautiful," Isobel exclaimed.

"Flora picked the color, and we all worked on the stitching," Joan explained. "But as I'm sure you guessed, Agnes did all the detail work herself."

"I will cherish it always," she said. Though she and Joan had not grown as close as Isobel had with Anna and Flora, they respected one another. Isobel also understood Joan's desires. She was two and twenty. She needed her own adventure, and she was happy Alex was giving her the opportunity to have one.

She looked at the man who would accompany Joan on her journey. Robbie stood by looking stoic with his arms folded across his chest. He was unreadable, much like Alex, but she sensed a darkness simmering beneath the surface. It wasn't that she saw evil in Robbie, but he seemed so removed from everything. She could only guess that it was intentional. *Perhaps I shouldn't have pushed for Robbie to take Joan to the Grahams. Perhaps he isn't capable of love.* Isobel did not want to see Joan brokenhearted. At the same time, love was worth the risk. If Joan and Robbie were destined to be together, love would find a way for them just as it had for her and Alex.

She hugged Flora, Joan, Anna, and even Murdoch goodbye. She waved to Robbie; he did not seem the sort who would enjoy a parting hug.

Alex hugged all of his siblings as well but lingered by Joan and Robbie. "Take good care of her, Robbie."

Isobel knew how relieved Alex had been when Robbie agreed to escort Joan. But then he hadn't noticed the tension between Robbie and Joan. Isobel debated at what part in their journey to Ireland she would bring up that observation.

"Joan, I hope you enjoy visiting with Mother's family," Alex said. "Send word when you are ready to come home. You will be missed."

"I will miss you all too," Joan said, her eyes welling with tears.

How bittersweet it is to satisfy our hopes and dreams, for pursuit of such things can take us away from loved ones. Isobel reflected on all she had lost since she left Edinburgh. *But I have gained a family.* As she looked around at Alex, his sisters, Robbie, and Murdoch, she knew it was true. *This is my family.* Joan was no longer the only one with eyes full of tears.

"Isobel, we should set sail. The winds are favorable," Alex said, coming to stand before her. "Are you unwell?" He touched her cheek where a tear had fallen.

"I'm just happy," she said.

Alex smiled and kissed her, then helped her board the *birlinn.* A crew of twelve men joined them. They pushed off from the bank, and the men set about adjusting the sail for the wind to carry them out to sea.

"Will you tell me about Ireland now?" Isobel asked, as she and Alex stood looking out over the waves.

"You'll see it for yourself soon enough," he said, wrapping his arms around her.

****

She did see and explore Ireland, and by their journey's end, Alex had one question for her.

"How would you describe it, my love?"

"I think you described it best, husband," she said, her eyes twinkling with mischief. "Like the Western Isles, but different."

Historical Note

The inspiration for this story began with one woman: Queen Margaret of Scotland. As the daughter of exiled Edward Atheling (son of Edmund Ironside, King of England), she was born in either 1045 or 1046 in Hungary. She and her family returned to England in late 1056 or early 1057 when Edward the Confessor named his nephew, Margaret's father, his heir. However, Edward Atheling died shortly after his and his family's arrival in England. Edward the Confessor then kept Margaret and her siblings under his guardianship until his death.

Margaret's brother, Edgar, did not have the necessary support to become king and upon his great-uncle's death, Harold, son of Godwin, became king. His reign was short-lived, with the Battle of Hastings giving way to Duke William of Normandy being crowned king in 1066, despite Margaret's brother's legitimate claim to the throne.

William did not view young Edgar and his family as a threat, and for a time, they remained in his care. Things changed, however, and the family sought shelter in Scotland over the winter of 1068. It is believed that Margaret brought the Holy Rood (a fragment from the cross on which Christ was crucified) with her at this time. She eventually married the King of Scotland, Malcolm, in 1070.

Queen Margaret is the only Scottish royal to become a saint and was known for her religious convictions. The Holy Rood (also known as the Black Rood) likely never left Scotland until it was taken by Edward the 1st of England (the Hammer of the Scots) during his reign in 1296. Eventually, it was lost to history. To this day, the whereabouts of Scotland's Holy Rood remain unknown.

King David (Margaret and Malcolm's youngest son) was indeed inspired by a vision to build Holyrood Abbey; however, other aspects of his life are invented in the story. Namely, Isobel herself. King David and his wife, Matilda (as I call her, Mattie) had two daughters, Claricia and Hodierna, and a son, Henry, Earl of Northumberland. Isobel Campbell is a completely invented character. In real life, David's grandson, Malcolm IV, did inherit the throne at (or around) age eleven.

Alexander MacKinnon is a fictitious character, but MacKinnons did inhabit Mull and Iona, though their early history is not well documented (at least not that I have found). MacKinnon abbots served at the abbey and MacKinnon warriors are buried in Reilig Odhràin, the burial grounds by Iona Abbey. Queen Margaret did travel to Iona during her husband's reign and initiated repairs on the monastery. She also provided the religious community with an endowment. However, she did not, by any known accounts, grant the stewardship of Iona to the MacKinnons.

During the period that my story is set, there would have been a Columban community on Iona (so named for the followers of St Columba, the Irish monk that founded a religious community on Iona in AD 563), but it was in decline. In 1164, Somerled, Lord of the Isles (also styled King of the Isles), brought an Irish abbot to Iona, but he died the same year and the community was not renewed again until 1200. At this point in history, Ranald, Lord of the Isles (Somerled's son), invited Benedictine monks to establish a community on Iona. An Augustinian nunnery was also founded, and Ranald installed his sister, Bethoc (Beatrice) to be the nunnery's first prioress. Here I played with the timelines to fit the needs of my story.

The Macleans did call Mull home. However, the first reference to a clan by that name does not come until 1367. Also of import to note is the title of Earl of Angus. It is considered one of the oldest mormaerdoms (a medieval term for a regional ruler) in Scotland. The title is associated with a region, not a clan, but I opted to pair the title to an invented clan for simplification. The title of Bishop of Edinburgh is real today, but it did not exist at the time of my story. Another invented title is the Duke of Lincoln. There is, however, the title of Earl of Lincoln.

Another adjustment to history is the gallowglass (or galloglass) men-at-arms and their swords. These individuals were elite warriors that existed between the early 1200s and the fifteenth century. I played with time to allow Uncle William to be one of these soldiers. The sword is also important to note, as this would not have been the weapon of choice in the isles at this time. Rather, an axe or bow would have been more commonly used.

My story is set after the Second Crusade (1145-1149). Scots on crusade is a fascinating topic, but one that I found to have little documentation. I first learned of Scotsmen traveling on crusade when I visited Pitlochry's Moulin churchyard in Perthshire, Scotland. In the graveyard, there rests an old, presumably medieval, flat stone with a two-handed sword engraved on its surface. This is thought to be the grave of a 12th century crusader. This prompted me to do research, and I found information about Scots going on the second crusade, including those that sailed for Lisbon, Portugal. Scotsmen are referenced throughout historical accounts of the crusades, most often (in such contexts) being referred to as "barbarians from the north."

As to who reigned over the areas described in the book, it is true that allegiance to the Scottish king was not common for islanders. The Lord of the Isles, Somerled, a Gaelic-Norse warlord, was indeed in control over much of the western isles. However, for the purposes of the story, I made Alex allegiant to King David and the Lord of Isles.

Throughout the book, I refer to places that existed at some point in history. However, these places may not have existed during the time of my story or my description of them may not be entirely accurate. For instance, construction of St. Andrews Cathedral did not begin until 1160, a few years after my story takes place. Another example of such adjustments can be seen with my reference to Stirling Castle as a stone structure. The first known reference to the castle comes in 1107-15, when Alexander I makes an endowment to a chapel at Stirling. While a castle (or fortification) would have existed in 1153, it isn't clear exactly how the castle would have looked at this time.

There is one food item I must mention, because it likely did not exist in the form I refer to within the story. Gingerbread, as a ginger-spiced cake, was not present until sometime in the 1400s. Prior to this time, the term referenced preserved ginger (in various forms). When I lived in England, gingerbread treats were readily available, and I would go so far as to liken gingerbread biscuits in the UK to chocolate-chip cookies in America. I suppose incorporating it into the story is a nod to my life abroad.

My goal, throughout the novel, was to keep things historically accurate wherever possible, while giving myself the license to bend timelines to suit the needs of my story. I hope the result is a tale enriched by the setting and history of medieval Scotland.

A word about the author...

Kate Forrest grew up in Western Pennsylvania, where she earned a BS in English and her MFA in Creative Writing. After graduate school, she and her husband relocated to Berkshire, England, and she spent two years traveling and gathering inspiration for her Scottish historical romance novels and nonfiction essays.

As a rolling stone, she enjoys exploring all the places in the world she has been lucky enough to call home.

~*~

Visit Kate at https://kateforrestauthor.com; follow her on Instagram @romancingtheforrest; e-mail her at Kate.Forrest.SL5@gmail.com.

www.ingramcontent.com/pod-product-compliance
Lightning Source LLC
Chambersburg PA
CBHW071527260626
47170CB00002B/537